DEAR ABBEY

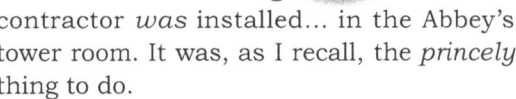

I0666187

FOR THOSE OF YOU WONDERING WHAT WE'VE BEEN UP TO SINCE YOUR LAST visit, I wish I could simply say *"life* goes on here at the Abbey." Only that's not quite true. I *can* say that planning this seventh ghastly gathering was a bit like snowboarding in Hell—difficult, but not nearly as much fun—because the work was frequently interrupted by unwelcome visitors. No, not you guys.

First, there was the county health inspector. He said I'd been warned about the problem weeks ago, and I now had only thirty days to take care of the rats infesting the Abbey. I really felt he was being unfair. I've been caring for these rats since the day we moved in. And how does one bathe and brush hundreds of rodents in such a short time frame? Well, I opted to just feed the li'l fellas. They absolutely love barbecued bureaucrat.

Then there was this guy who asked if he could hang vinyl siding over Nightmare Abbey's "ugly" stone façade. Trust me, no vinyl was installed, but a certain condescending contractor *was* installed… in the Abbey's tower room. It was, as I recall, the *princely* thing to do.

Next came an old lady collecting for charity. Why bother *me*? I swear, I've never had anything to do with Charity. If that witch is expecting again, it's probably Satan's kid. Ask *him* to support the brat.

Finally, and this was the last straw, this young man showed up on a bicycle. By then I'd *really* lost my patience.

By the way, is anyone in the market for a Schwinn?

On a more positive note, I believe Indy, my rowdy, 78-pound Siberian husky, and that rotting rascal, my dear Abbey, have finally settled their differences. (No, no, I did not. Read it again. I wrote *rotting*, not *rutting*.) Abbey has agreed to allow that carnivorous canine from Carcosa to occasionally gnaw on his bleached bones, as long as Indy promises not to bury him again. I'm all for that. I don't have time to be digging up old acquaintances—I'm too busy burying new ones. Besides, I still have the blisters from a previous bout of body snatching.

BEYOND THE INTERRUPTIONS and altercations, we also had one supernatural manifestion, a rather faded fellow searching for his long-lost liver, or some such nonsense. Alas, we haven't had a fresh liver since I stuffed last year's Christmas goose. So I exorcized the poor ghost and sent him packing with a few chicken gizzards.

Sigh! One might say the preparations for this 7th gathering were cursed. Nonetheless,

as unlucky as these fiendish festivities might be, we've once again assembled some great storytellers to dampen your spirits: Steve Rasnic Tem, Helen Grant, Simon Bestwick, Gary McMahon, and Steve Duffy are among the several party animals returning to Nightmare Abbey, along with our distinguished new guests, Stephen Volk, Michael Kelly, Jo Kaplan, and Johnny Mains…all showing their tails. Excuse me, *sharing* their *tales*. You'll encounter grim ghosts, ancient gods, hungry ghouls, and other grotesques.

Gee, that's a lot of Gs.

Have I reached 600 words yet? *No?*

Ah ha! You *have* been counting. Can't say I blame you, though. It's high time we got on with the ceremonies. And too, I see I'm nearing the end of the page, so I'll wrap things up.

Grab your robes, acolytes. Prepare the alter stone. Light the candles and bring out the first sacrificial scribe.

Welcome back to the Abbey. We've been waiting for you.

Tom English
Nightmare Abbey
New Kent, Virginia

NIGHTMARE ABBEY

GHOSTS, GODS, GHOULS & GROTESQUES

7

**COVER AND INTERIOR ILLUSTRATIONS BY ALLEN KOSZOWSKI
INTERIOR PHOTO ART BY NATU SHABBEY
EDITOR AND PUBLISHER: TOM ENGLISH**

www.DeadLetterPress.com   ISBN-13: 979-8-9862307-9-5

THE HADRIAN HORNPIPE

BY SIMON BESTWICK

"THERE'S SOMETHING I'VE ALWAYS WANTED TO KNOW," PAUL MANKTELOW SAID.

"What's that?" Sadie asked.

There were only three of us in the bar at the Station Hotel that night. I don't usually have lock-ins, but I'd made an exception that evening, as it was the night Paul had saved Sadie from a rapist called Ralph Brassland. Unfortunately, he'd killed Brassland in the process. But that's another story.

"When I decided to open a shop on Bone Street," he explained, "the first location I looked at was Number Twelve—It was the most recently vacated. But everyone I spoke to warned me not to take it. In a certain kind of film, I'd have pooh-poohed their warnings and come to a bad end, but I listened and set up at Number Four instead. Needed a little more fixing-up, but I've had no complaints. Keep shop there to this day—"

He stopped; we all knew he wouldn't be keeping shop anywhere after tonight.

I poured out a glass of his beloved *jonge jenever*.

"The strangest thing, though?" he said. "No one told me *why* I shouldn't take Number Twelve."

"That's weird," said Sadie.

"Not really," said Paul. "They didn't know. Only one person did."

He looked at me.

"I've never told anybody," I said.

"I'd guessed that."

I glanced at Sadie. "It's not a pleasant story."

She looked annoyed. "I'm a big girl, Tim."

Sadie was very small, with a delicate, big-eyed face; she looked about nineteen. I often forgot she was closer to thirty. It was only an excuse, anyway; the truth was, I just didn't want to remember. But you can never really forget some things, however hard you try.

BONE STREET'S nominally in Manchester, but you won't find it on any map of the city; nonetheless, people make their way here from all over the world.

People kill people every day. Accidentally, in self-defence, in war, in cold blood. Most of the time, that's all. But now and again— no one knows why—the Closers come after the person responsible.

Now, I don't know what the Closers look like; no one's ever seen one and lived. You *feel* them—well—closing in. And so you run. And after a while, if you're lucky, you won't recognise your surroundings anymore, and you'll find yourself stumbling out from under a railway viaduct onto a cobbled sidestreet full of above-doors flats and mostly-boarded-up shops. At the far end you'll see a square, dominated by the Station Hotel.

And that's Bone Street. The one place the Closers can't follow.

Unless you kill anyone else, as Paul had done. Which was why this was his last night, and tomorrow he'd have to go back under the viaduct, where the Closers were waiting.

So this was a kind of last request. Under those circumstances, I couldn't really say no.

However much I wanted to.

"EVEN ON BONE STREET, you need money," I said. "That, or something to sell. When I first got here, I didn't have either."

They both nodded. Paul had arrived with a well-stuffed money-belt, enabling him to rent some premises and start trading. Sadie, like me, had arrived in the clothes she stood up in, but she'd already been part of the oldest profession, and Dahlia's always had room for a new girl.

"I came out from under the viaduct five years ago," I said. "I was nineteen, had about two quid in change, and my only skills involved rifles and bayonets, which weren't much use here. I looked everywhere to see if anyone was hiring, but no one was, so it wasn't looking good."

Paul nodded soberly. Some of the buildings around the Square were derelict; the street's few really indigent inhabitants squatted there and begged for scraps. They rarely lasted long.

"Last place I tried was the mini-mart. Old man Polodski couldn't help me, but he told me to try the board. He didn't look at me when he said it."

The corkboard by the mini-mart's main entrance is still there. Items for sale. Items wanted. Index cards and slips of paper, most of them dusty and curled at the edges.

"There was this one card," I said. "Kind of old and yellowed, but it'd obviously been pretty fancy once. Cream-coloured, gold edging. The handwriting on it was very fine, very fancy. What they used to call copper-plate. You don't see it anymore. It said: *Boy Wanted—Strong, Reliable & Discreet. Room & Board supplied. Payment: 5s weekly. Apply: J. Hadrian Esq, No.12, Bone Street, Manchester 1.*"

"Old-fashioned," said Paul. "Like the script."

I nodded. "The shop was just across the street from the mini-mart. The sign's gone now, but if you look closely you can still make out what it used to say: *John Hadrian Esquire, Theatrical Supplies.* The door and windows were boarded up, but there was another little door beside them, for the flat above, with a buzzer and a speaker. I pushed the buzzer, and just as I was about to give up and turn away someone finally said 'Yes?'

"I asked if that was Mr Hadrian, and he said it was. When I told him why I'd come, there was a pause; then he said: 'Well, then. We'd better take a look at you.' And the door buzzed open."

I refilled my glass, then Paul's. Sadie sipped her liqueur glass of port, making it last.

"First thing I noticed," I said, "was the smell. Damp. Mould, mildew. Stale piss. Shit, too, I think. Food that'd gone off. And some sort of scent or perfume. A lot of that. Trying to mask the rest, I suppose. But it only made it worse."

AT THE TOP of the stairs was a landing with four rooms. There were two directly in front of me; the right-hand one was locked and the other's door stood wide open to reveal a bare room. Floorboards, stripped walls, and dozens of wooden boxes. All about a foot high and six inches wide, with a little brass plate on the lid. A few of them were open and empty; the rest were tightly shut.

At the end of the landing to my right was an open door, and I could see a sink and toilet behind it. All I could make out at the opposite end of the landing was the edge of a doorframe. "Hello?" I called.

"This way, Mr. Van Geldern," said the voice that had come out of the speaker. It was a very polished voice, and very much that of someone used to being obeyed. I was up on the landing before I knew it, making for the room at the end, and at the door before I wondered how he knew my name.

"Come in, come in," he said. "Closer."

There was a desk, two chairs, and two bookcases—one stacked with yellowed paperbacks, the other with heavy leather-bound volumes. Mr Hadrian sat up in a big brass double bed, on the table beside which an unshaded lamp provided the only light in the room.

The walls were covered with old playbills. *The Gaiety Music Hall Presents. For One Night Only. John Hadrian Esquire and his Marvellous Marionettes.* That sort of thing. He wasn't always top of the bill, and sometimes they were his *Performing Puppets* or *Dancing Dolls*, but the *John Hadrian Esquire* bit never changed.

There were two framed pictures of the man himself on the wall facing me. In one he was heavily made up with greasepaint, wore a blazer and boater and carried a cane, and was in the middle of a dance routine. A couple of tiny figures capered on either side of him: presumably his Marvellous Marionettes or Dancing Dolls. They were beautifully made and proportioned, with astonishingly detailed features. I couldn't tell if they were made from china or wood.

The second picture was a head-and-shoulders shot of him in evening dress without makeup. Dark, swept-back hair, a sardonic smile and pale, piercing eyes. Not handsome, but striking. Commanding, even.

The man in the bed was gaunt and frail, clad in a brocaded dressing gown, a nightcap and fingerless gloves, with a pair of half-moon glasses on his beaky nose. His thick white hair was the healthiest-looking thing about him; it might've been a wig, but to this day I'm not sure. I wouldn't have recognised him as the same man, except for the eyes; *those* hadn't changed.

"Well, boy?" he said. "There's a chair over there. Bring it over and sit down. Let's have a look at you."

The nearest chair was propped against the wall, and I pulled it to his bedside reluctantly; the smell in the flat was worst of all around Mr. Hadrian himself. But that was only part of it. Something about John Hadrian was, quite simply, *repellent*—it's the only word. Nothing specific; no one thing he said or did. He just made people feel that way.

He studied me, adjusting his spectacles, as though I were a piece of meat, trying to decide whether I should be a steak for the grill or fine shreds for a stir-fry. At last, he nodded. "Yes, Mr. Van Geldern. I think you'll do."

Before I could ask how he knew who I was, there was a scuttling, scratching sound from one of the walls. His head snapped round; his lips tightened in anger and loathing. "Rats," he said, almost to himself, then looked at me and smiled. "They afflict us, Mr. Van Geldern. In the walls, under the floors. Fortunately, they live and die, for the most part, out of sight. We put down poison, for all the good it seems to do. That will be one of your duties."

It sounded as though I'd got the job, at least, however unwelcome the thought of working here was. "We?" I said.

"Patrick is my—companion. He occupies the next but one room on the landing. He's unwell, poor lad. Can't do the work he used to. But he can take care of himself. He'll form no part of your duties. Those—along with rat-poisoning—will involve some cooking and generally assisting me. My vision isn't what it was, so I've been robbed of the pleasure of reading. You can read to me instead."

He took off his spectacles and polished them. "You'll also be entrusted with bringing in supplies. While the shop itself is no longer in use, I still have a few customers.

You'll make deliveries to them. I can't offer you accommodation here at the flat, but will pay for a room at the Station Hotel. You may help yourself, within reason, to whatever is in the kitchen, and add—again within reason—any items you have a particular craving for to the weekly grocery list. On top of that, you'll receive a wage of five shillings per week."

I'd already seen currency of all nationalities and ages changing hands on Bone Street; I'd no idea how far Mr. Hadrian's five shillings would stretch, but with food and housing paid for, I wouldn't need much. And I was mainly just relieved I wouldn't have to live here.

"I require considerable assistance," he added, "and sleep very little at my age. You'll present yourself here at six o'clock each morning, and be available until midnight. There will be no days off. You accept?"

He smiled; I suspect he knew very well I was in no position to refuse. "Yes," I said, telling myself I could tough this out till another opportunity arose, and forced myself to add "Thank you."

"You're welcome, Mr. Van Geldern. Now let us begin."

I'VE NEVER REALLY understood how time works on Bone Street. People have not only come here from every part of the world, but from different periods as well. It was 2014 when I'd arrived, but Paul Manktelow had made his way here sometime in the 1980s, and Sadie, as far as I could tell, had been a '90s girl, technically making her old enough to be my mother.

Mr. Hadrian apparently dated from Victorian or Edwardian times, as did his clients. Like him, they were generally music-hall entertainers, supporting themselves by performing in the Station Hotel's bar and passing the hat round, or staging a paying show at one of their homes. Most of Hadrian's customers lived in the less dilapidated Georgian houses in Bone Square, and took turns using them as ad hoc performance spaces. Delivering supplies of make-up, props, or whatever else they'd ordered was pretty much the most demanding part of my duties—physically, anyway.

Other than that, as the old man had said, I cooked, put down poison for the rats, and read to him. I'd been slightly afraid he'd try to take sexual advantage of me in some way, but thankfully he never did. He wouldn't use a chamber-pot or commode; that was one concession to his advancing years that he refused to make, so I had to help him out of bed—the only time I knew him leave it—and along the landing, while he gripped my arm in a steely arthritic claw. Thankfully, once in the bathroom, he never seemed to require my help. *Small mercies* was the phrase that sprang to mind. I've no idea what he did if Nature called between midnight and six a.m. Perhaps he just held it in.

I never saw the mysterious Patrick—in fact, I was under orders not to disturb him under any circumstances. I might have thought him dead, except for the occasional sounds of movement coming from behind his locked door. I was also banned from the room with the wooden boxes; that only made me more curious to inspect them, but while Mr. Hadrian's eyesight was failing, his hearing was almost bat-like; even with his bedroom door closed he'd hear the tiniest creak of a floorboard from the box-room.

I lived at the Station Hotel, but saw very little of anyone there; I was usually exhausted, collapsing straight into bed when I entered my room, and in any case, people tended to avoid me, with one very welcome exception. Occasionally, as a change from tinned soup and Pot Noodle, I'd spend some of my wages at Ahmed's Kebab House of Death, which had opened about a fortnight after I started working for Mr. Hadrian. I'd always liked '80s Goth music and the giant, bearded Iranian guy behind the counter played it from the speakers non-stop, all while wearing a black velvet shirt, wide-brimmed hat and guy-liner. Although a forbidding sight at first, he was a gentle and good-humoured man. And his chicken shawarma was truly epic.

"You look tired, my friend," Ahmed told me one night.

"Long hours," I said.

"I work long hours, too," he said. "My own business, and only me to run it."

"Well, if you need someone to help out..."

"Believe me, if I could afford it..." He glanced in the direction of Number Twelve. "Rather than you working there. I wouldn't do that to my worst enemy."

"I just appreciate seeing a friendly face, to be honest," I told him. "Everyone else around here..."

"Try not to take it personally, my friend. It's not about you. It's *him.* I don't know exactly what it is. I'm not sure there's anything—what's the word?—concrete. People just...don't like him."

I nodded wearily.

"Take my advice," said Ahmed, "and get out of there as soon as you can. I'll let you know if I hear of anything."

BUT I HADN'T the energy to look for anything new, and wouldn't have impressed any potential employers who'd seen me, either. I'd grown thin and grey-faced from the long hours and the foetid atmosphere of the place; by the time I'd been there a month, any hope of leaving Mr. Hadrian's orbit was a vague one, the kind that might be realised one bright day in the far, never-neverland future, like Heaven.

The one bright spot in my day was reading to the old man, as I could sit down and do something I actually enjoyed. Mr. Hadrian would have me pick half a dozen paperback story collections from the bookcase and lay them on the bed beside him. His finger would move from book to book as he murmured to himself, before finally selecting the day's text.

Unfortunately, Mr. Hadrian often chose to tell *me* stories instead, mostly about his glory days in music-hall. If I could've just let his droning monologues wash over me that would have been bearable, but he expected you to pay attention and provide a constant chorus of admiring "oohs" and "aahs."

"I worked with them all," he told me one evening. "Little Tich, Marie Lloyd..." he indicated a playbill where his name, indeed, appeared with theirs, and not far below them either. "I was due to play The Revue at the Tivoli with them in '02." When I failed to look suitably impressed, he added "To celebrate the King's Coronation. Ah, *that* would have been a spectacle."

"What happened?" I said.

"That's by-the-by," he said. "But I do regret His Majesty never got to see the Hadrian Hornpipe."

I must have looked puzzled, because he was quick to expand on the topic "It was my signature piece," he said. "Tich had his Big-Boot Dance. Lloyd had 'My Old Man Said Follow the Van.' I had the Hadrian Hornpipe. We'd all come on in sailor suits and dance to the Trumpet Hornpipe, faster and faster until it all turned to chaos." He whistled a few bars of the tune, which I recognised as what we'd used to call the *Captain Pugwash* theme, then chuckled and sighed. "Always brought the house down. I was the greatest entertainer of my time, Mr. Van Geldern. Or any other—"

Almost as if in answer, a chorus of scratching, scuttling sounds erupted behind the wainscoting; a look of fury crossed his face, and he flung one of the books lying on his bed at the wall. "Damned rats!" He took a deep breath and composed himself again. "Put down more poison, Mr. Van Geldern."

"Yes, Mr. Hadrian."

"I meant *now*, Mr. Van Geldern. But put the books back first."

By the time I'd returned the books to their shelves, he'd subsided back into the cushions, nightcap pulled down over his eyes, which I knew by now meant he was taking one of his infrequent naps. I padded to the door; by then I knew which floorboards creaked and which didn't. Mr. Hadrian didn't stir, which, as I crept out onto the landing, gave me the idea of finally satisfying my curiosity about the box-room.

There were dozens of boxes, as I've said. At close quarters, I could see the brass plates on their lids more clearly; they were all inscribed *Property of J. Hadrian Esq, 14 Balaclava Square, London* in that familiar copperplate script. I guessed this had been where the Marvellous Marionettes had been stored when not in use. All had locks securing them, but only three or four were still shut; most of them had been forced open at some point. I remember thinking at the time there was something odd about that, but couldn't quite pinpoint what.

I'll admit I was curious to see the puppets themselves, which I'd only glimpsed in black-and-white photos, so I opened a box, only to find it empty. I tried several others in turn, but they were, too.

"Mr. Van Geldern!" snapped a voice from the bedroom. "Kindly leave that room, which you know you are not to enter. And lay down more poison for the rats immediately, as you were instructed."

As I left, I decided Mr. Hadrian must have sold most of his beloved puppets over the years. It would explain why he kept the box-room off-limits: it contained his few remaining assets, not to mention being a painful and embarrassing reminder of his straitened circumstances. He'd probably lost the key to the boxes and had had to force them open, or get the mysterious Patrick to do so.

So why not just lock the door? But that was when I looked at it closely for the first time—it had been opened wide, flat against the wall, so I hadn't paid much attention to it previously. And I saw that where the door handle should have been, there was a ragged hole in the wood. As if it had been torn away. Maybe he'd lost that key too.

I GREW INCREASINGLY drained and exhausted over the ensuing fortnight, prompting more concerned comments from Ahmed whenever I went in for a shawarma. I didn't have the energy to exercise my curiosity; I only learned more about my employer by chance, when I made a delivery to Alfred Hennessy, a former actor who lived in one of the houses on Bone Square.

Like Mr. Hadrian, Hennessey lived surrounded by relics of his once-glorious past, including several photographs. He'd been handsome in his youth, but was now overweight and raddled, requiring large quantities of makeup and a regular supply of corsets to hold his girth in for performances. But he wasn't a bad sort. Just lonely and glad of company.

He'd always offered me a drink when I called on him—*a cup of tea or a little something stronger*, as he put it—and was touchingly happy when I accepted. Like Mr. Hadrian, he'd regale me with stories of his theatre days; unlike Mr. Hadrian, his stories were actually entertaining, as they didn't revolve around about how marvellous he'd been, but were full of hilariously indiscreet anecdotes about himself and other actors, famous and forgotten.

At one point, he took down a heavy tome from 1912, which turned out to be part of *Calladine's Almanac,* a sort of *Who's Who* of the great, good, and not-so-good of the entertainment scene, to show me his own entry there. It was a surprisingly long and complimentary one; by the sound of it his career had still been in full swing back then, before whatever had happened to lead him here.

Abruptly Hennessey got up, holding his stomach, and excused himself. I knew that meant he'd be spending the next ten minutes in the bathroom; it was only after he'd gone that it occurred to me that Mr. Hadrian might well be in *Calladine's Almanac* as well, and that this was even the very volume he should be listed in: HA to HE. If I wanted to know more about him, here it was on a plate.

I pulled my chair over to the occasional table where the *Almanac* lay and turned the book towards me. Calladine, whoever he was, had combined facts and salacious detail in equal measure, obviously hoping to appeal to both the serious historian and the sensationalist. The Edwardian entertainment scene had plenty of material for both, but John Hadrian, as it turned out, had provided far more scandal than any of his contemporaries. By the time Hennessey returned from the bathroom I'd put the book back as it was, and knew far more about John Hadrian, Esquire, than I'd ever wanted to.

I BROKE OFF at that point; all our glasses were empty. I poured Paul and myself a couple more *jonge jenevers*. Sadie, after a moment's hesitation, nodded when I indicated the port bottle.

"He hadn't lied about his career," I said, refilling her liqueur glass. "He'd been a big hit with his marionettes, and the famous

Hadrian Hornpipe. And he *was* booked to play the Revue at the Tivoli Theatre to celebrate Edward VII's Coronation in 1902. The part he'd left out was why he'd never kept that little engagement."

I sipped my drink; my throat felt very dry.

"About a fortnight before the Revue went on, a policeman found a naked child wandering in the street. She was in a pretty bad way—'mutilated,' according to *Calladine's Almanac*. They usually went into more detail, but that was all they said this time. Anyway, the child died shortly after they found her, but there was a pretty clear blood trail, which the police followed back to Balaclava Square."

"Number Fourteen," said Sadie. "Right?"

"Top of the class," I told her. "When they got there, they found another child, also dead and also 'mutilated,' plus evidence—again, the *Almanac* didn't say what—to link the house's occupants to a string of child disappearances over the past decade. The occupants themselves, John Hadrian and Patrick Sloane, his 'young male companion' had already bolted, and that was the last anyone ever saw of them. Except here, obviously."

I imagined them, as I had that evening, rushing through increasingly unfamiliar streets, possibly with Patrick Sloane tugging a handcart of some kind—how else could Hadrian have brought his puppets here with him, after all? Imagined Hadrian berating his luckless—lover? Servant? Brainwashed, terrorised dupe?—demanding he find the way to the docks and a ship to the Continent. Only for them to emerge, at long last, out from under the railway viaduct onto Bone Street.

"We've all got blood on our hands here, one way or another," I said. "But there are degrees. We all know that. And this was…"

"Worse than Ralph Brassland," said Paul, the first reference he'd made all night to the man he'd killed. I nodded.

"What did you do then?" said Sadie.

I shrugged. "I went back to the flat. I was on a kind of autopilot, I suppose. Like a trance. Numb. That's the part that frightens me most. Ahmed was right; that place was killing me. I don't know how much longer I'd have lasted."

"Were you planning to kill *him*?" said Paul.

I shook my head. "I already knew the Law. If I killed him, I'd have to leave, and that meant—" I stopped; we all knew what that meant.

"Meat for the Closers," said Paul, very quietly.

"I didn't know what I was going to do until I let myself into the flat," I said. "Then, suddenly, I did. I decided to talk to Patrick."

I'D COME TO PICTURE Patrick Sloane as utterly in thrall to Hadrian, quite possibly as abused and victimised in his way as the murdered children had been in theirs; someone I could at least get information from, and might even be able to recruit as an ally of sorts.

Silly, I knew: he was likely as bad as the old man if not worse. But the thought of confronting John Hadrian directly in any way, however frail and bed-bound he might be, was terrifying, which gives some idea of how reduced I'd become over the preceding weeks. Still, I had to do something, and Patrick was the softer option.

I heard Hadrian snoring as I climbed the stairs. He dozed from time to time during the day, as I've said, but only snored when fast asleep—and in that state, almost nothing would wake him. I couldn't have asked for a better opportunity to get into the locked room.

I heard the rats scratching and scurrying inside the walls and under the floors when I reached the landing, but they stopped as I tiptoed into the main bedroom. Mr. Hadrian snored on, oblivious; I scooped up the keys he kept on his bedside table and tiptoed out again.

I tried them, one by one, on Patrick's door; on the third attempt the lock clicked. I glanced back down the landing to ensure the old man was still asleep, then opened the door and went in.

Patrick's room was even barer than Mr. Hadrian's. A bed, a chair, and a desk; the only other items in the room were a scatter of small objects on the floor around the chair, and Patrick himself.

He sat in the chair, not quite facing me. His head was up, his glassy eyes open, but he'd been opened up from throat to groin, and was very plainly dead.

Or so I thought; it wasn't till I came closer that I realised Patrick Sloane had never really been alive at all.

Parts of him had. Close to, I could see the tiny delicate stitches with which John Hadrian had collaged the pieces of several children into something resembling a young man. The skin was hard and shiny, but I could clearly make out its grain, the tiny hairs, even moles and birthmarks. It no longer quite looked like flesh, but didn't look like wood or china either.

Inside he was hollow. A shell of bones and skin. The empty space inside was filled with machinery: rods, pistons, cogs. But the parts weren't metal. They were pale yellow-white in colour. Ivory-white, like bone.

Some of the items on the floor were tools of one kind or another. The rest were parts from inside Patrick. One, a ball of dark leathery material that I couldn't bring myself to touch, I eventually realised was a mummified child's heart. Either that had perished, leaving Mr. Hadrian unable to source a replacement without condemning himself to expulsion, or age had robbed him of the skills required to repair his servitor.

Either way, from the dust filming Patrick's skin and eyes, he clearly hadn't moved in weeks, which raised the question of what I *had* heard moving inside the room.

As if in answer, the scratching sounds—the rats?—suddenly burst into life, under my feet and in the walls all around me. And then they moved—*rushed,* in a surge, away from me and down the landing, towards John Hadran's room.

"What?" He shouted, suddenly awake. Then: "Van Geldern!"

Almost by reflex, I stepped back out of the room. Mr. Hadrian sat bolt upright in bed, glaring at me down the landing. The second he'd woken up he'd realised his keys were missing and knew what that meant. But it hadn't been me who'd woken him.

He fixed me with his eyes; as if hypnotised, I found myself moving towards him. As I drew level with the box-room, he opened his mouth to speak. I've no idea what might have come next, but then a loud, sharp crash sounded from his room. And it was a sound I recognised from my Army days, though it was thinner and tinnier and muffled by the floor and walls. It was the sound of dozens of booted feet crashing to attention.

The next thing I heard was a thin, fluting sound; a single note, whistled by dozens of mouths.

Rats, of course, neither stand to attention nor whistle, and they certainly can't carry a tune.

The tune in question was being whistled very slowly and deliberately, with none of its usual jauntiness. I wouldn't have thought it possible for the Trumpet Hornpipe—the *Captain Pugwash* theme of my childhood—to sound menacing, but it did. Especially when those tiny, booted feet crashed again, and then again, as if beating out a slow yet martial accompanying rhythm.

Mr. Hadrian's lips were white. His eyes darted back and forth, like a trapped animal's.

I looked into the box-room, finally realising what had seemed strange about the broken locks on the marionette boxes. The wood had been punched out, driving the lockworks from their housing—but from the inside of the boxes. And as I looked into the room, I saw that every single box now, at last, stood open.

The Hornpipe speeded up, and the stamping of their feet for their grand finale.

"Ingrates!" shouted Mr. Hadrian, as the tempo accelerated. "I made you immortal! I gave you eternity, you—"

He broke off, snarling and shaking his head, then glared at me again. "Well, *help* me!" he shouted.

The Hornpipe broke off instantly, and the dancing feet fell silent.

Mr. Hadrian stared at me, and I stared back at him.

Still held by his gaze, I moved forward to the bedroom door, and extended a hand. Then I grabbed the handle, pulled the door shut and locked it, and ran down the stairs as the Hornpipe started up again.

As I slammed the front door behind me, I heard him start to scream.

"I WONDERED AFTERWARDS if what I'd done counted as killing him," I told Paul and Sadie. "I was afraid, the next day, in case..." I trailed off, unable to meet Paul's eyes. "But nothing happened. He was a dead man, whatever I did or didn't do. If I *had* tried to help him, they'd have dealt with me too. But instead, I shut the door. I cut myself loose." I said it again, needing to believe it. "I cut *myself* loose."

"What happened to...them?" asked Sadie.

"Ahmed helped me board up the front door and the flat's windows the day after," I said. "People gave the shop a wide berth. If you stood close enough, apparently, you could still hear things for months afterwards. But no one's heard anything in a long time now."

"You think they're dead?" said Paul.

"I'm not even sure they were alive. But I'd hope so. But maybe they're just resting, like actors do when they're between jobs. Would you really want to take the chance?"

"I suppose not," said Paul Manktelow, smiling sadly.

"Well then," I said, and reached for the *jenever* bottle. "Another drink?"

Simon Bestwick is the author of eight novels, five novellas, and four full-length short story collections. His short fiction has appeared in Shakespeare Unleashed *and* ParSec Magazine *and been reprinted in* The Best Horror of The Year. *His novel* The Hollows, *as by "Daniel Church," was shortlisted for the 2023 British Fantasy Award for Best Horror Novel, his fifth nomination in all. His second Daniel Church novel,* The Ravening, *was published in September 2024. He lives on the Wirral with fellow author Cate Gardner and loves dogs, tea, and Pepsi Max. He also likes semicolons, to the dismay of editors everywhere. Lots of semicolons.*

ROCKET SCIENCE BOOKS

BLACK
Infinity ❾ FIRST
CONTACT

GEORGE PAL'S
THE WAR OF THE WORLDS

THE ORIGINAL
BATTLESTAR GALACTICA

RAY BRADBURY
MURRAY LEINSTER
ROBERT SILVERBERG
VONNIE WINSLOW CRIST
JAMES DORR • JEROME BIXBY
LEIGH BRACKETT • DAMON KNIGHT
JUSTIN HUMPHREYS • DOUGLAS SMITH
GREGORY L. NORRIS • JASON J. McCUISTON

V. DI FATE

NOT WANTED ON VOYAGE

BY STEPHEN VOLK

INEVITABLY, IN THE COURSE OF A PURSUIT AS UNUSUAL AS MINE, ONE IS ASKED QUESTIONS. Which is the most tragic ghost you have come across? To that I would have to answer, Mad Kate, the asylum girl wandering Chesil Beach *post mortem*, searching for her lost love. The most annoyingly persistent? I'd say Larraby Louth, burnt at the stake at a crossroads by Cromwell, and subsequently responsible for the restless sleep of many a guest of the Strabane Inn. The prize for the most perplexing would have to go to the eerie case of a pair of pince-nez through which a certain lady could, seemingly, look into the past, the facts of which only grow more fantastical with each telling. It hast to be said, these recollections were not easily drawn out of me. I tended to keep my private investigations close to my chest, not least because they often attracted a degree of pompous ridicule by those who presumed they knew better, in spite of having no knowledge or experience of the subject. On rare occasions, however, I shared them.

And so it was, at the captain's table one evening on board the *SS Arturus*, shortly after we had left the Aegean Islands on the return leg of our Mediterranean cruise, a vast indulgence for one of my insalubrious means, but thought to be a necessity after the nervous attack brought upon by my most recent case: one I do not, at present, feel the physical or moral strength to commit to paper. Mine was a medical crisis which, my doctor advised, could only be alleviated by the rest-cure of a sea voyage. And the air and sun had done its work. Or so I thought. I had no idea that the journey would provide me with one of the most startling and horrific encounters I have witnessed. If I witnessed it at all.

Thus I sat, over summer pudding drenched in cream, having been winkled out of my shell. The others had, by and large, talked of their jobs or wealth and the achievements of their sons and daughters, discourse presently thinning out to pastimes and hobbies. I gave mine, and was gratified that it elicited some raised eyebrows of genuine interest.

"You believe in ghosts, then?" asked Mrs. Faffenforth, a plump lady with an expensive necklace adorning her chest, as her husband's mayoral chain adorned his.

I gave my standard reply:

"First define your terms."

I pointed out I had no particular proof of an afterlife, Christian or otherwise. I did, however, believe that ordinary people had extraordinary experiences. Albeit, I said, that some such events, though utterly real to them, might nevertheless be largely a construct of the mind, especially under extreme pressure.

"Or extreme indulgence," said Mr. Faffenforth, lifting his port to his lips and tapping the glass with his fingers.

"Chemicals have their place," I said. "Are we all not constructions of chemicals when all is said and done?"

My remark was greeted with thoughtful laughter by all but one around the table. The man with his napkin tucked under his chin was looking at the dessert in front of him with something akin to disdain. Then I realized the disdain was aimed at me. He had not spoken all evening and now he did, in immaculate English with little or no trace of an accent, though we would soon find out he was Swedish.

"We know of chemicals, yes, but what is there we do not know? It is somewhat arrogant of the West to presume we are at the forefront of knowledge through the application of Science. But are there corners where Science fears to tread? Perhaps the ancient world with its gods and deities was closer to understanding the unknown forces of nature. Perhaps belief does not deceive the world but, rather, creates it."

"Bravo," I said. "I am all for a *perhaps*."

The others laughed, lightly, but the speaker himself did not, and covered his glass when Mr. Faffenforth threatened to refill it.

"Professor Krøyer is an archaeologist," said the captain. "He has just returned from an important dig in central Iraq."

"Eighty-five miles south of Baghdad."

"Where's that?" said Lady Hey. "Iraq, I mean."

"Don't worry." Her husband grinned. "I can show you on the map, dear heart, and it's all red. Part of the British Empire, fear not!"

"Quite so." Having been mute, the archaeologist now spoke with a quiet, if reluctant, authority. "When the British established the Hashemite king, the official English name of the country changed from Mesopotamia to Iraq. I've been interested in the land going back to the Lower Paleolithic, up to and not excluding the Caliphate in the late 7th century. It's an inexhaustible subject—historically, geographically. A great tangle of empires. Northern Mesopotamia became Assyria. Southern Mesopotamia became Babylon."

"As in the Bible?" piped up Lady Hey.

"Yes and no."

"The cradle of civilisation," I posited.

"If you can credit it with that," said the Swede.

The dinner guests proved united in wanting him to tell us more about his expedition, and, more through embarrassment than enthusiasm, he indulged us. In retrospect, from the comfort of my desk back in England, I now wish he had not.

"Taking the route established by our previous trips, I disembarked at Alexandria in the company of my sponsor and old friend Lord Tellisford, who had largely been the one responsible for ensuring us being jointly funded by the British Museum and the University of Pennsylvania Museum of

Archaeology and Anthropology, Philadelphia. The Americans, again, were present in the form of Whitney Hogan and his wife Amelia, who had drawn a detailed design of site RT50 on our first visit. I'm the custodian charged with getting the booty back home in one piece. Some went ahead with the coffin, for the sake of the family, to avoid delays, but I'll explain as I go along."

"Coffin?" I said. "You mean sarcophagus?"

"No. The sarcophagus is below. In the hold."

Mr. Faffenforth paused in lighting his cigar. "I read of Lord Tellisford's unfortunate death in *The Times*."

"You will not have read everything," said the archaeologist flatly, replenishing his water glass.

"Untimely."

Krøyer chose not to respond to that word. Replete as it was with suggestion.

"At Cairo we congregated with the rest of our colleagues, Doctors Valentine Bullen and Oscar Hamidi, our fixer Abdul Sharrukin and a translator, 'Hoss' Hossaini. The High Commissioner, Sir George Lloyd, guaranteed us safe passage and provided a few rifles to see us through rockier political terrain as we took the Ottoman rail system via Halep and Mosel to Hillah, where the possibility of unearthing a new tomb excited us immensely. So much so that Charlie—that is, Lord Tellisford—told me to 'keep a lid on it.' I don't think he wanted it to be common knowledge we might have the find of the decade, if not the century. Personally, sitting on my hands since we last turned over sand in the area had proven unbearable and I couldn't wait to feel the desert sun on the back of my neck."

"Did you know at that stage you were at the location of something important?" asked Mr. Faffenforth. "Or was it a case of hit or miss?"

"There were particular indications or clues. We had uncovered an enormous winged bull with the head broken off. These *lamassu* are Assyrian protective deities, similar to Chinese lions of Fo. Typically in pairs and invariably outside prominent sites, such as the palace at Nimrud, intended to exude power. Carved in situ from a single stone, it certainly exuded power to us. But, more importantly, was the discovery of a 'death pit' of some 67 attendants—the skeletons or part-skeletons of six men and sixty-one women—"

"Good gracious," exclaimed Mrs. Faffenforth, clutching the jewels at her throat.

"Undoubtedly servants, priests, soldiers. It could only mean they were intended to escort a king or queen into the afterlife. There was every indication they would have poisoned themselves or poisoned each other."

"Dear me," said Sir Nicholas Hey. "Is this a subject suitable for ladies?"

"Of course it is," said his wife. "Carry on Mr. Krøyer, if you please. And less of the interruptions, Nicky, if you don't mind."

"One compartment of the underground complex was particularly well-preserved and contained outstandingly high quality grave goods. A superb lyre with a gold bulls-head. Fluted goblets. A black stone sculpture redolent of the findings at Ur. Terence Oh, a Ph.D. candidate from Boston, detected cinnabar—mercury vapour—used to slow down decomposition during funerary practices, indicating this was indeed the tomb of someone special. But who?"

"Who indeed?" I interjected. "Sorry."

"The previous year we had found dozens of pieces of Iraqi glass, as well as over thirty cuneiform tablets which Hogan and Charlie unravelled as the story of Gilgamesh—half man, half god—but, most intriguingly, it read: *'Here another similar rests.'* Whatever were we to make of that? Only that several cylinder seals identified her as *nin* (meaning lady) and *erash* (the Sumerian word for queen). In Layard's treasure trove of bas-reliefs and clay tablets from the palace of Sennacherib we knew there were references to the burial place of Annunitum—also called Ishtar—but was it a person or goddess? A Temple of Ishtar had been excavated at Nineveh, but a tomb? The prospect was dizzying.

"We were reverent but meticulous, in that every person had a well appointed task. A representative of the Geographical Society, Mr. Lillistone, was in 'Alex', so we had to wait for him to arrive. The main thing was to exclude the curious and news-seekers. And to do everything to encompass preservation of artefacts. Breakages were common and to be avoided at all costs. M. Capon from Lille broke a ceramic vase on a previous expedition. He was not invited again.

"Mr. Lillistone cabled to say it was imperative to be present at opening, and that he was arriving on May 10th; 'Hoping no inconvenience, etc.' (which it was). The laboratory, magazine, and facilities being in order, we unpacked all materials, scientific equipment was fully tested. To start without the appliances in order would be foolhardy. We were reminded at every turn that in the desert day-to-day conveniences were arduous, tedious, and required pre-planning. This was not Europe. I instructed our translator to tell our labourers we intended to re-enter the tomb on Saturday 10th. Mr. Lillistone arrived by motor car, which caused some delight. Bright smiles all round.

"In the space of a day the carriers had uncovered the tomb entrance, which had been filled when we left it. The next day we opened the tomb by removing the watertight timbers we put in place the previous spring. A screen door led to a wooden door of passage, we removed the steel gate to the Ante-Room and Burial Chamber, which had a Union Jack flag pinned to it by some wag.

"A black blanket covered the sarcophagus, just as we'd left it. Small pieces of plaster had fallen from ceiling. Our lamps shone sufficiently, illuminating traces of slug like trails and a few wriggling fish-like insects we knew intimately from our tents and washrooms. The 2,000 candlepower electric lamps over the sarcophagus were turned on. Myself and Lord Tellisford removed the ground sheet, revealing the great gold incised block, which seemed even more striking than our first glimpse a twelve-month earlier.

"I crossed myself, nonsensically. Given that my own faith had nothing to do with that of the deceased occupant. Mr. Lillistone was present, as was Dr. Bullen and Dr. Hamidi. We had been screaming at the workmen for a week, but now they, and we, fell silent.

"We removed the sarcophagus and prepared to open the lid of the coffin within. We decided the handles were well preserved enough to do their job. Using leather strips all around (later calling ourselves 'reverse pallbearers') we lifted it out and placed it on a stretcher connected to a hoist and pulley system.

"Once it was in the tent, we removed the coffin lid, which broke only slightly at the nail-points. A humanoid shape revealed itself. We removed floral garlands, now decayed to the point of being unrecognizable. So brittle that our mere touch caused them to disintegrate. The face was masked with a headdress of gold feathers. It wore heavy gold earrings, a plated necklace. Gemstones scattered in the coffin like confetti. Amelia took photographic records before we proceeded. The coffin showed a degree of swelling due to humidity. I doubted it would last any sort of journey intact. Dr. Bullen commenced on the preservation work for the lid. I rolled back the covering shroud. A delicate operation. Due to its fragile nature, we could not remove the mummy from the coffin without risking considerable damage, so the examination had to take place in situ.

"At the end of each day we returned the coffin to the sarcophagus and the sarcophagus to the tomb. It was easier to protect that way. We still had the riflemen donated to us in Cairo. Tomb robbers are rare, but there was no reason to be lax. I had enough to worry about with the problem of transporting a sarcophagus that took eight men to lift. In a rare moment of conjecture, I calculated the worth of that pure bullion and shuddered when I considered the toil and pain of the stone workers, peasants, and water carriers who had worked on the creation of the tomb. Let alone those who had died for it. Willingly.

"The work was laborious. Layer by layer. Dr. Hamidi made a longitudinal incision down the centre of the wrappings, but even peeling away the outer layers it was still impossible to extract the mummy from the coffin. We could only get close to knowing the incumbent by the gifts, figurines, and amulets left in the tomb, gold furniture, bas-reliefs, an alabaster box of ointment of spikenard, all painting a vivid picture of devotion and supplication. We did not dare remove the mask with its eyes of argonite and could only look down upon the childlike body swathed in linen darkened by some ritual libation. A golden rope lay on her stomach like a coiled umbilicus, next to a scroll of high office inscribed with the face of a lioness and inlaid gold bands which bore texts edged with beads: *In the company of greatness.*

"At that moment I shed all doubt. I shared with camp my conviction that the body was indeed that of Ishtar. But Ishtar was the name of a goddess, came the reply. 'Meddling with something of a deity, eh?' Whit Hogan said with a large grin. I didn't find such irreverence funny. I am sure it was only his bombastic American sense of humour, but I wondered how he would feel if his own God had been joked about as 'something of a deity'?

"Irrespective of that, I had become aware that, as we celebrated our historic find, the workers had become twitchy, a sense of their past having been breached being something of a double-edged sword. Kings and queens of the past still being kings and queens, to their eyes, even as they counted their wages and took gainful employment from unbelievers.

"Our team would sometimes talk of ancient religion over thick black coffee. Whit Hogan was a 'We turn to dust' sort of person. 'When our soul departs what is left is no more sentient than the leaves in this pipe.' Nevertheless, from the very day we brought the mummy up into sunlight, every one of his wife's photographs had emerged fogged. We had no explanation for why that should be. But we had other concerns.

"Over days, not hours, we strove to remove the external trappings, which were semi-deteriorated due to the holy wood-pitch oil used in embalming. We prayed it would be in better condition nearer the corpse. Sometimes we reached a level so rotted it had to be cut away. It was extremely strange to have tiny fragments of dust or dirt on one's hands or sleeve which last saw the light of day hundreds of years before the birth of Christ.

"Meanwhile Hogan and Hossaini were beavering away with wooden trays and props, making sure the tomb ceiling didn't collapse before we were finished, while humidity, in spite of our best efforts, was getting worse. It was they, paradoxically, who found an opening into a rock-cut corridor, little more than a tunnel, with the warning: *Beware the Gatekeeper of the underworld.*

"'Always good advice,' said Whit, cheerfully.

"We had a final tally of over three hundred objects which would be cleaned and restored in London. Blistering in the heat, we envied the more congenial work that would face those curators in the British Museum who would place them in glass boxes for the gawking eyes of the public. But these things were magnificent, and if our work was for nothing but that end, it was no bad thing, as I saw it.

"Lest you think it was all drudgery, that was far from the case. We formed friendships. Cast iron ones. We celebrated birthdays, lit candles and blew them out. Had sing-songs around the campfire—English, Swedish, American—and cultivated an air of normality where we could. The work was never morbid. Not morbid, that is, until we were visited by death."

It's true to say that a dreadful pall fell over the table.

"Please," said the captain. "Please don't feel you have to continue, if—"

"No," said Krøyer. "I do have to continue."

"We all know that Lord Tellisford died."

"You do, but you do not."

"Captain," said Lady Hey, "We owe the man to finish his story in the way he feels fit."

"Story?" said Krøyer with mild but pained amusement. "Story. Indeed." His lips tightened and he chose not to meet our eyes as he spoke. "It was said that the cause was illness. He caught an infection. Perhaps from water. Perhaps from one of the dreaded insects. Or snails. He was a strong man. A fit man. I saw him playing rugby and riding his cherished foxhunter like a man twenty years his junior. At RT50 I watched a fever breaking on his brow. I heard him ranting about poison in his veins. The local men started gossiping the instant they heard of his sickness. He had touched the gold umbilical. What had we all touched or not touched?"

I felt decidedly uncomfortable as the man looked increasingly ill at ease. His own brow glistened, but the whites of his eyes remained the colour of dirty dishwater, and his voice took on a disturbing tremor.

"On the third night I could not stand his raving any longer. He sounded in physical pain. The piercing shrieks denied me sleep. In anger and distress I ran to his tent, half to slap a wet flannel on his forehead, half to strangle him. To my horror I found him with cuts over his hands, as if he had defended himself against some assailant. He was gibbering. It was a pitiful sight. Nobody was in the tent but he and I. Not even a shadow. The flaps had been tied from the inside. Dr. Hamidi said the beat of his heart was racing. He suspected a stroke and predicted another might be imminent. We had to get him to the nearest hospital. None of the local men would drive him. Whitney Hogan leapt behind the wheel but the car would not start. According to Hoss, our carriers were saying an evil spirit was responsible for the failure of the engine. I told him to shut up. A sandstorm rose and all dispersed except for my most intimate colleagues. Within ten minutes Charlie endured another spasm and died in my arms."

None of the dinner guests could speak. Nor could I. The archaeologist raised his coffee cup to his lips but barely sipped it.

"One Iraqi said he had seen a demon, part cat, part man, part donkey. I punched him on the chin. The Chief Inspector of the district told me that had been foolish and we would be wise to leave before hostilities erupted. I had no wish to do otherwise. We hastily catalogued what we had removed, and departed. The thorax of the mummy was bared to the skin. I removed the collarette from its throat. By then even the most loyal of workers would not come near it. The rest of the torso would have to be examined in London. With his last words, my dear friend had made me promise to get the treasures to England. I was glad to oblige.

And glad to bid the Royal Necropolis farewell."

"Hear, hear," I murmured. A sickly feeling had permeated my body which I don't think was related to the undercooked beef we'd eaten earlier. "You'd lost your friend, and it is entirely understandable that you might feel the country and its superstitions responsible."

"To Lord Tellisford, poor fellow." Mr. Faffenforth raised his bubble of brandy. A couple of the others raised their own glasses half-heartily. The archaeologist did not. Mr. Faffenforth pointed to the floor. "So his body is, am I right in thinking...?"

Krøyer shook his head.

"The Americans accompanied the coffin by rail. Charlie's daughter was working in Istanbul for the Foreign Office and wished to accompany her father home. I volunteered to journey by sea. Penning the telegram had been agony enough. Now I have to return and face his widow. And though I shall tell her the truth, I shall not tell her the whole truth." He set about arranging his cutlery meticulously. "I shall not tell her of that very last night I spent in the desert, when a shadow circled my tent, and I was not entirely certain it was a man."

My sickly feeling was accompanied by a throbbing headache at the back and front of my skull. My ears felt blocked and my vision was blurred. But not so blurred that I could not make out the storyteller's eyes were fixed on me.

"So, Mr. Venables," He said, taking off his napkin and dabbing the sides of his mouth as he rose to his feet. "Forgive me if I do not see the entertainment in ghost stories. Ladies. Gentlemen. Goodnight, and sleep well."

"Well, really." Mrs. Faffenforth appeared startled by his sudden exit.

"Dash it all." Her husband was more aghast at the Swede's rudeness.

Sir Nicholas stroked his moustache in lieu of any opinion at all, and Dotty Attwood's Aberdeen All-Stars struck up a spirited rendition of "Lilac Lover Boy" in the dance hall.

"Do excuse me, all," I said, hastily following Krøyer and catching up with him at the stairwell leading down to the second-class cabins. He did not slow down when he heard my footfall behind him.

"I say, Krøyer." He did stop and look down at my hand on his elbow when I placed it there. "Look, I'm sorry if, well…what I said in any way offended."

"It didn't," he replied stiffly. "Not in the slightest, I assure you. I shall just be glad to get back to England and civilization, that's all."

"Listen, I understand the impact of such…experiences. I really do. The superstition of a tightly-knit community can be contagious. That's one thing I know about superstition. You mustn't let it—"

"I'm very glad for your wisdom." He slowly removed my hand from his sleeve. "I hope it keeps you warm at night. Now, excuse me."

Without much choice in the matter, I did.

THAT NIGHT the seas churned around me and the previously becalmed seas in my head churned also. The tale told over dinner had intrigued and, yes, finally disturbed me somewhat—but no more, I told myself, than many an anecdote I had heard over the years. I was unsure why it unsettled me so. Perhaps that was the very reason. It was a reminder of the dozens of stories I had compiled, the horde of unearthly beings that weighed down upon us in our daily lives, whose maws and moans seemed an endless reason to forego sleep in favour of waking terror, in a cabin where I could barely stretch from one side to the other, where the creaking of the hull and woodwork proved to be a constant lullaby, and the blind barely covered the porthole which separated me from black and ghastly depths. Consequently, my eyes had no intention of closing.

A knock on the door made me consult my watch. It read 2 a.m. Beastly hour. My imagination, surely? But no. I heard it again.

"Yes. Who is it?"

I opened the door to find Krøyer standing there in a silk dressing gown, his braces dangling and his shirt collar missing, greyish bags under eyes like the small coals used in the face of a snowman.

"Can't sleep."

"Ditto," I said.

"Care to join me in a snifter?" He tantalizingly produced a bottle of Johnnie Walker Red Label from behind his back. Most of it was gone, but the allure of a pure single malt was irresistible. "You'll have a little glass for your toothbrush. I've brought mine."

Minutes later we were sitting side by side on my bed watching our glasses fill and seeing the surface of the amber liquid tilt with the movement of the ship. I had no time for "bottoms up" or "down the hatch" before my uninvited guest had emptied his receptacle and refilled it. To the brim.

He began talking about the dig, not requiring any contribution on my part and not really adding much information or detail to what I'd already heard. Almost completely repetition for repetition's sake, as if something different might catch or emerge or break through and make a difference, suddenly making everything clear. He rubbed his runny nose in his cuff and took out a stereoscopic viewer into which he slotted a number of photographs of the dig which had been taken by Amelia Hogan. Her name was written on the tiny labels glued to the corners of each slide. I held the contraption to my eyes and saw a smiling Lord Tellisford wearing puttees and a kepi, standing next to Krøyer in his white suit and pith helmet. The images of the coffin on the bier were clear enough, but the mummy itself, once the lid was removed, was indistinct, the chemical in the development process rendering it smoky, as if a storm cloud had descended.

"It doesn't convey the place," Krøyer said inconsequentially, then: "I thought you, for one. Might believe me." Which was a far cry from what he'd said at dinner. The whisky seemed to have opened him up into quite a different person than he was in company, and I felt both privileged and sorry for the burden he carried.

"You have suffered a great psychic wound," I suggested. "And, not unnaturally, you are looking for meaning. But sometimes a death is just happenchance. There is no meaning or reason."

His eyes were dead and dry.

Eyeing my Scotch, he said: "Are you going to finish that?"

I shook my head.

He helped himself and knocked it back in one.

I said: "Think of what it'll be like when you get to London. It'll be all over the newspapers. It's a great national triumph. I know you'll have wanted your friend to be with you, but he'll have wanted you to enjoy it. You'll be fêted for what riches you have brought with you."

I squeezed Krøyer's knee and shook it, but he didn't seem to want to wake up from his dark thoughts.

"It's not what I've brought with me," he said. "It's what has come with it."

THE NEXT MORNING the Mediterranean sun shone brightly, as if punishing us for our indulgence. The Johnnie Walker had done the trick in my case, and as soon as Krøyer had left my cabin and my head had hit the pillow, I was out like a light. As I strolled the deck under the nattering of sea birds, and I told myself to be careful it didn't become a despicable habit. I was certain my doctor, who was a teetotaler and Quaker, would not approve.

The choice for breakfast was ludicrously profligate. I do not know anyone who could face mutton or kidneys and bacon at such an early hour, or soda and sultana scones for that matter, but they were on offer, and many tucked in with abandon. They had booked for luxury and were determined to get every ounce of it every step of the way. I couldn't even face the lurid-looking kippers and made do with dry toast. Even that was an effort. But if I was a little shaky, it was nothing compared to the archaeologist, who looked distinctly green around the gills.

The other chaps at the table were lively enough, animatedly comparing their golf handicaps, and I tried not to glaze over, whilst Krøyer sat with his hands supporting his chin or cradling his forehead as a startling picture of abject melancholy. When somebody vacated the seat next to him I moved over.

"Hair of the dog?"

"I can take my drink, thank you."

A solitary trickle was running down from his forehead to his cheek and his skin was paper-white. I said he didn't look well and he apologized for that with a tone of great sarcasm. I suggested if he was sickening for something he should see the onboard doctor. He said he had. He'd complained of gut-rot and sweats soon after we'd left port. The quack had given him powders but it hadn't made much difference.

"I know that feeling."

"He put it down to foreign climes. Told me to eat light and lay off the alcohol. Ha, the alcohol! The alcohol is all that keeps me..."

He didn't complete the sentence.

I asked if he wanted to talk about it.

"No, damn it. I don't want to talk about any of it. What on earth good does talking do? I just want to be done with it."

He had raised his voice considerably and a number of other passengers were looking up horrified from their poached eggs and kedgeree, the perfect illusion of civilized society having been disrupted. I became aware that Krøyer was not only shaking but actually sobbing.

"Go. Leave me. Go, please. There's nothing you can do. Please."

As he attempted to brush me aside, he happened to sweep a fork from his place setting onto the floor, where it clattered. He bent over to pick it up.

I looked down and saw his fingers grip the utensil, but they were trembling exceptionally. Unnaturally. So unnaturally that my throat tightened.

Krøyer was utterly frozen in position, apparently staring at something under the table. I placed a hand on his back but he immediately crabbed away on all fours, almost hitting the occupants of the table behind me and tripping up a waiter. Quickly realizing the stares he was attracting from every direction, he shot to his feet, eyelids pulled back.

I REACHED THE gentlemen's washroom, where I found him with his head under the tap, towels scattered, water cascading, a lake spreading across the chess board tiles under foot.

"What did you see? Krøyer! What in God's name did you see, man?"

"Nothing!"

"Tell me."

"Tell you? Why on earth should I—?"

"Please."

"All right! All right!"

He lapsed into a coughing fit, supporting himself against the sink with straightened arms and head bowed, almost as if afraid to look at his own reflection.

"An…an old lady's foot. That's what it was. That's what it *should* have been, poking out from under the hem of her dress—but it wasn't. *It wasn't!* It was deformed, I tell you. It was huge and bent and gnarled, with these yellow…" The coughing turning into a spluttering wheeze, he formed one hand into a crooked claw, every finger bent into a hook. "It was the talon of an eagle."

"What? What do you mean? What lady?"

"The old lady. The old lady with a halo of white hair."

The residue of Johnnie Walker curdled in my stomach.

"There was no such lady," I said. "Not at our table. I swear. Come back if you don't believe me. You're having some kind of—"

"*Don't!* I know what I saw!" He pawed my hand off him. He was sobbing again and I felt dreadful.

"Look, if you're taking medicine, if you're suffering from some kind of fever, this is an hallucination. I'm no expert, I'm no doctor, but the explanation is quite rational."

"I need to get to land. It'll be all right if I get to land." The archaeologist shivered as water dripped down his face onto his shoulders. "I just need to get off this ship."

The very thing that, it transpired, would be utterly impossible.

AT NOON THAT DAY, the intercom system asked all passengers—many of whom were settling down to lunch—to gather in the dance hall, where Captain Shawcross made an announcement at the microphone usually reserved for crooners and band leaders supplying the evening's entertainment. We could see immediately from his expression this was not entertainment.

He announced we would not be docking at the quay in Venice today as per the schedule. A number of the crew had been put in isolation, along with their roommates, as a precaution, after reporting the symptoms of a stomach-related illness. Erring on the side of caution, as his duty bade him, the captain instructed us to minimize contact with other passengers while tests were undertaken. We were, in effect, in a state of quarantine. He urged us to report any symptoms such as vomiting or diarrhea. We were told to wash our hands thoroughly before and after handling food. We should drink only bottled water whilst the source of any suspected infection was investigated. We should restrict our movements and remain in our cabins wherever possible, and, if contact with other individuals was essential, we were instructed to maintain a distance of three feet. Meals would be delivered to our door and, for the time being, the dining room would be out of bounds. We would be informed of any changes, but for now, for our own safety and for the safe running of the ship, it would be appreciated if we obeyed these instructions to the letter. Thank you.

A hum circulated amongst the passengers as the captain left the stage. Cigarettes were lit and puffed. Some people laughed. The most haughty and devil-may-care brigade. Others looked seriously worried and absented themselves almost immediately. Sheets of paper were circulated by the purser, lest we forget any of the directives issued, but nobody needed reminding.

We were unable to land in Venice was the long and the short of it. On board there had been detected a suspected case of…what?

Within minutes some were saying there was nothing to worry about, it would blow over. Others assumed as a given that we were having the wool pulled over our eyes and there was more going on that the captain was willfully keeping from us.

"Such as?" I inquired.

"Yellow fever. Pneumonic plague. Cholera."

The industrialist George Faffenforth, who, to my knowledge, had no medical expertise but was clearly a doctor of philosophy in suspicion, peered over at the figure of Professor Krøyer, who was lurking—somewhat in isolation himself—near the door. At the very periphery of the captain's announcement, as if he didn't need to hear it.

I saw Sir Nicholas Hey stare off in the same direction, saying out of the corner of his mouth: "Cholera be damned."

UNSURPRISINGLY, talk of vomiting and diarrhea did nothing to make the joys of a Mediterranean cruise more pleasurable. On top of which I was not sure if it was that or the vestigial memory of my encounter with Krøyer in the washroom—and mention of the mysterious, non-existent woman with white hair—that made me feel tense and off-colour. People seeing things that I didn't tended to have that effect. But I knew it took little for me to succumb to my innate hypochondria and one reason for the holiday was to attempt to remove the sticky pain my body carried which had peaked as a feeling of unassailable dread. I told myself to buck up. I wasn't ill and wouldn't be. And nothing was inexplicable. To misquote Robbie Burns, all was right with the world, except for my thinking it otherwise.

The decks were swabbed and disinfected, possibly more to rid us of the foul smell that some believed to be the source of the disease. Opinions abounded, and passengers had begun to think nothing of being disruptive. The first casualty being their trust in the captain, which I thought ludicrous as anything other than a futile expression of their dissatisfaction. But the entitled classes were used to getting their way and did not like being told what to do when it didn't suit them. Tea and tiffin had to be at three o'clock and, by heavens, if it wasn't, a crack in the earth might open up and swallow us all, so some blighter had better account for it.

Not being born to that particular and boorish echelon of society, I kept my head down, venturing out only at dusk when I thought I might catch a glimpse of Krøyer and, hopefully, see that he was all right. The less I saw of him the more I feared such a presumption was not the case. I saw a

husband and wife playing badminton, and admired their ability to put the strictures of quarantine out of their minds while they enjoyed themselves. I wished I could do likewise, but of Professor Krøyer there was no sign and I was unable to relax.

BY THE FOLLOWING DAY, tempers were wearing thin and the natives were restless, to coin a phrase. The corridors were eerily deserted. I kept to the deck and kept my distance. Conversation which had been congenial was now sparce, even spiky. Men gathered in huddles conspiratorially, egging each other on with a shared disgruntlement.

"Who's responsible for this infection getting on board, anyway?"

"Not us. We're English."

"I'd put money on the archaeologist. He's a foreigner. And, dash it, he was sweating like a racehorse at dinner the night before last." The speaker was George Faffenforth. "He's just come back from some armpit in the sand dunes of who-knows-where."

I felt duty-bound to interrupt. "That is not a fair accusation. The man has not been told to isolate, or, presumably, he would have done, and wouldn't have been there listening to the captain's announcement. It's far more likely one of the crew."

"Oh, you defend him, do you?"

"Don't be silly. I merely think it's best to avoid idle speculation, abide by what the captain asks, and stay calm."

"Calm?"

I sensed a brewing playground altercation with bullies.

"I paid good money for this cruise," said one of the other men, his finger jabbing at my chest. "And I intend to enjoy it."

"I very much think you won't enjoy it much if you grow sick and die," I replied. "In fact, I guarantee it."

With that, I returned to my cabin. Agitation from the confrontation restricted me to my quarters for the rest of the day. No symptoms, but a restless night nonetheless. What the subsequent days would bring if the passengers became more fractious, I dreaded to think.

I dreaded to think, also, what had made the footsteps I heard at night. The ones not from the deck, above, but from below.

MY CONCERN INTENSIFIED when Professor Klas Krøyer had not been seen for forty-eight hours. More worryingly, he had not responded to my knocking, and I had it on authority from the kitchen staff that food and drink left at his door had gone untouched. I asked if the captain had been informed, but did not get a satisfactory reply. Meanwhile, in uncanny response to my interests, almost as if designed for my ears specifically, a harrowing series of observations of a seemingly preternatural nature were circulating in the form of gossip.

The same galley porter who removed the tray told me meat had been taken from the kitchen and trailed down the walls of first class. He said a Canuck engineer told him he'd only seen such a bloody trail when a black bear had killed a deer and dragged it away through snow. But the nearest thing we had to a wild beast on board was Lady Pape's Jack Russell, and that was blind as a bat and toothless.

At a game of quoits, a garment factory owner from Nottingham told me his wife had been unable to sleep and, hearing noises like the shifting of heavy furniture and the grunting of a bull, she stepped outside her cabin and saw a man walking down the ill-lit corridor away from her, wearing a skirt and so hunched over she could not make out his head. Just very large hands, as large as winter gloves, hanging at his side in the flickering light, as the generator lost its power then came on again. Fingers ending in long, pointed fingernails.

He asked me if any other passengers were losing their minds. I didn't know if an affirmative answer or one in the negative would give him reassurance.

WORRYINGLY, the chaplain gathered the faithful at 8 a.m. the next morning, a Saturday, for a service of "sanctuary, salvation and hope." I heard voices raised in the usual hymns but had no intention of attending, having been frightened off the Church by the slow-drip torture of Sunday School in the provinces. Nevertheless, I couldn't avoid overhearing the man in the dog collar talk of the need to find the resilience and faith to overcome ungodly forces when they threatened our wellbeing, in whatever form that should take. I thought it was time I sought out Captain Shawcross and apprised him of the situation, psychological or otherwise. By now I very much thought "otherwise."

"The amateur supernaturalist."

"Sir, if I may..."

The captain made no secret he was busy. We would have to walk and talk since he was needed on the bridge. Consequently I saw more of his back and broad shoulders of his uniform than the hewn face and salt and pepper beard.

"I trust we have no ghosts, on top of everything else."

"I'm not sure what we have, sir."

I told him many of the passengers were now fired up with the suspicion that the disease on board had been carried by Professor Krøyer—and originated, more directly, as preposterous as it sounded, from the ancient mummy being carried in the hold. I said it was more than a possibility that Krøyer himself was being adversely affected, to the point of madness, by the presence of the artefact, since he held it peculiarly responsible for the death of his oldest friend.

"Poppycock," said the captain, turning to me as he ascended a metal staircase. I saw that the fingers of his hand were bandaged and exuding yellow pus.

"I do not disagree. However, I foresee trouble if nothing is done."

"And what do you propose *should* be done, Mr. Venables?" Brass buttons, beard, and piercing gaze suddenly gave me one hundred per cent of their attention. Disarmingly so.

I took a deep breath and said I thought the only possible solution was to dispose of the sarcophagus thought by many to be instrumental in causing our ill-fortune. I said with pulleys and the expertise of eight or ten crew members, I did not see it would be difficult to raise it to the deck and easier still to consign it to the ocean.

The captain laughed and said I had conveniently circumnavigated the fact it was someone else's property. The property of the

British Museum, no less. I answered I was sure that, in maritime law, under exceptional circumstances, the decision of the commanding officer usurped all others when it came to the safety of life and limb. And this circumstance was nothing if not exceptional. The captain's decision was justified. Besides, it could be achieved with all the appearance of an unfortunate accident.

"You do not believe this nonsense."

"It does not matter what I believe," I said.

"Then let me make myself plain, sir. I will do nothing—absolutely *nothing*—and you would do well to pretend this conversation never took place, and, if I may be so bold, keep your vivid imaginings in check." He gave a grimace as he felt a spasm of pain and squeezed his fingers tightly. "Now that will be all. When medical authorities give us 'all clear' we will be moving. That is all you need to know."

AFTER THAT, things came to a head hideously quickly.

At nightfall a storm rose up and an insistent rain lashed the portholes. Everything appeared to shake, whether it was bolted down or not. My whole cabin rattled and sighed for hours on end. When I heard raised voices I presumed it was the crew battening down the hatches, but when I shuffled out to explore, I saw it was a mob of nine or ten middle-aged men—Faffenforth and Sir Nicolas included—hammering their fists on the door to the Professor's cabin, insisting on being let in. I was terrified what they might do if they were.

"Krøyer! We know you are in there. Come and face us like a man and explain what the hell is going on!"

No reply forthcoming, the ensuing silence only led to further eruptions of the most ungentlemanly invective. When I saw one of the chaps pick up a fire extinguisher with the clear intent of breaking the door down, I was compelled to intervene, telling them on impulse that was the cruise line's property and any damage would see them end up in court. I followed this up by blurting I had sent for the captain five minutes ago, which was a lie, but had the desired effect.

I told them to go to bed and go to sleep before they did something they would regret. Luckily, they saw the light of reason and sloped off back to their holes.

Once they were out of sight I rapped the door lightly with my knuckles.

"Krøyer. It's me. Venables. Open up, old chap."

At first—nothing. Then a rustling sound. Then Krøyer opened the door no more than an inch to reveal a flickering eyeball and unshaven chin.

"Snifter?" I said weakly.

No whisky was on the cards and I wouldn't have drunk it if there was. The ship lurched and the wind whistled. Krøyer lurched too, back in the direction of a chair in which he huddled under a tartan blanket. I gazed around the room. My own cabin was plain, drab, taupe, but here all the walls were covered in cuneiform writing. Pictograms. Squares. Symbols. Naturalistic designs drawn in curved lines. Years later I'd see similar images from the reign of Gudea of Lagash in the 3rd millennium BC, but at that moment they made me feel only that I had stepped into a tomb.

"What—what are these? What does it mean?"

Krøyer did not answer. Or could not. Pain creased his eyes into slits.

"Don't you hear? The demon is here. The storm-demon. It will destroy me. It protects her. That is its purpose." He gave a guttural cough. As the weather battered the hull he pressed the palms of his hands to his temples. "We are trapped. It will destroy us all."

I knelt in front of him. Prised his hands away and cupped mine to his cheeks. They were burning like embers. "You must be strong. Be strong, please."

"But I'm not strong. I'm not. I'm not. I'm not. I am going to die."

I cannot remember the rest of the conversation, but he would not be shaken. I was bereft but could do no more. The atmosphere in the cabin was stifling and airless. He picked up the stereoscopic viewer and stared through it. There were no slides in it, so he was looking straight at me. I am not sure what he wanted to see.

He leaned over and took a small object from a drawer at his elbow. It was a small clay tablet incised with symbols by a stylus. "You have been good to me. Take this. It is supposed to protect you from evil. But what is evil? And what is good? I thought we were doing good. I thought we were good people." He looped the leather thong attached to the amulet around my neck.

"Do you want me to stay with you?"

The archaeologist moved his head from side to side.

"Are you sure?"

"I must face it alone. If it takes me, the rest of you may live. That would be a good thing, don't you think? That would make me a good person, wouldn't it?"

THE WALL LIGHTS flickered as I walked back to my cabin. I would not have been surprised if the storm caused a power outage. The movement of the vessel played merry hell with my inner ear. I had to cling to the walls for balance.

The pills coming to my rescue, I tried to sleep, knowing I wouldn't.

I stared at the amulet of inscrutable design. How dare it mock my learning! I hung it on a coat hook. For half an hour it tapped the wall with the regularity of a clock. I got up, coiled it in its leather strap and buried it in my suitcase. Then took it out and put it round my neck.

I lay back on the bed and stared at the ceiling. Nothing there but shifting shadows reflected from the endless sea seeping in from behind the blind. I could not get the Professor out of my mind. What he had said. What appalling strangeness he believed.

I must face it alone. If it takes me...

What did he mean—*Takes me*?

With a gasp I raised myself up on my elbows. I was a fool. A damned fool. It was obvious. I planted my bare feet upon the floorboards.

He meant to take his own life. I was sure of it—and I had listened like a dumb tit while he told me so!

I pulled on my socks and shoes. No time for shirt or jacket.

I ran to his cabin, breathless by the time I got there. Hoping against hope I was in time, but the door was already banging off its hinges. Unlocked. Open. I held it fast so that I could look inside, only to see in an instant that the room was empty.

"Krøyer?" I had little faith in hearing a response. My second shout was louder, rattling the fitments so delicately designed in the Art Nouveau style. "Krøyer!"

Nothing.

Could I stop him even if I found him? I had no idea, but I had to try.

I swung this way and that—to the left or the right? Which way? Which blessed way, I asked myself?

There! A hundred yards. Another door banging off its latch. The door to the stairway to the deck. God in heaven...

Dangling potted plants swayed. One falling to the floor and spilling its dirt and petals. Neptune was having a field day.

I sped up the steps, careful not to lose my footing. Water was flooding down, soaking me to the skin in seconds. I stumbled up the foaming rapids. Fell flat on my face more than once. Clipped my chin and drew blood from biting my lip. I tripped again on confronting the cold night air and thought I had broken my elbow as I was thrown into the hail and dark.

"Krøyer?"

Again—nothing.

The seawater blasting my face was a great, heavy blanket. I had entered hell, if hell can be a tempest the like of which could only be called Biblical. A wave higher than a three-storey house crashed onto the deck before me, the explosion of spume knocking me back so hard my feet slid as if on an ice rink and I had to cling to a lifebelt fastened to the wall, my wet fingers spidering for grip. The vessel itself rose twice as high as that, then plummeted, head-first, a bucking bronco of a whale. I left my stomach up there, somewhere in between.

Sheet lightning shone on the surface of the water like the silver of a shattered mirror. Lights in the portholes flickered off and on. Electricity out and electricity in, battling each other, heaven versus the paltry toys of Man. Was there really any contest?

I looked over my shoulder to the bow

and then to the stern, the way my body was pointing.

Nothing. No one...

No, wait. A figure. No—*two figures*. At the rail at the stern. Next to the flag.

"Krøyer!" I howled, my teeth turning to blocks of ice.

Neither figure moved. If figures they were. They seemed barely even that now. Merely silhouettes lacking definition, though one was taller, stooped, with shaggy hair and the other animated. Then an impenetrable wall of rain, grey, vast and swirling, obscured both.

I have never felt more impotent. It was the Professor, I was sure of it. The smaller figure was him, but he was not a small man. And he was not alone.

Hanging on for dear life, my own life, I observed within the maelstrom there were gaps of a few seconds where the wind would change and the force would be behind me not against me. I decided to take full advantage of the fact. At each periodic lull I scrambled towards the stern and the flagpole. Perhaps three feet, perhaps four. As far as I could to get the next hold, the next sure footing. This I did two or three times, taking me nearer by a factor of forty or fifty yards—a journey that would have taken me a minute under normal circumstances now taking considerably longer.

A cry: "It's here! You see it?"

With my free hand—the one not ice blue—I scraped water from my eyelids and looked again.

The archaeologist's silhouette was facing me. I could make out his face. A blur of pinkness. The brown moustache. The dots of eyes.

"Come inside! It's not safe!" I cried.

He did not reply. Or did not hear, swathed as he was in wrappings of lashing rain. As was the figure that stood next to him, and over him. For its form was much the greater than that of a human being. It's stance powerful, steady, resolute, and unadorned with any semblance of agitation. Oddly, there seemed a state of grace between them. An acceptance. A completion. No indication of the act I was about to witness when the wind changed and a wrenching wail came from the ocean that I was not sure was the protest of the ship or the chorus of the deep.

In a brief half-second of clarity—so bright under the glare of a lightning bolt it might have been one of the stereographic slides the archaeologist kept in his cabin—I saw it in all its glory. The body and limbs of a man, but lion-headed, nostrils flared, its puffy snout wrinkled to advertise massive fangs bared in a silent snarl. Its mane shook droplets of copious rain. Donkey ears pointing skywards. Eyes chalk white. In its right hand a long, curved dagger was raised, and fell—and fell, and fell, and fell...into Krøyer's chest.

With each blow the lightning reigned, the thunder roared, and his name no longer came to my lips.

The figure crumbled. For there was only one figure now. And it lay motionless.

IT IS NOT to my credit that I fled, locking my cabin door after me and barricading it with a chair.

I held my weight against it, fearing the creature might come for me. And so it did. I heard its scratching footsteps upon the stair. I heard its talon tread, heavy as stone, along the carpet outside my room. My ears followed it as it paused inches from my door. I clutched the amulet I wore as a necklace and prayed as best I could.

I heard it walk away. The footsteps grew quieter, and I knew they had descended to the hold.

THE NEXT MORNING a blue sky unfettered by the indignity of clouds made the onslaught of the night before seem like a delusion. Weather could change abruptly at sea, but it seemed like an impossibility to me that the storm had passed.

I had neither slept nor undressed, and, in that ragged state was told Captain Shawcross wanted to see me. I did not ask why. I had a feeling I knew. His ashen complexion confirmed as much as he asked me to sit down. He fidgeted with the objects on his desk as he told me he had some very bad news.

"I'm sorry to have to tell you the body of Klas Lindell Krøyer was found in the early hours of the morning by members of the crew. There is no easy way to tell you this, but it had been mutilated in a most unsightly fashion. I ordered it to be moved immediately to the medical bay, lest it be seen by any of the other passengers. It was not a fit sight to be seen by anybody. I served on a dreadnaught during the war, and I saw many things, but I never saw worse. I wanted to tell you personally because tongues wag and you appeared to be his friend."

"Not friend," I said. "Acquaintance."

"It's a most bizarre occurrence. The wounds, so severe...I can only imagine he fell off and was drawn into the propellors, and, what with the harshness of the storm, the waves threw him back onto deck. It's an unlikely thing, but unlikely things happen."

I said they did.

"Can I ask you, in the strictest privacy, did he ever talk to you of suicide? Of taking his own life?"

"Yes," I said, to my shame and regret. Coward that I was. "Yes, he did."

SHORTLY AFTERWARDS there was a further announcement. Test results confirmed the crew members with dubious symptoms had been battling gastroenteritis. They were now recovering and the *Arturus* has been given all clear to dock.

With quarantine lifted we were free to explore Venice. Many couples made the most of their liberation, fleeing onto dry land to devour the narrow streets around the Piazza San Marco, visiting the Palazzo Ducale, or enjoying a bracing boat trip to the glassware foundries of Murano. I did not join them, preferring my own company. After what had occurred I was in no mood for convivial social banter, so went from one sort of isolation to another, secreting myself in small cafés or *osterias*, taking an *espresso* as I wrote up in my journal what I had seen—or thought I had seen. Sampling a bowl of *spaghetti vongole* or the local delicacy of *fegato alla Venezia* to the sound of waiters chattering in a language I didn't understand, accompanied by the cooing of pigeons, was all the excitement I desired.

When it came to returning to the ship, the prospect of continuing the rest of the journey on board proved increasingly hard to contemplate. The smells, the tastes, the very atmosphere of the liner would be torture. So, while others snored in their cabins, I booked into a small, family-run hotel in Cannaregio, the city's most northerly *sestiere*, near the Santa Maria Mirácoli, not far from the Ghetto, returning only once, to inform the captain of my plan to discontinue my voyage by sea and instead return to England by rail, via Simplon, via the Orient Express to Paris and Calais. He shook my hand and said that he understood how the journey had been painful for me. He himself had been upset to see the state of Professor Krøyer's cabin. "But then," he added, "he was very much insane."

MONTHS LATER, when I went to see the long-anticipated finds from Iraq at the British Museum, including the remarkable sarcophagus, it was extraordinary and strange to behold the mummy of Queen Ishtar-Annunitum first-hand. The word picture created by Krøyer "made flesh" so to speak. The gold mask with its eyes of argonite had been removed, the corpse itself resembling that of a charred and withered child. The scroll of high office was relegated to a separate display cabinet. The golden umbilicus, another.

I had planned to leave the museum in the afternoon in time to catch a matinee showing in Piccadilly of Charles Chaplin in *The Gold Rush*, but something made me stay longer. The exhibition extended into another gloomy hall which showed incredible reliefs depicting an Assyrian lion hunt. The cinematic nature of the images rivalled anything I was likely to see in the Haymarket, and held me more than the antics of a mere comedian in a bowler hat with a wibbly-wobbly walk. The violence of the friezes quickened my heart, but nothing prepared me for the huge bas-relief on the wall nearby. The stillness of it, or the sense of awe that struck me when I stood before it.

Nineveh, Iraq, 640 BC.

The notation described it as an Akkadian deity, one of a species of *ud*-demons who represented "supernatural intervention in the affairs of Man." It featured, they said, on protective amulets and apotropaic yellow clay or tamarisk wood figurines from the first millennium BC.

One of 11 monsters (storm demons) created by (child of) Taimat, the sea, mother of the gods, on the reverse tablet of the Epic of Creation.

I was dwarfed by a giant half-hewn body in cracked stone the colour of the desert. Eyes and teeth the colour of sand. Mane of shoulder-length hair. Right arm raised high.

Gate keeper of the underworld. Servant of Nergal. Mesopotamian hybrid creature.

Lion's head, donkey ears, human body, eagle talons in place of feet.

I recognised it well.

Tomb guardian, I read. *Big Weather Beast*, they called it. *Ephemeral and insubstantial as the air, its face could transform from male to female on a whim. From a man to a woman with messy white hair.*

And its weapons were always the same. In its left hand it held a mace. In its right a dagger. Its name was Ugallu.

Suffice to say that I did not return to London with my nervous debilitation cured, nor a healthy constitution restored. If anything, the voyage had served only to amplify all my doctor said was responsible for my morbid and fearful thinking. Before I'd embarked, he'd told me I must shed my illusions of a malevolent universe beyond human perception. Of devils and spirits in the ether operating under some Manichean laws. Yet, what had I seen during my time on the SS *Arturus* to disprove it? In the grey mist of Chelsea at dawn, it occurred to me that the exact opposite was true. That the engine of all human beings was fear, and we fought it at our peril. The embrace of it was all we could hope for. That, or denial.

Klas Krøyer's funeral took place in Wimbledon, his adopted, suburban home. I attended, though did not make myself known to his family. I paid my respects to the man, and when I placed my hand upon the cold tombstone, I felt we were two fearful men in communion. At least one of us was at peace.

Under his name and his dates it read:

I Nattens Mörker

I later found out that in Swedish it meant: *In the darkness of the night.*

Whether they were his words or those of another, I have no idea, but I found wisdom there. Somehow they defined something I'd been grasping for as a great truth but never found expressed.

*In the darkness of night...*when we shall all meet our demons. Be they believed or unbelieved.

Stephen Volk is best known as the creator of BBC TV's notorious Halloween mocku-mentary Ghostwatch *and the award-winning paranormal drama series* Afterlife. *His other screenplays include* The Awakening, *the miniseries* Midwinter of the Spirit, *and Ken Russell's cult classic* Gothic *starring Natasha Richardson as Mary Shelley. He is a BAFTA winner, a two-time British Fantasy Award winner, a Shirley Jackson Award and Bram Stoker Award finalist, and the author of four collections of short stories:* Dark Corners, Monsters in the Heart, The Parts We Play, *and* Lies of Tenderness. *His acclaimed Dark Masters trilogy consists of three novellas featuring Peter Cushing ("Whitstable"), Alfred Hitchcock ("Leytonstone") and Dennis Wheatley ("Netherwood")—with a guest appearance in the latter by Aleister Crowley. His most recent books are* Under a Raven's Wing, *featuring a young Sherlock Holmes and Poe's Dupin, and* The Good Unknown and Other Ghost Stories. *Visit www.stephenvolk.net for more information on Stephen's work.*

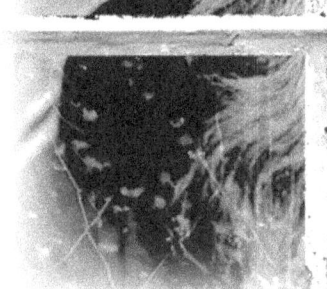

JOLLY

BY STEVE RASNIC TEM

GREEN AND RED PLEATED PAPER BALLS HUNG FROM THE STORE'S CEILING, WHITE PLASTIC GARLANDS WRAPPED THE COLUMNS, SHINY MYLAR balloons floated free and unmoored. Candy canes adorned the walls like a spray of upside-down J's. Over the intercom system Bing Crosby sang *Silver Bells*. A large banner suspended over Wallace's head said WELCOME TO THE NORTH POLE!

Wallace needed to remember so many things: to call them "children," not "kids," that Ho's always came in threes, and to never promise what he could not deliver. *It'll be a surprise and you're going to like it.* He practiced these words in his head again and again.

On Christmas Eve the line of kids and parents waiting to see Santa wound through the toy department and out into appliances and bedroom furnishings. Wallace thought it might be the longest line in his thirty years playing the part. He wished he could say it was because of his skillful portrayal, but his best years as Santa were long behind him. These days his biggest concern was masking the booze on his breath. He switched to vodka days before the job began—clear liquors were the least detectable—and he had a strong curry for breakfast. He chewed on garlic and mints all day, and after dinner he gargled cider vinegar. He'd pay for all this contamination tomorrow, of course, but his usual Christmas Day was spent alone, sleeping until noon, and watching TV the rest of the afternoon. *Not such a sad way to spend a holiday. I prefer it that way.*

A lot of the smaller kids were tired and anxious, barely holding it together. He knew the feeling. Too much wanting, too much excitement, hurt. No child should be crying on Christmas Eve. He always tried to whisper something consoling when he had them on his lap. It rarely helped. So many were terrified of the jolly old elf. He understood that. Santa wasn't human, but he had to pretend to be. Kids sensed that, and it made it worse.

The skinny elf behind the camera glanced nervously at the line, no doubt wondering if they were going to get through all these children by closing. They hadn't been prepared for so many. Last year the store cancelled because of the pandemic. That made for a meager Christmas. Santa and his three elf helpers all needed the extra cash. Wallace got by on a small pension plus social security. Since retirement this was his only consistent part-time gig.

Some of these kids had been in line for over an hour. Jackson, the store owner, liked to overbook the Santa line. He wanted that twenty-five bucks per photo with Santa. Children got to sit on Santa's lap and spill their guts for free, but if their parents wanted photos—and many did, even if their child was bawling—they had to pay the fee.

Those steps up to the gold and red Santa chair were harder to negotiate with each passing year. Wallace had bad arthritis, and if he was inebriated he required at least two elves to help him make the climb. He knew the teenagers who played the elves hated that part of the job. *I'm sorry, I'm sorry. I know I'm just an old drunk,* he thought but never said.

Wallace went back to "Santa School" every few years for a refresher. They taught you things like executing a proper ho ho ho and how to maintain a curly and super soft beard so that when the little tykes grabbed it their stubby fingers slipped through without pain. Recently the course added instruction on handling active shooter scenarios.

Every two hours the crew got a ten-minute break, enough time for Wallace to take a leak and fortify himself with some liquid Christmas spirit. "What's in the bottle?" Jack, the new elf, asked. Jack's costume was still pristine, a sparkly green. He asked lots of questions.

"Eggnog. It's good for you. It's got eggs in it."

"Doesn't look much like eggnog."

Annoyed, Wallace wiped his mouth on his sleeve. "It's a special formula for my ulcers. You're not planning to aggravate my ulcers are you?" Jack was smart enough to walk away. When his break was over, Wallace tried to hurry back, in his rush knocking over a large stack of jigsaw puzzles. He overheard Jack make a jeering noise.

Back on the Santa chair he tried to maintain his standard of giving each child

focused attention, but the parents were getting antsy, and they were the ones rushing their children through. Kids were giving him a couple of sentences and then leaping from his lap. He was supposed to give each kid a lousy packet of four jellybeans when they climbed up. He usually gave them two or three of those packets. The candy would be stale by next year anyway.

His Santa suit stank. The kids who scrunched up their little faces obviously noticed. *Sorry kids.* It was worn almost to transparency in spots. Every day on his way to work he froze waiting for the bus. It wasn't leather, or silk, or any material he imagined the real Santa suit was made from. But he was required to supply his own, so it had to be one he could afford.

Wallace no longer needed a padded suit. Now he had his own bowl full of jelly. His jiggles were getting a bit out of hand, and some days his face was as red as his suit, his jaw, and cheeks sore from all those forced ho-ho-hos. By the end of the shift his knees and finger joints would be swollen, and he'd be breathing hard from the pain.

When the next kid plopped down hard onto his lap Wallace farted. The hardest part of the job some nights was trying not to fart. "Don't worry, that was just Rudolph," he whispered. The little boy giggled. Wallace prided himself on his relationships with children. This was perhaps unjustified.

It appeared someone placed an ugly doll at the front of the Santa line. Wallace looked for Jack, thinking he must have been the prankster. The doll didn't move, and the children stuck behind the figure were beginning to complain. "Do we still get our turn?" said a small child near the back of the line.

Wallace had no idea what this toy was intended to represent. He didn't keep up with the latest TV shows and he couldn't afford to go to the movies. He couldn't quite make out its features. It was late, he was tired, and he'd had too much to drink.

The doll appeared to be naked or wearing some sort of tight red outfit. Its face was covered with scruffy, dirty-looking fur. An ugly, awful thing—what child would want such a toy for Christmas? Wallace wouldn't have allowed one in his house.

"Psst, Santa. Are you awake? We're getting short on time."

Wallace looked up at the Jack elf tugging on his sleeve. He realized there was another moppet sitting on his lap, staring up at him with big green eyes. "I'm sure you'll get everything you want, sweetheart," he said, and kissed her on the forehead.

"Hey! You're not supposed to do that!" Jack exclaimed, but the child was gone and another, almost identical youngster had taken her place. This rotation continued unabated for another half hour, Wallace performing exactly as he'd been trained. Now and then he would scan the crowd, looking for the ugly doll.

It occurred to him then that it might not have been a doll at all. Sometimes there were children with disabilities. Although they were often moved to the front of the line, they or their parents sometimes insisted they be allowed to queue up like everyone else. Wallace felt ashamed the word *ugly* had popped into his head. He'd been tired and the figure had caught him off guard. He hadn't looked at it the right way. There was no such thing as an ugly child.

An older boy slid onto his lap, poking Wallace in the belly with his sharp elbows. He had a list in his hand, a long one. He began reading it. The kids weren't allowed to do that. To save time they were supposed to tell Santa their top four or five. Both Wallace and Jack tried to interrupt, but the boy wasn't having it. He talked over them. It was the usual wish list of outrageously priced electronics. Wallace gave up, looking around the store, not bothering to listen.

That different-looking doll child, now lively and quick, was bounding about the Christmas displays and eventually landed on top of a toddler's head, ripping off the kid's red- and green-striped stocking cap and running its gnarled fingers through the kid's blond hair, picking things out and eating them. The poor toddler began to wail.

Wallace screeched and leapt to his feet, dumping the older boy from his lap. The boy rolled down the steps screaming, his alarmed parents running to his side. There was blood. Wallace tried to explain about the strange child, or doll, or whatever it was, but it was nowhere to be found.

Dash away dash away, all.

IT HAD SNOWED quite a bit during his shift. Wallace shivered waiting for his bus to arrive. He wished again he'd brought a change of clothes, or at least a heavy coat. Jackson fired him on the spot, making a big show of it, perhaps thinking that might avoid a lawsuit. Adults were screaming at him, and all the children were crying—that was the worst part. How do you comfort a child who's seen Santa fired on Christmas Eve?

His Santa career was over. The bus was late, and Wallace was convinced he would die if he didn't get out of the cold right away. When it finally arrived, he jostled past the people in front of him and climbed aboard.

"Hey, Santa isn't supposed to be a jerk!"

Wallace didn't bother turning. "It's the twenty-first century. *Anybody* can be a jerk."

There were two other Santas already on the bus. Wallace wondered if they might have heard about his firing, but they didn't acknowledge his presence. He understood. When you were in the role you needed to convince yourself you were the real one.

As the bus passed the downtown shopping centers he saw several late-night Santas ringing their bells beside cardboard chimneys. Maybe he could still get one of those jobs.

The neighborhoods proclaimed their joy with colored lights and huge displays. Quite a few houses had Christmas lights along the edge of their roofs, the colors racing. More suitable for a used car lot than holiday decoration, in his opinion. There would be fewer tomorrow night, and many fewer by the weekend, although there were always people who kept their lights up until mid-January, which always felt a little desperate to Wallace.

He saw increasing numbers of Santa Claus inflatables in the yards with reindeer, a giant Frosty the Snowman, an elf or two, beginning to collapse under the weight of the fresh snow. Most would be a sad pool of vinyl by morning.

One of the other Santas had fallen asleep and was now snoring. Wallace had never allowed himself to do that in public while in costume. It didn't matter if you were a fat Santa or a skinny one, a solemn one or a crazy one. But a certain air of mystery had to be maintained. Santa's alienness was key. Whether you considered him an elf, a supernatural being, or even a demon in disguise, the one thing he was not was human. Could a human being deliver toys all over the world in a single night?

Wallace was beginning to sober up. That was quite an achievement for him on Christmas Eve. He heard a persistent tapping on the roof of the bus, then scrabbling as someone, or something tried to hold on. Maybe it was a squirrel attempting to hitch a ride. There were lots of squirrels in this area. His neighbor called them tree rats. He heard the noise again, followed by a thump. It was probably just a low-lying tree branch scraping the roof as they passed beneath it. People didn't trim their trees adequately.

He'd have a drink or two when he got home, sitting in front of the Christmas tree. Maybe he'd start a fire in the fireplace. He hadn't done that in a couple of years. Liquor and a warm fire, maybe Christmas music on the radio. He'd feel better, at least better than this.

He managed to get off the bus and halfway down the block without slipping and falling. He counted that as a victory. Wallace felt two snowballs hit him squarely in the back. It ought to have annoyed him, but he thought it funny, given the evening he'd had, and he admired their aim. He'd fire back at them if he weren't so tired. "Damn street urchins!" he shouted and began giggling uncontrollably. He had to be careful. If he fell over and they ran away he might not be able to get up and he'd freeze in place. But that sad mental image made him giggle even more. What were those kids doing out anyway? It was late to be throwing snowballs.

The squirrels were active this evening. He could hear them jumping from tree to tree. They were having much more fun this Christmas than he was. Snow fell from a branch and onto the back of his Santa suit, sliding down his neck. The sudden chill made him shake uncontrollably.

He recognized his house by the decayed string of lights wrapping the bush by the sidewalk. They hadn't worked in years. At least it saved him money on electricity. He kicked his way through the snow and lifeless vegetation covering the flagstones, his yard a frozen dead jungle.

He struggled to climb the steps onto the porch. A big letter J hung by his door. He used to paint it every year to look like a candy cane. Now it was striped in different shades of gray. When he was a kid he made a wreath out of painted popsicle sticks and pipe cleaners. He still hung it on his front door every Christmas.

He juggled his keys, dropped them into the snow which had blown across the porch. "Shit!" He bent over, freezing his fingers scraping them on the boards until he found them.

Someone snickered behind him. He turned around, imagining himself jumping off the porch and giving chase. Of course, that wouldn't happen, and he didn't see anyone. The squirrels raced across the porch roof, their chatter sounding like laughter. *To the top of the porch, to the top of the wall.* Next week he would buy himself some rat poison, or maybe a handgun. Call it a Christmas present.

A FOUL SMELL hit him in the face as he entered his home. It had been there awhile, but so far he'd been unable to track it down. A dead animal, or maybe just food spoilage. *You get used to it.*

His little Christmas tree leaned far enough to the left the ornaments on that side kept falling off. It was a terrible tree, but he felt sorry for it and couldn't bring himself to take it down. He'd left it up, with its handful of ornaments, for years. Of course, it was long dead. But at least there weren't any needles left to shed.

He'd left that plate of lime Jell-O he'd had for breakfast out on the table, a spoon still in it. It now had a couple of bugs stuck to the surface, but he could eat around those. He sat and took several bites. He loved the lime taste, and green was his favorite color. He'd come to hate red.

He glanced around the dining room at his collection of snow globes, displayed on narrow shelves attached to all four walls. They were the nicest things he owned.

He could hear Christmas carolers out on a sidewalk a few houses over. It was kind of late for them, but he liked hearing the music and their failed attempts at harmony. They'd skipped his house ever since the scene he made five years ago. For some reason he'd thought they were trying to break in.

He'd always wanted a Christmas village with tiny figures of Victorian shoppers, their arms full of packages. But the good ones were so expensive. He'd been saving up, but after tonight that dream was probably out of reach.

He made a jam sandwich and placed it on a table by the fireplace along with a warm beer. He scrawled FOR SANTA on a piece of paper and stuck it under the edge of the plate. It was ridiculous, of course, but he did this every year. At least Wallace now had a snack ready for the morning, assuming the mice didn't grab it this time.

He took off his wet socks and hung them from the mantle. He needed to remember to take them down. He'd burned up quite a few pairs over the years. He looked for matches to light a fire but couldn't find them anywhere. Realizing he was too tired to engage in a lengthy search and still a little intoxicated, he sat down in his greasy upholstered chair and stared into the cold, blackened firebox.

He heard the squirrels clattering on his roof again. Or something larger than a squirrel, a racoon maybe—some of those thumps were loud. A narrow stream of soot and ash drifted down into the firebox. Whatever it might be was messing with the chimney. It would regret that. Every couple of years Wallace used brushes and a vacuum to clean off the smoke shelf above and behind the damper. There were always a few skeletons, birds and squirrels and remains he could not identify.

He used to watch his father perform that chore when he was a kid. That's when he realized Santa couldn't possibly be human. Not only was the flue too narrow for a jolly fat man, but how did he get past the smoke shelf and the damper? Santa was either the

greatest contortionist ever or some sort of alien.

Wallace fell asleep in his chair before midnight, as he did every year. In his dreams he was the real Santa, travelling through both time and space in his mission to save every single child the pain of disappointment. Santa's bag was depthless, with room for everything. At one house he pulled out an eight- by ten-foot swimming pool. Chimneys were no obstacle. All he had to do was touch the side of his nose and he became thin as a worm, and so long his head was poking out of the fireplace while his boots were still on the roof.

Wallace wasn't awake when Santa came.

MUCH TO HIS SURPRISE there were presents beneath his dead tree for Wallace to open Christmas morning. He usually didn't have any Christmas presents unless he wrapped something for himself. Even more surprising, the jam sandwich was gone. So was the can of beer. *Well, God bless us everyone.*

He fell to his knees beside the tree, overcome by the memory of childhood excitement. The packages were haphazardly wrapped using pages of old newspapers, magazines, and random trash. He felt jittery opening them, but he was too curious not to. Inside the first was a delicate bird's nest containing a small skeleton. In the next one he found one of the fake candy canes the store used as part of its decorations. In the final package was a red- and green-striped stocking cap, the right size for a tiny child. Wallace remembered it from last night's Santa line, and the terrified toddler who'd worn it.

He got up and walked around the house looking for any other indications of stirring creatures. He thought he heard a sighing, wheezing noise, and entering the dining room he saw the large feet sticking out from under the table. They were blocky and covered with black hair, the toenails yellowed and untrimmed. He got down on one knee and peered under the edge of the tablecloth.

All tarnished with ashes and soot. The creature was the one he'd seen in the store the night before. Its head was large and bulbous, covered with dirty, knotted white hair. *No rosy cheeks here.* Its thin lips were barely visible beneath the mats of hair. At first glance Wallace thought it was wearing a red jacket, but upon closer examination he was convinced it was the figure's leathery crimson hide, although it was possible body paint was involved. There were spots, creases, where the redness faded into dirty gray, particularly under its arms and little round belly. Lying crushed in one of its simian paws was the beer can. It kept its genitalia tucked between its legs. *As all decent Santas should.*

Its eyes snapped open. They were like green jewels. It jumped to its feet, and immediately Wallace understood this was no jolly old elf.

It rotated its head as if looking for an escape route. It leapt up on the table with a single bound, and there began the most amazing transformation, its belly spreading, ballooning into a huge sack with a mouth-like opening. *Do I really have nothing to dread here?*

This vision of Santas gone bad reached out and grabbed what it could, sweeping Wallace's collection of snow globes off their shelves and into its moist fleshy bag. Wallace tried grabbing horrible Santa's feet, trip him up or pull him down, but he was too slow and clumsy and Santa too quick. Once the snow globes were gone Santa bounced through the rest of the house, snatching what it could and shoveling Wallace's things into its sack. By the time Santa returned to the fireplace it was practically waddling.

Santa turned to look at Wallace, opened its mouth, and emitted a mournful noise, reminiscent of foghorns and ships sinking into a watery grave. At the end it inhaled deeply and was sucked backwards up the chimney.

Wallace moved as quickly as his unhealthy body would allow, stumbling out the door and down the porch steps. He kept looking for Santa on the roof or Santa in the trees but could find no trace of him.

Three kids on bicycles raced by, almost running Wallace down. He spun like a top and attempted to give chase, shouting curses when he could not keep up. In his exhaustion he began to laugh, and although he tried his best, he could not stop.

Steve Rasnic Tem's writing career spans over 45 years, including more than 500 published short stories, 17 collections, 8 novels, miscellaneous poetry and plays. His collaborative novella with his late wife Melanie, The Man on the Ceiling, *won the World Fantasy, Bram Stoker, and International Horror Guild awards in 2001. He has also won the Bram Stoker, International Horror Guild, and British Fantasy Awards for his solo work, including* Blood Kin, *winner of 2014's Bram Stoker for novel. Earlier this year he received the Horror Writers Association Lifetime Achievement Award. Visit his website at:* www.stevetem.com

MATT COWAN'S HORROR DELVE:

THERE'LL BE SCARY GHOST STORIES: 13

OF THE SCARIEST CHRISTMAS HORROR STORIES EVER!

ALLEN K. '91

"There'll be scary ghost stories and tales of the glories of Christmases long, long ago."

THIS VERSE FROM THE RELENTLESSLY CHEERFUL CHRISTMAS SONG, "IT'S THE MOST WONDERFUL TIME OF THE YEAR" (1963), has been the source of much confusion over the years. After all, why mention "ghost stories" in a song primarily espousing the joys of "parties for hosting," "much mistltoeing" and "loved ones" being near?

I suspect writers Edward Pola and George Wyle included that line in reference to an old, largely forgotten holiday tradition. Back before the modern conveniences of whole house indoor heating, television sets or radio, families had to find something to keep themselves entertained during the long, frigid winter nights of Christmastime, so they would gather around the fireplace to regale each other with stories. What better sort of story could one tell in such an environment than the horror tale? While this practice became quite popular in Victorian England, it fell out of favor in Puritan America.

Christmas stands alone as the holiday most steeped in tradition, history, and lore, so fodder for the crafting of truly terrifying horror stories is plentiful—just look at its origins. Many of the traditions we hold most dear actually originated from pagan celebrations such as Saturnalia and Yule, but which have been re-skinned to fit our modern sensibilities and beliefs. For instance, no one knows the actual date of Jesus's birth, but while attempting to convert pagans to Christianity, choosing a date (December 25th) around one already popular with the public of the time, such as the Roman's Saturnalia (December 17th–23rd), made sense. There are several more pagan traditions we have absorbed into our modern celebrations as well, including the Christmas tree, hanging mistletoe, and caroling (Wassailing).

Of course, no discussion of Christmas ghosts would be complete without invoking the granddaddy of the festive haunting tale, Charles Dickens. The enormous success of his seminal novel, *A Christmas Carol* (1843) struck such a chord with the general public, reverberations from it are still being felt today nearly two centuries after its initial publication. This iconic tale of the miserly Ebenezer Scrooge being visited in the hours between Christmas Eve and Christmas Morning by three spirits (not to mention the specter of his deceased former business partner, Jacob Marley) has enjoyed countless film and television adaptations over the years, and I personally make a point of watching one each season to help get me in a festive mood.

Another important figure who helped carry forth the Christmas-ghost-story-telling tradition would be M.R. James. While serving as Provost of King's College, he regularly wrote bone-chilling horror stories which he read to a group of friends and colleagues during the holiday season. You may notice James is not represented in the stories I've listed below. That is because only one of his stories actually takes place at Christmas and it isn't exactly overflowing with details regarding the festivities. The stories I compiled for my list here are heavily focused on containing both terrifying chills, as well as rich descriptions of the season.

Assembling this list was difficult. I've spent more than a decade putting together my annual Suggested Christmas Horror Story Reading Lists over at my website, HorrorDelve.com, so I have a huge store of favorites to pull from. What follows is my attempt to create an ultimate list—a best of the best of terrifying Christmas horror stories, if you will. My initial list was 31 possible stories long. Needless to say, I had to make some difficult cuts. "The Water Ghost of Harrowby Hall" (1894) by John Kendrick Bangs (1894) was the first Christmas ghost story I ever read (in the pages of Alfred Hitchcock's Haunted Houseful anthology, which I checked out repeatedly from my elementary school library). It holds a special place in my heart, but unfortunately other, more frightening tales took its spot. A few more I really wanted to include but ran out of space for, included classics such as: "Jerry Bundler" (1897) by W. W. Jacobs—where a ghostly prank goes horribly wrong, and "Florinda" (1956) by Shamus Frazer—involving a wraith which resembles a creepy doll; as well as more modern masterpieces such as "Visiting Star" (1966) by Robert Aickman—where a bizarre troupe arrives in a small town for a Christmas performance, and "The Stars Are Shinning Brightly" (2020) by Joana Parypinski—involving a creepy group of carolers who sing unsettling songs every night leading up to Christmas.

So LIGHT A FIRE, grab some eggnog, and treat yourself to some horrifying, festive chills.

13 OF THE SCARIEST CHRISTMAS HORROR STORIES EVER!

(in Order of Publication):

1. "Number Ninety"
B. M. Croker (1895)

At Christmastime a man who adamantly disbelieves in ghosts accepts a challenge to spend the night in a house so haunted its caused both its neighboring residences to remain empty as well. Once there, he finds himself invited to a phantom Christmas dinner party full of unwholesome guests. A demonic presence pervades the bloodthirsty house. Mrs. Croker crafted a superbly creepy haunted house tale with this one. It's a favorite of mine!

2. "The Shadow"
E. Nesbit (1910)

The tradition of telling scary stories at Christmas is on display here as three young ladies coax a shy housekeeper into telling them a ghost story during the wee hours of a Christmas party. The housekeeper tells them of her personal encounter with one from her youth that took the form of an amorphous, deadly shadow. Nesbit is always excellent at creating frightening tales with malignant supernatural forces. Incidentally, she also penned a cracking Halloween story in "Man-Size in Marble" (1887).

3. The Step"
E. F. Benson (1926)

A shrewd businessman mercilessly evicts tenants who owe him money without a second thought to their plight or the fact that Christmas is so near. As things go from bad to worse for the family he tossed out, he begins to hear disembodied footsteps following him. The protagonist here is similar to Ebenezer Scrooge, but the horrors he encounters at the story's conclusion are far more terrifying. E. F. Benson has long been one of my favorites horror writers and this story helps prove why.

4. "Smee"
A. M. Burrage (1929)

A group plays a game on Christmas Eve. It's similar to hide and seek but done without knowing who they are seeking. Each participant is given a folded piece of paper. Most are blank, but one has the word "Smee" on it. That person will be the hider sought by the other players. The lights are turned off, and the one designated Smee sneaks away to hide. Once the signal is given, the search begins. Whenever another player is encountered they are asked if they are Smee. If they aren't, they say so. If they are, they don't answer, and the one that found them joins Smee while others seek them out. The group playing inside the darkened house of this tale come to find that they have somehow acquired an additional unknown player. This one is a true classic!

5. "Lucky's Grove"
H. R. Wakefield (1940)

A tree is placed in a wealthy man's house to serve as their Christmas tree. It was taken from an area considered sacred which is referred to as Lucky's Grove. The gathered family and workers begin to see ominous creatures lurking about, and they start having disturbing dreams as well. Some even become deathly ill during the holiday celebrations that follow. One young boy fashions a beastly-looking snowman for reasons he himself doesn't understand. Wakefield's ghost stories remain a masterclass in evoking terror and dread.

6. "Christmas Reunion"
Sir Andrew Caldecott (1946)

A wealthy, young man who's staying at a friend's house for the holidays becomes noticeably upset after receiving a mysterious telegram from Australia.

He inherited his fortune from an affluent uncle whom he had been forced to abandon in Australia to die following an unfortunate accident. The young man becomes even more unsettled when the visiting store Santa Claus the family hired arrives with tidings he doesn't seem to appreciate. A section from "Stories I Have Tried to Write" by M. R. James is directly referenced here, likely as a nod to this story's genesis.

7. "A Christmas Game"
A. N. L. Munby (1949)

A medical student returns home to celebrate Christmas with his family and is surprised to find an older gentleman named Fenton there. His father knew Fenton from years before and upon hearing he had no one with which to spend Christmas, invited him to join them. The family enjoys dining, playing games and opening presents together until evening arrives and they darken the room for father to tell his annual scary story while objects are passed around to represent gory things related to it. This game has an unexpectedly terrifying effect on Fenton. Here we have an excellent Christmas horror tale, full of descriptions of festive celebrations as well as nightmarish ghostly manifestations.

8. "The Waits"
L. P. Hartley (1961)

A wealthy family is visited by two carolers on Christmas Eve, but when the daughter offers them money, they refuse it, telling her it isn't enough. This result is repeated when other family members offer them more. The carolers say they want the father to come see them, then they sing a twisted version of "God Rest Ye Merry Gentlemen." Hartley also wrote another strong Christmas horror tale in "Someone in the Lift" (1988), but I find this one more horrific, so it claims a spot on this list.

9. "The Hanging Tree"
R. Chetwynd-Hayes (1979)

A precocious young girl becomes fascinated by the shadowy figure watching and beckoning to her from a bench by a large tree across the street from her family's house. None of the others attending that Christmas Eve dinner are able to see him. This is a top notch, spooky tale with a rich Christmas setting. As a side note, Amicus Productions made two feature films adapting stories by Chetwynd-Hayes, *From Beyond the Grave* in 1974 and *The Monster Club* in 1981.

10. "The Christmas Eves of Aunt Elise"
Thomas Ligotti (1983)

During a Christmas Eve family gathering at his wealthy Aunt's house, Jack listens in on her true tale of a house that used to exist across the street but which was torn down brick-by-brick at the former reclusive owner's wishes following his death. Later, a young antiquarian, who'd always been fascinated by the place and didn't know it had been removed, returns to town and notices it standing there all decked out in Christmas lights during a heavy fog. Unfortunately for him, he accepts the oddly smiling former owner's invitation to come inside to look around. This is an outstanding, very eerie story. You really can't go wrong with anything by Ligotti. His vision and style are so unique you become enthralled by the grim worlds he manifests.

11. "Wish You Were Here"
Basil Copper (1992)

This novella follows a successful writer who's working on repairs to ancient Hoddesden Hall which he recently inherited from a reclusive aunt. To his dismay, he begins receiving musty smelling, Victorian-era postcards in the mail with obscured postmarks and the hint of women's perfume to them. Each card from this mysterious sender is from progressively closer European destinations, saying she will be there by Christmas. While delving into this mystery, he discovers that the aunt from which he inherited the place disappeared and has never been found, and the cousin who took possession of it before him fell down an open well and drowned. The increasing nearness and frequency of

ALLEN K. '93

these postcards unsettles his sanity as Christmas approaches. Although long, this is an intriguing Christmas horror/mystery with a great finale.

12. "The Decorations"
Ramsey Campbell (2005)

A boy, visiting his grandparent's house with his parents for the holidays is disturbed by his grandmother's obsession with the lighted plastic Santa on their roof. She seems to think something evil inhabits it, which she calls "The Worm." Ramsey has penned quite a few excellent Christmas horror tales, and each one is masterfully done, but I find this one the scariest and its ending is epic!

13. "The Merry Makers"
Paul Finch (2020)

This tale follows a man who has a car accident while attempting to drive to a meeting in the snow on a frigid Christmas Eve. With his car disabled, his cell phone dead, and not knowing where he is, he sets out seeking help and shelter from the cold. He heads toward a place with light coming from it and is granted admission into the house by a mute woman and her odd, older brother. The man of the house says they don't celebrate Christmas even though everyone thinks the do because the house is named Mistletoe Hall. The man appears to be working hard to keep the stranded motorist from leaving before morning. Despite his initial claims, Christmas is indeed recognized in Mistletoe Hall, only in a horrific, bizarre way. Paul, who writes a new Christmas horror story every year, proves his mastery here.

That wraps up this volume's look at festive fear. So, my fellow fiends, until next time, when we'll continue to *delve* into all things *horror*.

"The air was filled with phantoms, wandering hither and thither in restless haste, and moaning as they went."
—Charles Dickens,
A Christmas Carol

THE SORROW OF STONES
BY JOHNNY MAINS

THE EFFORT OF THE HIKE BIT DEEP INTO HER LUNGS. DRY PINE NEEDLES CRUNCHED UNDERFOOT. Branches bent heavily into her and pinged away as she forced her way through the trees. Classical music soothed her as she tramped, a slow, poignant symphony that had been her father's favourite. She smiled gently as a memory of them sitting in the lounge listening to it on a dark Sunday afternoon, played out in her mind as she pushed onwards.

Jill Berlin paused when she saw the felled trunk in the clearing, sunlight prodding in through the upper branches of the surrounding trees. She took her air pods out from her ears and pocketed them, unhitched her small bag from her front, then her rucksack, and placed both gently onto the forest floor. She removed the tripod that was attached to the side of the larger pack and assembled it. Then she unzipped the smaller bag and took out the Panasonic 4K camcorder and locked it into place. Jill regarded the newness of it amongst the surroundings of the woodland; ancient objects to be recorded on modern tech.

Next, she attached the fluffy microphone to the camera, removed the lens cap, lined everything up, walked to the felled tree, sat on it, and checked to see if her eye-line was good enough. It was a mechanical process, one that she did without thinking. Once she was happy, she went back to the camera, pressed record and sat on the tree, gave herself a three count, smiled and started to speak.

"Hi, and welcome to another episode of *The Wild Wanderer*." Her soft North Yorkshire accent was crisp and clear. "This week I've decided to find a new place, so I've driven up to a location in the Highlands of Scotland. This area is completely unknown to me, and I'm really excited by what we're going to discover. This will be an overnight stay and as part of this new film, I'll be making my shelter from my surroundings only. However, my caveat remains, if there are no branches to make a bed, the tent goes up! So, don't forget to hit that like button. If you're new to me and my channel, be sure to subscribe and you'll get new content as soon as it's up. You can also become a member. To join, follow the link in the description below. If you follow me, there's exclusive content—stuff that won't be shown on the channel." Jill smiled, then twitched, and continued as a pigeon broke free above her.

"So, are you ready for me to work up a sweat and find my spot?" She kept on smiling.

"It's a bit chilly today. The forecast for this evening says were going to see a bit of a dip in temperature, so I'm going to have to put some extra effort into making a fire, possibly a 'long fire' if you're lucky! My backpack is solid, around twenty-seven pounds, and man alive, it's maybe a little too heavy for the kind of exploring I'll be doing. It's fair to say that by the end of this video I'll either be fitter or dead!"

Jill laughed, then fell silent for fifteen seconds, got up and ended the recording. She put on her backpack and picked up the camera and walked a few yards further and set up some establishing shots of her walking with the full kit on. She was starting to feel tired now.

THE TREES BECAME SPARSE as she reached the end of the forest. Once she was out, the landscape seemed to have shifted; there was no longer any grass, or moss. There was scree above and flat slabs of granite. Jill took her time, hefting her tripod up and over her shoulder. The rucksack felt impossibly heavy on her back. The granite was wet, and even though she had absolute faith in her boots and capabilities, she had heard horror stories from other walkers who found themselves on their backs within seconds. Broken legs, shattered vertebrae. Air Ambulance called out. Mountain rescue to the more impossible spots.

Like this one, she thought to herself as she looked at her surroundings. There was no way that a helicopter could land here, it would slide down the granite.

It was too far for her to turn back, though. The peak was a twenty-minute climb, and once there, she could have a quick look over and then make her way back to the forest, set up her tent, spend a couple of hours making a spot for the night. She could build a fire and do some establishing shots of getting ready for bed. All good footage. Then, once that was all filmed, she'd go back to the car, drive five miles away to the cosy hotel room before setting off back to the tent in the morning to film some

footage of her getting up, making a cup of tea and dismantling the camp. There was the odd post from her three million subscribers that what she did was faked to a certain extent, but she blocked them as soon as they popped up. She put her head down and started to walk up the steep incline.

Of course, she didn't have her camera on when the eagle swooped above her, before it tumbled off in the air currents then darted way off to the right, into the ground beyond the farthest reaches of the forest.

Once over the peak, she looked into the valley below. The view took her breath away. At the bottom of the hill, in the place where the other mountains and hills joined, was a round patch of ground. There were what appeared to be standing stones, twenty to thirty of them, two of which had fallen over.

Jill had a big decision to make. Commit and make her way down to do the video there and stay the night, or go back to the car and return the next day. She looked at her watch. It was an hour and a half to sunset, and it would take as long to get there and return to this point, if not longer. She'd be walking back to the car in the dark, something that she didn't want to do.

She decided not to go back to the car. The stone circle held too much promise. She brought out her phone and opened the Google Maps app. Surprisingly, there was good reception.

She started the slow descent, worried that the heaviness of the backpack might tip her over and send her flying down the steep incline. But she found that if she shuffled sideways, her dominant foot out first, followed by a slow slide of her other, then she was able to make her progress down better than if she'd walked down without anything on her back.

She hoped that there was going to be a flat space for her to put up her tent; there was nothing worse than finding a patch of land and seeing that there were hidden rocks, lumps, in amongst the grass.

It took a while to get to the bottom of the mountain and when she stopped to look back up her whole body reacted with shock. What she had come down was sheer and perilous and much more dangerous than she'd had any awareness of during the journey. So dangerous that she didn't quite know how she was going to get back up. It looked impossible—what had seemed to be an awkward downhill scramble now left her in doubt about whether she could get back up. She knew she would have to sacrifice her rucksack, that was certain. But perhaps she could make her return with just her car keys and the camera bag. Still shaken, she dropped her bags and started to look around the clearing.

She didn't think it would take long to cross and then she could reach the standing stones in maybe five minutes. She got the camera out and placed it at the bottom of the steep incline. Her hands shook as she pressed record. Jill turned and began to make her way up a good fifteen foot of slab. She slipped, scree loosening underfoot, but managed to anchor herself with a knee. A rock tore through her trousers, and she swore in frustration before rising slowly to continue. It took a few minutes before she was in the correct position to turn to record the establishing shot but then she descended confidently, smiling.

"What a place! Now, obviously, I don't want to give the location away, but if you know where it is, you know how beautiful it is in real life—absolutely stunning." She walked towards the camera and crouched before it, hoping that the autofocus worked as it should.

Jill paused for a few seconds, then let her smile drop. She reached for the camera and did a few slow pans of the scenery. *There's a good chance this could be one of my best videos*, she thought, regardless of her current predicament. It really *was* the perfect spot.

She started walking towards the stones, leaving her heavy rucksack at the base of the incline.

As she approached the stones the light began to change, almost imperceptibly, but enough for Jill to feel her nervousness return. Though dusk wasn't due for hours yet, the atmosphere was sombre, tenebrous.

Finally, Jill came to the first stone. It had fallen and was covered by lichen. She took her phone out and started to take photos of it. It had no markings, but a chunk, about the size of her fist, had been removed from it at some point. On closer inspection, the gash looked angular, perhaps a sharp implement like an axe had once hit it.

She moved to the next outlier stone, this one standing up. It was over six foot tall and had the shape of a large hand roughly carved into the stone at the same height as Jill's head. She placed her own hand in the carving, and for a millisecond it was as though hers had been pulled deep into the stone. She shook it off. Of course, her senses were heightened, unnerved by the atmosphere and she was letting her imagination get the better of her.

Her hand felt cold for longer than was natural. It was still cold as she unscrewed the camera from the tripod and took it free-hand to film the stones one by one.

"This place is remarkable, certainly not recorded on any maps that I've seen of this area, and I chose this place carefully. I wonder how long these stones have been standing here for. Thousands of years? It's a beautiful place. I've never seen anything like it in my life."

It was at that moment she heard the noise. A heavy, purposeful scraping sound that was being carried to her by the wind. Stone on stone. She couldn't see what was scraping. It was strange; the further into the stone circle she was walking, the more she felt that it was closing in on her. Her peripheral vision and sense of place felt as if it was warping.

"Hello?" she shouted, but of course, there was nobody there. Probably a goat rubbing its horns against one of the stones, she thought as she took another step into the circle. There were standing stones on either side of her; one of them had been smoothed so much it looked as though it had been polished. She touched it. It was like marble and as cold, if not colder. The next stone was as rough as if it had just been lifted from its original resting place. It had the faint scratchings of a simple leaf design in the middle of it, but as she looked closer it could be that it was just an illusion, a quirk of the stone. She was overwhelmed by a single thought: how did these stones get here in the first place? It seemed a virtually impossible task, even today. And how long had they been here?

Her camera startled her with a loud, frantic beep, indicating the battery was low. She hadn't thanked her sponsors, and she had less time now than she was comfortable with. This was a better place than any to do it. Evocative. Primeval Boots would be over the moon with this piece to camera.

She flicked open the tripod again, then changed the battery on the camera and set it to a wide lens that got her and a long line of stones.

"Today's sponsor is Primeval Boots. You can see the ones that I'm wearing now, these are the latest model, the Primeval Ante, for women and men—these are super comfortable and have handled a month of hard tramping through bogs and forests. They were easy to break in and are completely waterproof. Almost as good as wellies. If you go to their website, follow the link in the description below and order a pair. Use the code 'BerlinPrimeval20' and you'll get 20% off your first order. They post worldwide and have a dedicated and loyal fanbase. I think they are the future of wilderness footwear, why don't you give them a try? Thanks again to Primeval…"

That scraping sound again. Much louder, much *closer*.

She spun around to see what she thought were two stones, one much larger than the other, almost touching. Then she saw the smaller stone move.

Jill screamed. The stone, caught, froze. It had a face.

"Oh," it said.

Jill's heart trip-hammered in her chest, like a bird trying to escape its cage. Her hand went straight to the knife that was attached to her belt.

She took another step forward, then remembered her camera. She unclipped it from the tripod. Her hand shook as she approached the thing at the stone.

It was a man, a *very* old man. He was wearing a tattered black oilskin coat that could only be held together by magic, so much of it had gone. His face looked as punished as the rock he was scraping. Jill saw

that he was no threat. She almost started to laugh from the adrenaline. She raised the camera in front of her face.

"Look who I've found in the middle of nowhere. Can you tell us your name?"

The man said nothing and continued to scrape.

Jill took another step closer.

Her mind flitted to Barbara Hepworth. She'd seen a YouTube video of the sculptor chiselling a hole in a marvellous lump of wood, using her mallet like a conductor uses a baton. She was gouging the wood out, not stopping till a circle around the inside circumference had been removed. The old man was doing the same, with a pointed nub of granite, scraping round and round the hole in the stone. He had got quite a way in, but he had a while to go to make his way through.

"Are you an artist? Are you allowed to do that? Are you hungry?" she asked as she saw how thin he was beneath his rags, her humanity taking over. He gave no response. She turned the camera off and placed it on the ground, taking a good look at the man. If she was being honest with herself, she thought she was looking at a ghost. He seemed to glitch in and out of focus, even though he was only a few metres away; the aphotic quality of the light was certainly making visibility different. And again, that shift, the stones getting closer, the feeling that Jill was being drawn into something.

She took out her phone and unlocked it. There was no signal. She cursed and tried to walk away from the old man.

"It's Muriel, it's Muriel tha's oan the ither side o' this stane. Ahm trying tae git tae her." His Scottish accent was broad and coarse, but Jill understood it.

"What do you mean, on the other side of this stone?"

"It's a grief stane, the first person tae git through the ither side can bring back thir loast wans. Ah loast ma Muriel in the Holiday fire. If ah can git through, she'll return, ah know it."

Jill peered into the hole.

"How long have you been doing this for?"

"The fire wiz Christmas Eve, ah came doon here the next day. Ah took ower frae someone who wiz trying to bring back thir child."

A horrendous memory came crashing down. Jill's father, in her arms, dying of the cruel one-two punch of throat and brain cancer. The pleading in her father's eyes for the pain to stop. "I'll write a note to say that I asked you to kill me," he had whispered, his voice destroyed by the chemotherapy. She had been too scared. He was in agony till the last day when he was given morphine of such a high dose it would "speed things up."

"And they come back perfectly?"

"Tha's the way the story goes, aye."

"And the person who you took over from, did they come back? Try and stop you?"

The old man's brow furrowed. He was trying to think.

"Naw, they didnae."

Jill stood staring at the man as he scraped into the stone, round and round, like a schoolteacher drawing a perfect "o" on the blackboard.

"What date was the fire?" she asked.

"Christmas Eve, nineteen twenty-seven."

The old man turned slowly and looked at her. His was a body of wretchedness.

"She wiz burnt tae a crisp. As black as coal. Ah could only identify hir by hir teeth; she loast wan o them thi week afore, tripped ower and hit hersel' against the mantlepiece. Wiz an awffy whack, that ah kin tell ye."

Jill cried, aghast at realisation of the widower's plight, ninety-seven years spent scratching away at the stone. Big fat tears made their way down her cheeks. She was filled with an unbearable longing to see her father again. And as awful as the predicament was before her, if she had a chance, just one single chance to change that, no matter how long it might take, it was worth doing, wasn't it?

One last question.

"How old were you when the fire happened?"

"Sixty."

Jill reached out and snatched the stone from the man's fist. He screamed at the injustice, a wail of utter devastation, unlike anything Jill had ever heard in her life. He tried to grab it back but couldn't; every time he swiped at Jill it was as if he was swiping through a ghost.

"I'm so sorry," she whispered. She turned to the stone and started to scrape. She was younger, so she would be able to scrape through to the other side of the stone. *I'll do it for a couple of hours*, she thought, *before having a bite to eat*. And if it rained it wouldn't matter, she had the very best clothing, even if the boots were a bit flaky. She could always go back to the car to change into her spares.

It wasn't long before she forgot what a car was. She only remembered the last day with her dad. Over and over.

Around and around.

Her arm never tired. She was driven by singular determination. She would be the first to break through. She could hear her father calling out to her.

THE OLD MAN was pulled backwards to a space in the stone circle. He saw the young woman scrape away, and as she scraped, the colour drained away from her clothes. He tried to walk back to her but felt an overwhelming heaviness creep over him. He was frozen, arms trapped by his sides. His lungs stopped working as they turned to granite. Within minutes he was a small, unassuming standing stone, joining the others who had tried to make their own way through the grief stone.

Johnny Mains is an editor and author. As editor, his first book, Back From The Dead: The Legacy of the Pan Book of Horror Stories *(2010) won Best Anthology at the British Fantasy Awards. He has since edited* Dead Funny: Horror Stories by Comedians, Best British Horror, *three anthologies of "lost" stories by Victorian authors, edited two books for Tartarus Press by Tod Robbins and A.L. Salmon, and two anthologies for the British Library:* Celtic Weird *(2022) and* Scotland the Strange *(2023). His latest anthologies are* Bound in Blood *(2024, Titan Books) and* Halloweird *(2024, British Library). As an author he has written three collections and two novels. Mains is slowly working on his fourth collection and his third novel.* ∎

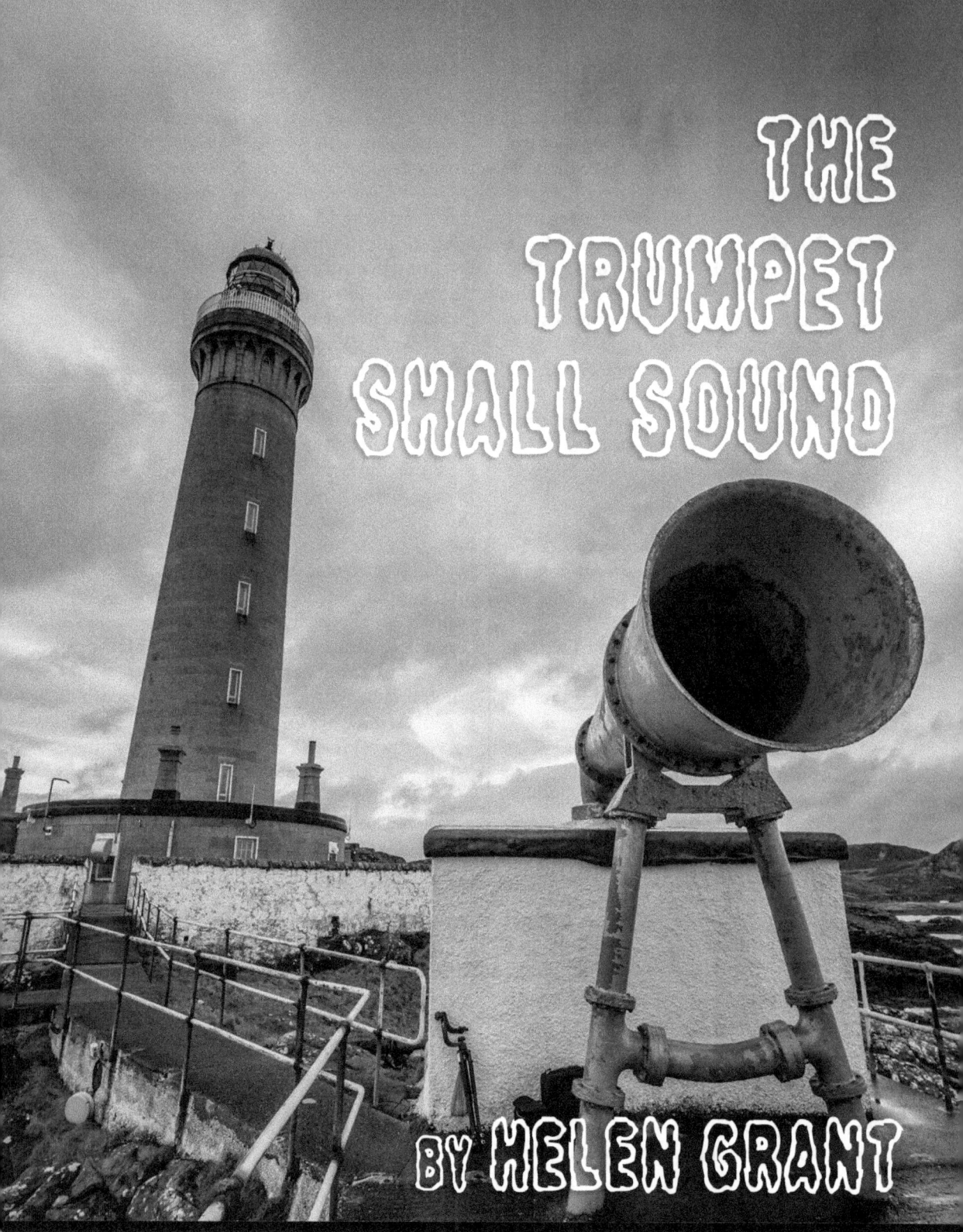

THE TRUMPET SHALL SOUND

BY HELEN GRANT

TWO DAYS AFTER ANGELA LEFT, MATT'S MOBILE PHONE STOPPED WORKING: **NO MOBILE RECEPTION.** There'd been no WiFi connection since the day before. The power still seemed to be on but the router obstinately showed a red light regardless of anything Matt tried.

Being quite alone, he had plenty of time to think. It wasn't raining at present, so he pocketed the useless phone and went and stood at the gateway in the perimeter wall. He gazed down the road that wound away from the lighthouse, as if looking would make Angela reappear. He asked himself whether he should have gone with her. It was a pointless question, since the decision was made, but he was a person who liked to think that he was in the right. Angela had taken the car they had both arrived in, so if he wanted to leave now, it would have to be on foot. It might eventually come to that, but Matt was not particularly keen. It was a pretty long way to the nearest small village, let alone a town, and he hadn't walked that far for years. Besides, the last broadcast before the screen was filled with grey snow had explicitly told viewers not to go anywhere.

He'd argued with Angela about that. They weren't supposed to leave the holiday accommodation. It wasn't as though the next people were going to come and claim it, under the circumstances. Of course they'd only paid for the two weeks, but if anyone came after them for more money (which seemed very unlikely) they could point out that they'd been following government guidelines.

Matt had had an uneasy sense about why Angela had resisted his arguments, and he had pushed a little harder. Eventually she had snapped and said, "Matt, I need to get back—" and then stopped. The way she had spoken indicated that there had been something more—"I need to get back *because*"—but she had bitten it back at the last moment. He'd known then, though. They had no children to get back for, not even grown up ones, no pets, no business that couldn't wait. Angela wanted to leave because something else was pulling her— or in fact, someone. Someone she wasn't telling him about—yet.

She hadn't said much after that. He'd watched her moving about, emptying the drawers and the wardrobe with reckless haste. She'd pushed past him and gone into the kitchen, where she'd taken about a third of the provisions, the non-perishable stuff.

Matt supposed he ought to be grateful to her for leaving so much. When the car was loaded up Angela had paused for a moment with her hand on the door handle and they had looked at each other. That had been the moment when he could have said, "Don't go" one more time or she could have said "Come with me" but instead she had given him a taut distracted smile, and got into the car.

Matt had stood and watched the car following the serpentine track that led away from the point. He was able to see it for a long time: it was all open country, with very few trees. He thought that Angela accelerated as she went along, as though growing in confidence. Finally the car had vanished over a rise in the land. Now he was standing in more or less the same place and the road was still deserted. In a distant field he could make out dark shapes that were undoubtedly cattle, but that was all. He wondered whether Angela had safely arrived wherever she had been heading for.

After a while he went indoors and looked again at the diminishing supply of food. There were a few jars and cans and some perishable stuff: tomatoes, an onion, a single aubergine. Enough for a day or two, but not much longer. They'd been approaching the end of their stay at the lighthouse, and running the stocks down.

On the kitchen surface there was a tray which had been full of tea bags, coffee sachets, packets of sugar and single servings of milk in tiny foil-topped pots when they had arrived—a sort of welcome pack. There had been individually wrapped biscuits and flap-jacks too, all of which had been consumed in the first couple of days, back when Angela and Matt had been blithely cavalier about food, and Matt had still believed they were here to save their marriage. It seemed unlikely that whoever did the changeover brought supplies with them every single time; more probably there was stock some-where in the accommodation, and the logical place was behind the locked door at the far end of the kitchen.

Matt searched desultorily for the key. Then he kicked the door down. It took a couple of attempts, and he had a nasty feeling he'd pulled something in his leg, but when he was inside the pantry looking at shelves full of carbohydrates he felt like Rambo. He thought fleetingly of Angela; she should have appreciated him more—he was a man of initiative. A man of *action*. He helped himself to handfuls of chocolate chip cookies in plastic wrappers.

After he'd eaten enough of the biscuits to think that a little variety in his diet might be pleasant, he began to think of other possibilities. Between the keeper's cottage where he and Angela had been staying and the engine room there was a small ticket office and exhibition area, and he was fairly sure he'd seen a chiller cabinet in there, stocked with soft drinks. Under the circumstances, nobody could blame him if he helped himself to those too.

It took him longer to break into that part of the building, but he was rewarded with a considerable quantity of cans and bottles. He cracked open a can of Irn Bru, the hiss loud in the silence, and wandered about, sipping the fizzy orange liquid.

There were display panels on the walls, with grainy photographs of the lighthouse's early days, the keepers unsmiling in buttoned jackets, caps and carefully knotted ties. A lonely life, thought Matt. Only one other, or perhaps two other, people to speak to most of the time. The sea, the sky, the light. No wonder they sometimes went nuts. He didn't like to dwell on that, so he went through into the engine room and looked at the diesel engines instead.

When they'd first arrived at the lighthouse they'd done all the touristy things—they'd been up the tower, they'd been down the cliff path to gawp at the foghorn, and they'd watched the staff running the engines for the tourists, a process which was remarkably loud. Once they'd run them when Angela and Matt were in the keeper's cottage drinking coffee, and the sound had been thunderous even through the wall.

Angela had found the engines interesting for about ten minutes, but she wasn't technically minded. Matt was an engineer, and he found them fascinating. He'd watched the staff closely while they were running them, and he was fairly sure he could do it himself. The engines were there to power the foghorn, which was a tourist attraction rather than a navigational necessity these days. They drove the air compressors, which charged the receivers, and then a valve was opened to transfer the pressurised air to the tanks in the foghorn house, where a mechanical timer controlled the blasts. Matt and Angela had heard the foghorn sounding; it was loud, resonant and somehow melancholy. It made Matt think of a lonely sea monster, bellowing out its sorrow to the empty sea.

That night, when Matt was lying on his side of the double bed, still not quite accepting that he could have starfished across the middle of it with impunity, he realised that the lighthouse was still operating. The room was very dark, as there were no lights on inside or out, and the floor length curtains were thick ones. However, there was a small space at the top of the curtains, between the heavy rings, and as he lay there sleeplessly he saw it light up for a second or two. For a moment he thought he'd imagined it, that his brain was playing tricks in the darkness, but then it came again, a pulse of brilliant light that lasted for a beat or two and then died.

It was strangely reassuring; his phone, the WiFi, the TV had all stopped functioning, but the lighthouse kept flashing every twenty seconds. He wondered how long that would last. Then he recalled the banks of solar panels on the flank of the promontory. Perhaps the light would keep going indefinitely, until something actually broke down. He watched for the flashes for a little while, and then he turned over and went to sleep.

TWO DAYS LATER he cracked. Mainly it was the diet of biscuits. Matt wasn't a particularly healthy eater but now he found himself fantasising about grilled chicken and salad. Steak and kidney pie. A burger and chips. A nice piece of fish. Anything, in fact, but bloody biscuits.

He emptied out the backpack optimistically purchased for clifftop walks, and put a couple of extra bags in it. With no mobile reception and no TV there was no weather forecast, so he went outside and looked at the sky. No clouds, a little wind. He probably didn't need to bother with waterproofs. He locked the keeper's cottage carefully and stowed the key in his trouser pocket. Then he set off, swinging his arms as if to display confidence, though there were only seabirds to see it. The backpack bounced against his shoulders.

For perhaps half a mile, the road went downhill, and then it rose until it reached the point where Matt had last seen the car with Angela in it before it disappeared. As he slogged up the rise, greedily sucking air into his lungs, he glanced right and left at the fields. The one on the right was empty; in the one on the left there were several cows close to the fence, silently staring at him. They pressed against the wire and Matt wondered uneasily whether anyone was caring for them, doing whatever you needed to do for cattle. He recalled seeing the others clustered together at the far end of the field, invisible from where he was now. Probably they had a water trough up there.

He kept walking, sweating a little. He topped the rise and as he began to descend again a small bay came into view. Matt and Angela had passed it several times at the start of the holiday—first when they drove up to the lighthouse, and later when they went into the distant town. Each time there had been people camping there in tents and campervans; he had seen them lounging in picnic chairs or wading gingerly into the cold sea. Matt did not expect to see anyone there now, but to his surprise there were still campervans parked up on the grass. He stopped and counted seven of them.

For a moment he considered going down and speaking to whoever was there; in fact he took a couple of steps that way. Then he thought better of it. He wanted food, nutritious food, after all, and he doubted anyone who was camping would have spare provisions for a stranger. Still, he stood there looking and gradually he began to notice things. There were several open doors, though no sign of anyone bustling around getting in or out. By one of the vans there were two overturned picnic chairs. And protruding from behind the same van was what might have been a pair of legs.

Matt stared for a long time but he could not be one hundred per cent sure that that was what he was seeing, not at that distance. It might have been a pair of discarded wellington boots, perhaps. Or if those *were* legs, the owner might be lying on the grass, innocently sunbathing; it was just about warm enough. They were very still, but that might mean the person was asleep.

Matt began to walk again, putting distance between himself and the turning down to the bay. Every so often he turned and looked back, but he never reached a point where he could see behind the van. There was no sign of anyone else moving about down there. He thought there were sheep on the hillside beyond, but no people.

Eventually he saw the first dwelling place ahead of him: a white block of a bungalow set back a little way from the road. There was no vehicle outside it. As he approached, he saw that there were two empty parking spaces right in front of the house. A holiday home, he guessed, although it looked a little shabby for that. Or perhaps the owners had been away when the catastrophe had struck.

There was a glazed porch at the front of the building and as Matt drew level with it he saw that the outer door was open a little way. There was a large crack in the pane of glass set into it. He stared at the open door, and then he stared at the road ahead. It was still a fair distance to the next house, let alone the nearest village. A man of initiative would not have hesitated.

The garden path was short; half a dozen steps took him to the door. When he pushed it gently it swung inwards with no complaint from the hinges, and he stepped inside, listening. The only audible sound was his own breathing. He put out a hand and grasped the knob of the inner door. It opened easily.

Matt put his head inside and looked about. He saw a blue-carpeted hallway lined with closed doors. Directly to his left was the kitchen, visible through glass panes, and done out cheerfully in shades of green and yellow. He began to feel confident that the house was empty. However long he listened, he heard nothing, and besides, at least some of the doors would have been open if there were anyone there. All the same, he took care to open the kitchen door quietly. The room was empty. There was another glazed door on one side of it, leading presumably to a dining area. That was closed too.

Matt went into the kitchen, removed his backpack and took out the extra bags. He opened the fridge door first, but soon realised his mistake when the smell hit him. There were no solar panels here, and the power was off. He began opening and closing cupboards, looking for non-perishable foods. Pretty soon he hit paydirt: a cache of tins, jars and packets. Simply reading the labels made his mouth water: *Chicken Curry. Irish Stew. All Day Breakfast.* Moving swiftly, he piled as many as he could into his backpack and others into the bags. He was thinking that he would have to stop there because of the sheer weight he'd have to lug back to the lighthouse when he spotted the wine rack.

Just one, he thought.

He went over and was actually in the act of stretching out a hand to grasp the neck of a likely-looking bottle when he became aware of something out of the corner of his eye, and turned with a sickening jolt of shock. Close at his elbow was the glazed door leading into the next room, and on the other side was a woman.

She was perhaps seventy-five, with white hair cut short and as fluffy as a baby bird, and she was clad in a dull but respectable burgundy acrylic twinset and slacks. Matt noted very clearly the gold sleepers in her papery earlobes and the gold bracelet watch on her liver-spotted wrist. He also saw that she was dead.

Her eyeballs were milky white—statue's eyes, Matt thought queasily—and her skin had the grey-green tint of early decomposition. There was a mangled looking injury at the side of her neck and blood smeared all over her lower face, staining her teeth. She was indubitably dead but she was *not* lying down. She was pawing at the door between them, thumping at the glass panels with the mindlessness of a bluebottle buzzing at a windowpane. Matt saw with horror that several of her fingers were missing.

It took him several seconds of paralysed horror to realise that she wasn't able to get through the door; she lacked the ability to turn the handle, although Matt supposed she might manage it eventually purely by accident. He backed away very slowly, and almost fell over his backpack. He picked it up with one hand and kept moving, leaving the other bags where they were. As he crept out of the kitchen he could still hear that *bump-bump* behind him as she mindlessly pushed against the door. Then he heaved the bag onto his back and fled.

Outside, he drew in great lungfuls of clean air and then swore, over and over. He wasn't sure whom he was swearing at: the government broadcasters for not being more specific about the danger, or himself for having nearly walked into it. Then he threw up. When his cramping stomach was empty of the last crumbs of chocolate chip cookie, he wiped his mouth on his sleeve.

A virus, they said. What kind of bloody virus does that*?*

He thought of his last sight of the car as it vanished over the hill. What had Angela found at the other end of her journey? Had she even had enough petrol to get wherever she was going? If not... Matt realised he felt sorry for her, whether she'd cheated or not. He also reflected that other people would have done what she'd done—a lot of them.

He turned his back on the road leading to the village, and started walking back to the lighthouse.

When he came to the place where he had seen the cows, Matt at first thought they had gone—ambled back up the slope towards the rest of the herd. Then he saw that one of them was still there, lying on the coarse grass with its velvety brown back pressed against the wire fence. He was focused on getting back to the light-house, but it still struck him as a little odd—was it sleeping there? As he drew level with it, its body seemed to shudder and it crossed his mind fleetingly that it might be hurt. He paused uncertainly, and the same convulsive movement occurred again. Then, as he watched, something appeared on the cow's flank—a reddish object which fluttered and then settled. Fingers. A hand.

Someone was behind the animal, just out of sight.

Matt became aware of sounds—*wet* sounds. A terrible image filled his head, of someone crouched behind the cow, tearing, chewing, swallowing. He walked on, his hands clamped over his mouth, moving swiftly but not running because he feared to draw attention with rapid movements. When he came to a curve in the road he risked a look back and saw that it was not some*one*, a single person, feasting on the cow. There were two of them—no, three. The third was small. They had bare calves and forearms and where their clothes were not dyed crimson the fabric was bright and colourful: holiday outfits.

Matt did not want to see them at closer quarters, particularly not the small one. He put his head down and kept moving, only glancing behind him occasionally to check that he was not being followed.

LATER THAT DAY, Matt went back into the ticket office and located the keys to the tower. Then he climbed the spiral staircase to the lantern room, and looked out. On one side there was sea, grey-blue waves with ripples of white foam. There were no craft to be seen anywhere, but that might have been the case at any time; lighthouses were usually positioned in places where you didn't want ships to come close in to shore. From the other side he had a good view of the land he had walked across earlier that day. He stood there for a long time, peering out. He could see the field where the cows were but from this distance he couldn't really make out any detail. Close to the road was a dark blot that was almost certainly the cow lying against the fence. At the top of the field, near the cliffs, were more dark shapes: cattle crowding around a drinking trough or feeder. He could not see the people in the colourful shirts and shorts anywhere. Where were they?

A terrible, gnawing dread settled over him. Would those people—those *things*—come here? He'd seen no intelligence in the old woman in the bungalow but clearly some instinct, some urge to feed, remained in those affected. Whatever strange tides they drifted on might bring them here, to the lighthouse. Supposing the light drew them, like moths?

Matt looked at the lenses set up on a stainless steel stand in the centre of the room. In daylight, unlit, they were as glossy as tear-filled eyes. When darkness fell they would be dazzling, flashing every twenty seconds with a brilliance that drenched the landscape. He wondered if he should pick up the chair the staff had left up here and swing it at the lenses—try to smash them to smithereens. He doubted any retribution would fall on him if he did.

He touched the back of the chair, thoughtfully.

In the end, he didn't do it. The engineer in him revolted at the thought; once smashed, the light would probably never be repaired, not now. He would do it if it became necessary, he decided.

Matt descended the tower, following the stairs round and round, and went back to the keeper's cottage, where he looked at the provisions lined up on the kitchen surface. He regretted not bringing the other bags now; what he had managed to carry back looked pitifully little. He supposed that if he alternated between meagre tinned meals and packets of biscuits he might last a week or ten days. And then... He decided not to think about that.

When night fell he simply went to bed, switching off all the lights in the cottage. He lay there for a while, watching the gap at the top of the curtains light up every twenty seconds. Outside, everything was silent, and eventually he slipped into an uneasy sleep.

THE FOLLOWING MORNING, Matt ascended the tower again. When he left the keeper's cottage, he looked out and checked left to right first. There was no sign of anything untoward. The only moving things were the sea birds wheeling overhead and the wind ruffling the grass beyond the wall. He went up to the lantern room again carrying a flask of tea and some of the tiresome packets of biscuits. In addition he had a pair of binoculars which he had found after some considerable searching, in a cupboard in the ticket office. He positioned the chair so that it faced the landward side. Then he sat down and watched.

He finished the tea and a bottle of Irn Bru before he saw anything. Then it was far away, so far that he had to use the binoculars. As he brought them into focus he saw that it was one of *them* (he didn't like to name it any more clearly to himself) moving along the road in a stumbling, haphazard way. When it came to a bend in the road, it just ignored it and staggered on over the grass. Matt calculated that if it maintained its current trajectory, it would miss the light-house compound altogether, and if it did not have the intelligence to stop, it would keep going until it went over the cliff edge and plummeted into the sea.

It would also encounter a cow. The animal was standing almost in its way. With sick fascination Matt watched the distance between the two narrowing.

"Run," he muttered, but the cow simply stood there. He even saw its head turn slightly; it was clear it could see the thing approaching it. He held his breath, but then to his astonishment the shambling figure moved past the cow without reacting to it in any way, and continued its uneven progress across the grass.

Matt lowered the binoculars. Why hadn't it attacked? He thought about that for a long time as the thing struggled onwards, drag-ging its feet over tussocks. He remembered the one in the bungalow, with her milky-white eyes. Perhaps they couldn't see clearly with their decomposing eyes, especially if something were motionless. The dead cow he'd seen them feasting on might have moved suddenly and deliberately, attracting their attention. Or perhaps it had simply been bad luck: the things had literally stumbled on it. He remembered those terrible wet tearing sounds, and shuddered. There was no doubt—poorly sighted or not, they were extremely dangerous. You wouldn't want to find yourself cornered in an enclosed space.

At any rate, he thought, this might mean the lamp wasn't a problem. He ate another packet of flapjacks, thoughtfully, and then went back to watching.

• • •

FIVE DAYS LATER, Matt opened the last tin of food. It was the *All Day Breakfast*, which in his imagination had become a lavish and mouth watering fry-up. Instead he popped the ring pull and found himself looking down into a congealed cylinder of beans, sausage and egg. It looked disappointing, but once heated through it was reasonably tasty. It was also gone far too quickly, and the prospect of going back to living on chocolate chip cookies was not attractive; something would have to change, and soon.

He had been spending most of his days in the lantern room, watching the things which had been people through the binoculars. Considerably more of them had appeared, although he was coming to the conclusion that their migrations were undirected and mindless. There had been no sign of them gathering outside the compound after a night of the lamp flashing and he suspected that their sight really was poor or non-existent.

It had also become apparent several days ago that a change was coming over them. Earlier, Matt had seen some of the things stumble past the lighthouse and drop unresistingly into the sea. Now, increasingly, they simply seemed to … stop. It was like watching a battery-operated toy run out of power. They would move more and more slowly, as though dragging their limbs against an unseen current, and then the next forward step just wouldn't happen. Some fell to their knees, and others pitched forward onto what was left of their faces. Gazing through the binoculars, Matt saw that one of the nearest was—or had been—an older man of perhaps seventy, with thick white hair, and clad in a neatly tailored shirt and trousers with that same terrible maroon stain on the front of them. He stood still while the wind made the grass around him undulate like waves. His hands shivered and his jaw worked convulsively for a little time. Then he stopped moving.

Are they dying? Matt wondered. He adjusted the focus and studied a thin woman in a fluttering summer dress that had once been white with blue flowers on it. As he watched, she listed to one side and then fell gracelessly into the grass, where she lay unmoving. He lowered the binoculars. *Can something die if it's already dead?*

He imagined himself walking out of the lighthouse compound and heading off down the road, taking little detours around these stricken horrors. Matt had an uneasy feeling he was being craven not to try it, but he didn't trust them not to shudder back into terrifying animation and attack him.

After a while he turned his back on the rolling landscape with those ugly figures dotted about in it, and gazed out to sea instead. There were still no boats to be seen, but there were sections of coastline visible to the south so he spent a long time scanning those. In one place a column of brown smoke rose indistinctly into the air but at that distance it was impossible to know what was burning.

Matt decided he would try again that night, after dark. He would see whether there were lights anywhere along that stretch of land. If the power was still on, that might mean other survivors—somewhere to aim for if he left the lighthouse.

Not if, he reminded himself uneasily. *When.* One day, even the biscuits would run out.

AT TWILIGHT, Matt ascended the tower again.

He'd brought a blanket and a flask of tea with him, anticipating some long cold hours of watching from the lighthouse's metal gallery. He couldn't imagine watching from the lantern room itself when the light was operating; he was afraid he'd burn his retinas out. It was a clear, dry night, but when he stepped out onto the gallery the sensation of cold air moving all around him was vertiginous and for a few moments he remained with his back against the wall. Above him, the lamp suddenly burst into dazzling life. At such close range it was like a silent explosion and Matt squeezed his eyes shut.

This was a crap idea, he said to himself. All the same, the alternative of watching from somewhere down on the cliffs, with those dead-but-perhaps-not-dead bodies lurking in the grass like landmines was unthinkable. He steeled himself, and when the light had died again he walked cautiously round the tower to the side which faced the sea. As he did so, he counted to twenty under his breath, and closed his eyes as the flash came, pressing his face into his elbow to shut out the glare. Then he gazed out to sea.

Whatever had been burning earlier must have gone out; Matt couldn't see any sign of a conflagration in that direction. In fact he couldn't see any lights at all. He thought he could faintly discern the distant coastline as a dark stripe between the leaden sea and the velvet of the night sky, but that was all.

He stared with such desperate concentration that the next flash took him unaware, and left him blinking into a flaming afterglow. Matt cursed and pressed his hands over his face. He felt a little sick.

Nothing on that coastline? Not one light?

He began counting. When the next flash had been and gone he looked again, but there was nothing to see. In all that dark vista, the only light was the one that pulsed so brightly above his head every twenty seconds. The landward side was the same, though he could hardly have expected otherwise, since the nearest houses were out of sight. All the same, he felt terribly alone. When the light came it bleached the landscape briefly and Matt saw the unnamed things standing like sentinels in the long grass; then it would fade and for twenty seconds he felt like the only creature in all of that vast darkness.

He drank the tea from his flask and pulled the blanket close around him. For a while he looked at the land, and then he felt his way round to the other side and gazed at the sea. He did this for a long time, until his eyelids began to droop. He swayed on his feet, his eyes sliding closed, jerked awake again and saw a light.

He'd lost track of the count and a split second later the world was bleached into invisibility. Matt covered his face again and waited. When he was sure his eyes had recovered he lowered his arm and ventured to look again.

There really was a light. It wasn't on the land—it was far out to sea, in a place where there was no distant land mass.

A ship, he thought. *Or at least a large boat.*

Excitement flared in him. It might be a military cruiser—something huge and well equipped, with stores and a canteen. Company. Safety. *Food*. That was precisely the kind of craft that might still be sailing the sea, biding its time. Perhaps even looking for survivors.

Matt experienced about a minute and a half of unadulterated joy, thinking *I'm saved!* and then his mood plummeted. How would anyone know he was here? The lighthouse was undoubtedly visible but it was automated, as anyone versed in nautical matters would know. It was probably a useful landmark but nothing more—not something worth investigating.

He stared at the distant light until the count of twenty was up and he had to hide his eyes again. He found he was almost in tears, imagining all the people, all the resources, just sailing away. His lips parted as though he were going to scream after the distant ship, but he knew he'd have been wasting his breath. Nobody could possibly hear a single cry at that distance.

The foghorn. They'd hear that alright.

The thought had barely passed through his brain before he was back inside the tower and running down the spiral stairs. He stopped himself when he got to the bottom, and made himself open the door cautiously and look right and left before crossing the courtyard, for fear one of those *things* might have got inside. It was deserted. He went in through the ticket office and into the engine room. There he waited for the flash from the lantern before switching on the lights, trusting that the flash would camouflage the sudden illumination.

The diesel engines waited, prosaic yet beautiful to an engineer's eyes, finished with green paint and gleaming metal fittings. A strange calm came over Matt. He remembered what to do to get the engines running, and he set about doing it. He did not allow the urgency of the situation to unnerve him. The foghorn *must* sound before the ship had a chance to get too far away. He worked fast, and he did not make mistakes.

The engines clattered into life, one after another, roaring and knocking. The sound was tremendous. Matt remembered how it had been when Angela was still there, how they had been able to hear the racket through the thick walls of the cottage. It was earsplitting close up. He knew he had to wait until the correct air pressure was achieved before turning the valve to let air down to the foghorn, but he was feverish with impatience. What if the ship sailed out of range?

Please God, he said to himself, although he had never had any particular faith. *Please God let it be near enough.*

He fidgeted and sweated, shifting from foot to foot. At last there was enough pressure, and with some effort he turned the wheel that opened the valve, hearing it scream from disuse. Then he ran the short distance to the tower and went up the steps two at a time, followed by the roar of the engines. As he emerged onto the gallery, the lantern flashed. Everything turned dazzling white. Even after it had faded all Matt could see for several seconds was a throbbing afterglow. Then he went to the seaward side of the tower and gazed out, counting under his breath.

As his eyes adjusted properly to the dark, he realised he could still see the light.

"Yes," he said under his breath.

At the same instant he heard the foghorn sound below him. In the cool night air it was loud and very resonant, rolling out over the dark sea. Whoever was on the ship *must* hear it, he thought in sudden jubilation.

Nineteen, he counted, and covered his eyes.

He was opening them again when he heard a clang. It was distinct enough from the clattering of the engines and the fading blare of the foghorn that he briefly wondered what it was. Still he kept gazing at the light, out there on the sea. He was convinced it was very slightly bigger—that it was getting nearer. Or at any rate, *nearly* convinced. Matt held onto the railing, the metal cold under his hands, and strained his eyes.

Clang.

There it was again, that curious sound, and this time it protruded far enough into his consciousness that he nearly forgot to shut his eyes during the flash. Afterwards, he focussed on the light again, willing it closer, but his concentration was broken. He couldn't think of a good reason for that clanging sound. He didn't want to stop watching the far-off beacon of hope, but a feeling of unease was creeping over him.

Holding onto the handrail in the dark, he made his way round the tower, listening. The foghorn sounded again, vast and forlorn, and as it died away he heard another clang, and then another. It seemed to him that the sounds were coming from the landward side, and specifically from the gate, which lay deeply shrouded in darkness.

Matt shaded his eyes as best he could and waited for the next flash.

Nineteen...

The light bloomed above him, and swept over the ground in a dazzling white tide. In those few brief instants of illumination Matt saw a heaving, pullulating mass of activity on the other side of the gate. Limbs were thrust between and over the bars, groping at the air. Exposed teeth gleamed brilliantly—bone too.

Darkness closed in again. Matt clutched the rail, his mouth dry.

No, he thought. *No, no.*

Almost instinctively, he began counting again. He wanted to believe that the next flash would show him an empty gateway—that the whole horrible vision was the product of his imagination. But in the darkness he heard more of those dull clangs and knew that others were coming, hurling themselves mindlessly against the metal bars and the press of bodies already clustered there.

Flash.

The gateway was choked with bodies and beyond them Matt saw more scarecrow figures stumbling up the road towards the lighthouse. Their movements were graceless, uncoordinated even, but they were horribly fast. With enough of them pressed up against the gate, it would eventually burst open—he could see that.

The foghorn was sounding again, with a long sonorous note that seemed to vibrate through his bones. Matt saw a reaction amongst the things at the gate, as though their frenzy suddenly intensified.

Darkness.

Sound. Oh God, it's sound. How could I have been so stupid?

For a moment he stood there, paralysed with horror, and then he started feeling his way around the gallery until he was on the other side. Knowing that the flash was coming again in a few seconds, he stared desperately out to sea. The light from the ship was there, but it was still a long way away. Even if it came, he knew, there was nowhere to land a boat at the point where the lighthouse stood. The nearest place was probably the bay.

Flash.

Matt dropped his gaze, shielding his eyes, and below him he saw the clifftops leading down to the foghorn. Things were crawling over them, drawn by the sounds. They moved oddly, because some of their limbs had been mangled or broken by falling over the cliff edge, but still the sound drew them, even if they had to claw the ground and drag their shattered bodies along.

Darkness.

A whimper escaped Matt's lips, but it was lost in the long blare of the foghorn. Then he lunged for the doorway, one thought in his mind: *turn the engines off.*

As he followed the spiral staircase round and round, going as fast as he dared, another flash bloomed through the window. Matt didn't stop to look out. He was almost within sight of the ground floor when he heard the gate burst open: there was a very loud clang and the dull sound of bodies falling. He froze, his hand clutching the rail.

Over the muffled roar of the diesel engines he heard other sounds start: bumping, shuffling, dragging.

Matt measured the distance to the ticket room door in his head. He knew he couldn't get to it, and into the engine room, before those things swarmed over him. He backed up a little, slowly, caught between the mad desire to try and shut off the noise that was calling them and knowing he'd never make it. Outside, the foghorn sounded again, too loudly.

Matt turned, trembling, and went back up the stairs. Thoughts crackled in his head like breaking glass.

How long before the diesel runs out and the engines stop? When the noises stop, how long before those things go away? Will they go away?

As he reached the gallery and stepped outside another flash turned the whole world a brilliant white.

Matt was dazzled for a few seconds but when the next explosion of light came he was ready, hands shielding his eyes. He found himself looking down on a scene from Hieronymus Bosch. The courtyard was filling with writhing, grasping, snapping bodies. The doorway to the ticket office and engine room was already crammed with them and those unable to force their way in were mindlessly attempting any other opening. A window smashed as hands that were more bone than flesh thrust themselves through it.

Matt thought: *dear God, is the tower door closed?*

As the darkness closed in again, he realised it wasn't. He could hear them already, crashing about in the limited space below, clawing at the walls, hurling themselves at the staircase. There was no escape, he knew. Pretty soon they'd be crawling up the stairs, and he had nowhere to go.

Matt wondered whether it would be any use to stay still and silent on the gallery and hope he'd somehow escape their attention. It was a desperate plan, but it was all he had. He turned to close the gallery door, holding his breath, feeling for the handle in the darkness. He could hear that the things were close; they were ascending the spiral stairs far more quickly than he'd expected. Had he made some sound they had heard, even over the racket below? The sickness of extreme terror was on him and he couldn't tell. In spite of it, he was counting the passing seconds, automatically.

Nineteen.

When the flash came it showed him the loathsome things that were crowding their way up to him, things that still wore the remnants of suits and summer dresses and holiday clothes. Hanks of hair hung over empty sockets or eyes that were milky white. There was still meat on some of the phalanges clutching at the air.

And then—he thought he saw Angela amongst them. There was no time to question whether it was really her or not; it was the hideous sum of all his fears. As the darkness swept over him Matt screamed helplessly, and he was still screaming when he felt their teeth in his flesh.

Helen Grant writes Gothic novels and short supernatural fiction. Her new novel Jump Cut, *about a notorious lost movie, was published in September 2023 by Fledgling Press. The* Independent *described it as "a chilling, highly atmospheric tale."*

Helen's short stories have appeared in Weird Tales, Supernatural Tales, All Hallows *and various anthologies including Egaeus Press's acclaimed* Crooked Houses, Swan River Press's *Uncertainties* 2 *and Titan Books'* *dark academia volume* In These Hallowed Halls. *Joyce Carol Oates has described her as "a brilliant chronicler of the uncanny as only those who dwell in places of dripping, graylit beauty can be." A lifelong fan of M.R. James, she has spoken at two M.R. James conferences.*

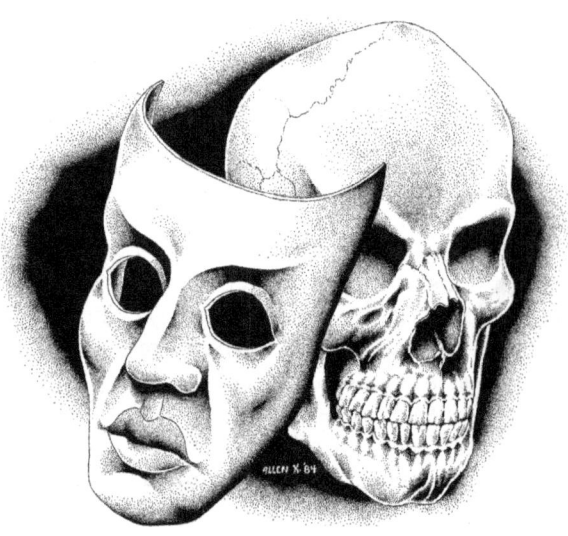

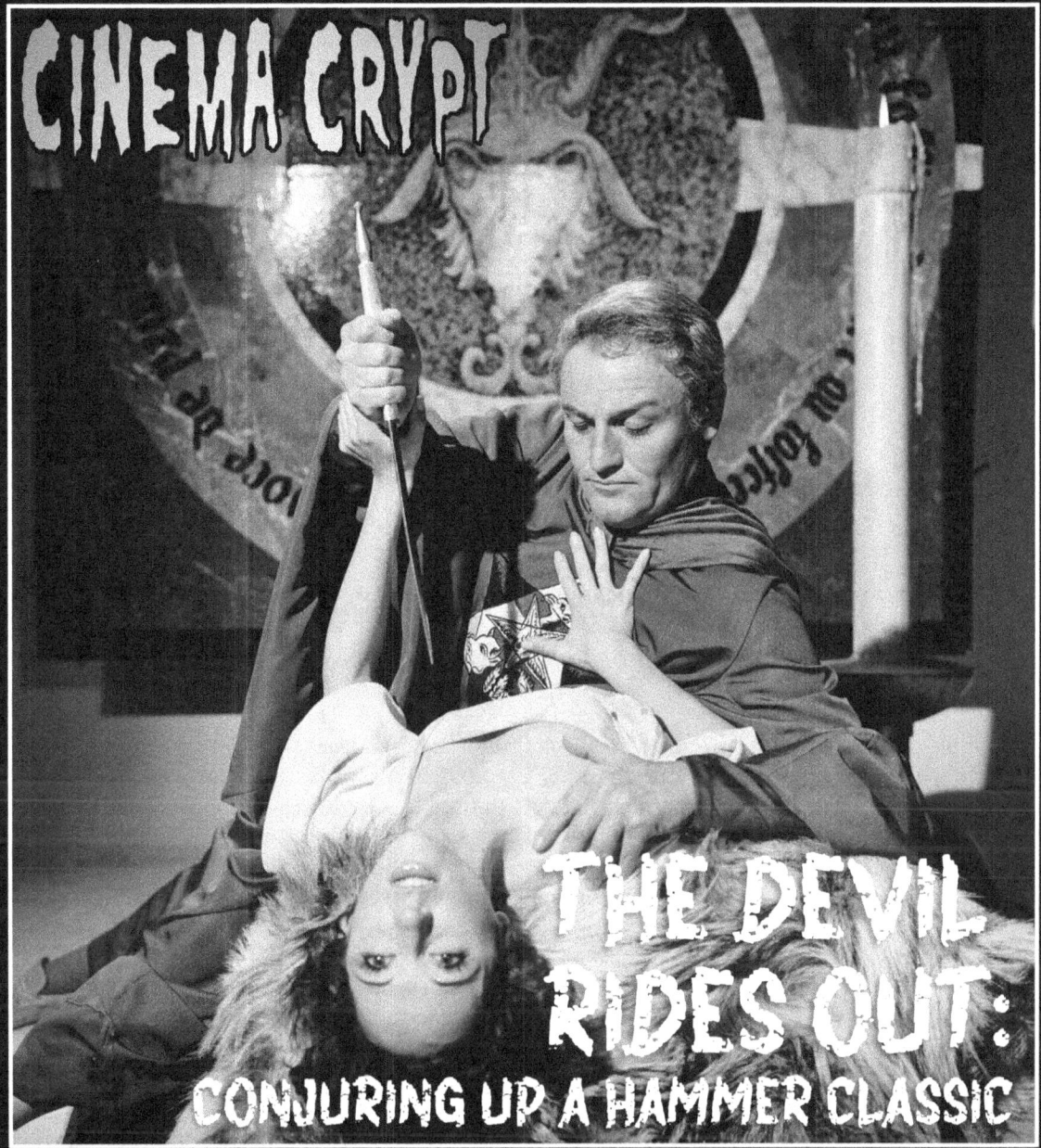

JOHN LLEWELLYN PROBERT'S

CINEMA CRYPT

THE DEVIL RIDES OUT:
CONJURING UP A HAMMER CLASSIC

IT'S GENERALLY CONSIDERED TO BE ONE OF THE BEST FILMS MADE BY BOTH HAMMER FILMS AND ITS DIRECTOR, TERENCE FISHER. It was based on a book written in 1934 that was still a worldwide best seller fifty years later yet despite that the title was changed for its initial release in the United States. Its author, Dennis Wheatley, was a renowned writer of both pulp thrillers and novels of black magic, but one of the many reasons it is such a magnificent film is because of a tremendous piece of screenwriting by Richard Matheson. It's 1968's *The Devil Rides Out* (US title *The Devil's Bride*), a movie that may have seemed a little out of step with current trends when it was released (possibly accounting for why it didn't do as well as everyone was hoping), but whose reputation has deservedly grown over the years.

The Devil Rides Out (1968) and all associated images copyright © 20th Century Fox and Warner-Pathé

We open to James Bernard's threatening bombast of a score. Bernard would often use the syllables of a Hammer movie title as inspiration for his music, and *The Devil Rides Out* is no exception. It's also worth pointing out here that Hammer were well aware of the kinds of audiences that attended their movies, and knew that, far from the quiet and respectful art house crowd, they were more the type who needed the crash bang wallop of James Bernard to announce "the film is starting so shut up and pay attention!"

The titles unfold over cabbalistic symbols and a smiling Baphomet. We'll be talking about the cast more in a bit, but for now let's just enjoy the sight of familiar Hammer crew names like director of photography Arthur Grant, production designer Bernard Robinson and editor James Needs. Let's also take note of the name Michael Stainer-Hutchins, the man credited with providing the film's special effects. We'll come back to him in a bit, but for now let's allow Richard Matheson's screenplay to unfold at a pace that's going to crack along for most of the picture.

A biplane lands. It's piloted by Rex Van Ryn, looking every inch the dashing Wheatley hero ready for action with his three piece suit already on beneath his flying garb.

He's played by Leon Greene, who had been a bass singer with the D'Oyly Carte Opera company, acted and sang in Richard Lester's film version of *A Funny Thing Happened on the Way to the Forum* and also appeared for Hammer as Little John in the same year's *A Challenge for Robin Hood*. Known in part for his distinctive voice, Hammer nevertheless decided to have Patrick Allen dub him. If you want to hear what Greene would have actually sounded like in the film, you can still hear his voice in the trailer.

Rex is picked up by the Duc De Richleau, played by Christopher Lee who needs no introduction to readers of this publication. In the novels the Duc is French, but Lee quite sensibly makes no attempt at an accent.

What many people don't appreciate is that Dennis Wheatley's novel *The Devil Rides Out* was in fact a sequel to a book called

Leon Greene,
Christopher Lee,
and Patrick Mower.

Below:
Gwen Ffrangcon-Davies

The Forbidden Territory, in which all the main players (excepting the antagonist) were first introduced. Therefore, while the follow-up mentioned their previous exploits in passing, readers were likely expected to already be up and running with who they were. Matheson appreciated this wouldn't be the case with cinema audiences and with great economy sets up the group of friends by mention of their names in conversation here, and a little later, mentions the fact that Rex has flown over to attend their reunion.

One of those friends is Simon Aron (Patrick Mower, who would go on to appear in Gordon Hessler's somewhat unsatisfactory *Cry of the Banshee* as well as Robert Hartford-Davis's ill-fated *Incense for the Damned*) whom the Duc hasn't seen for some time. He has, however, bought a house with an observatory, so they call in there, gate-crashing a party whose attendees would tick numerous diversity box requirements of many a modern major studio. Here, though, the reason is to emphasise the exoticism of Simon's new lifestyle. Amongst the guests is Peter Swanwick, who was probably best known for playing the Supervisor in Patrick McGoohan's classic television series *The Prisoner*. Our heroes meet the Countess (Gwen Ffrangcon-Davies who was also in Hammer's *The Witches*), Tanith (Niké Arrighi

who would return to Hammer for a more minor role in Peter Sasdy's *Countess Dracula*) and, most important of all, Mocata. The Mocata of the novel is a pale, bald, almost grub-like black magician, allegedly modelled (as pretty much every fictional black magician of the period was) on Aleister Crowley. In Hammer's film he's played magnificently by Charles Gray, who takes less in the way of inspiration for his character from the novel and instead plays him rather more as a silky, satanic Bond villain. Little wonder, perhaps, seeing as he had just come off working on *You Only Live Twice* and would indeed go on to play Blofeld in 1971's *Diamonds are Forever.*

Simon claims he has forgotten about their reunion. Two more people turn up and Tanith is spooked because there should only be thirteen people present. Then it's the Duc's turn to look worried as Rex haplessly blurts out that they weren't invited and just popped in. Unsurprisingly they are asked to leave, but not before the Duc insists on going upstairs to take a look at Simon's observatory, which is a fine piece of production design overall, but especially the satanic mosaic on the floor.

There's a rattling from the cupboard. It's two chickens! One is black, the other white, and now the Duc's suspicions are confirmed. Poor old Rex is still none the wiser, so the Duc has to spell it out for him, calling black magic "the most dangerous game known to mankind." The Duc tries to convince Simon to leave with them and when Simon refuses, the Duc resorts to that good old standby of 1930s fiction and knocks him unconscious. They carry Simon out. The Duc punches the butler. Mocata is not pleased. We are barely ten minutes into the film at this point, a lot has happened,

and we as an audience are not at all confused. Well done, Richard Matheson.

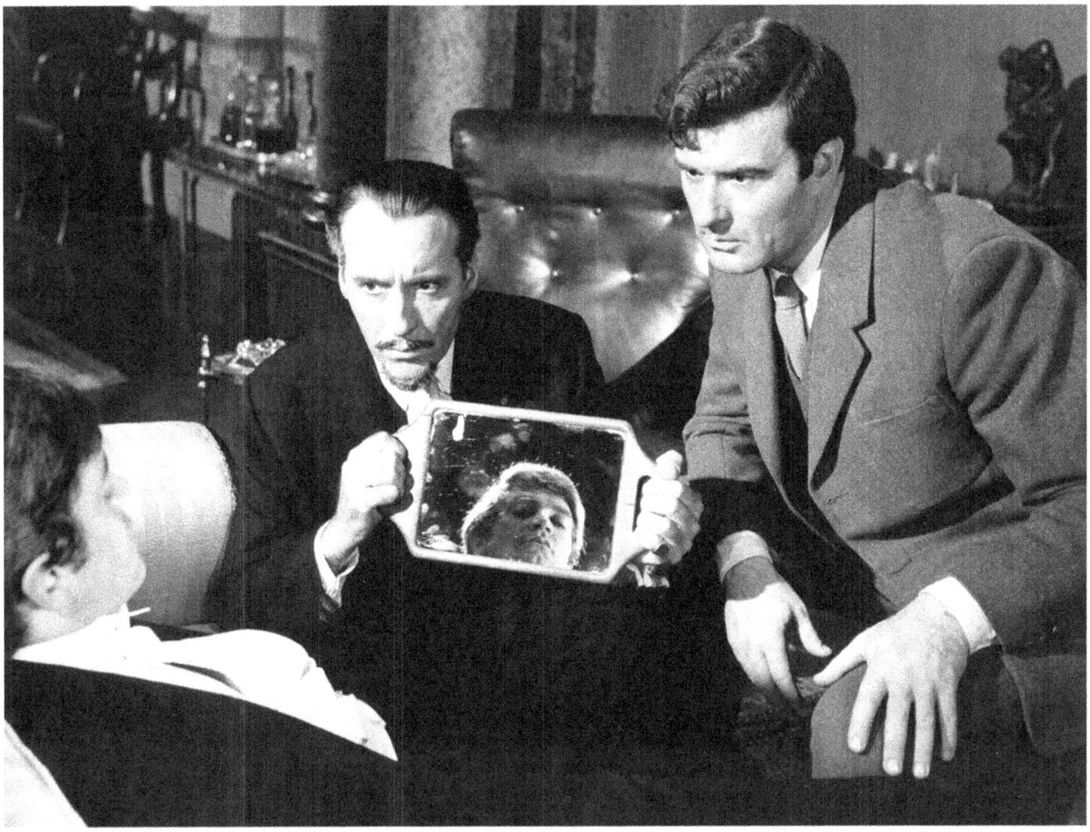

Back at the Duc's place Simon gets hypnotised and is sent to sleep. The Duc puts a crucifix around Simon's neck. In the novel it's a jewelled swastika but this was understandably changed with World War II having intervened between book and film. Simon goes off to bed while the Duc authoritatively informs both Rex and us that the power of darkness is "a living force which can be tapped at any given moment of the night."

Meanwhile up in the Duc's bedroom we get one of the loudest crashes of soundtrack music ever to accompany someone opening their eyes. As in the novel, Simon begins to choke from the chain around his neck. It's removed by Max the butler. Max is played by Keith Pyott who, like Peter Swanwick, doesn't receive a credit in this and was also in *The Prisoner*.

Simon is gone. Rex and the Duc head back to Simon's house where there's a handy open window to let them in. The house is in darkness and the satanists have likely skedaddled. We get a beautiful, eerily lit wander through the house, culminating in the observatory, where it turns out the chickens are fine but our heroes might not be, as the lights dim, the temperature drops, and something begins to emerge from that satanic design on the floor. The sight of an African man in a red loincloth may well not have had much effect on even audiences of the time, but those eyes are still rather spooky.

Rex looks at them despite the Duc telling him not to. It must have made a change for Christopher Lee to be the one lobbing a crucifix at something, which is what he does here to get our heroes out of trouble.

In the car, the Duc explains that Mocata must be a powerful sorcerer to conjure such a demon, and that he may even be an ipsissimus. The word is actually the superlative of the Latin *ipse*, meaning self, but it has been used to describe a master of the sorcerous arts. It turns out it's April 29th, meaning our heroes have only one more day to rescue Simon (and, it turns out, Tanith) from their Satanic baptism. In more economical scriptwriting, Tanith is found "at a London hotel," picked up by Rex and driven off into the country to the home of the friends we heard mention of at the beginning of the film, with almost all of the above taking place offscreen.

Richard and Marie are Paul Eddington (also in *The Prisoner* but later much more famous for starring in the BBC sitcoms *The Good Life* and *Yes, Minister*) and Sarah Lawson (aka Mrs. Patrick Allen, who starred with him in the same year's *Night of the Big Heat*). Their daughter, Peggy, who is going to play an important part in the ensuing proceedings, is played by Rosalyn Landor, who in a couple of years' time would appear

in Lionel Jeffries' classic children's ghost story *The Amazing Mr. Blunden* (1971) and a few years after that in an episode of *Hammer House of Horror* (Don Sharp's "Guardian of the Abyss").

With his classic car and his "poop poops" as he pulls up to Richard and Marie's house, Rex is a bit like a dashing version of *The Wind in the Willows*' Mr. Toad. He certainly displays Mr. Toad's lack of common sense by leaving Tanith in the car so she can steal it. Rex gives chase in Richard's red roadster. Mocata's power turns the windscreen white, but Rex is a 1930s hero, so he punches through the glass. However, the fog that subsequently appears proves rather less negotiable. The car crashes and Rex has to resort to pursuit on foot.

It does seem terribly convenient that the country house the satanists are all meeting

up in is so close to both Richard and Marie's and (as we shall see in a minute) the Duc's London residence as well. Mind you, it does boast a very nice triple-headed serpent gate mount.

Off all the satanists drive to their sabbat, with Rex hidden in the boot of one of the cars. The sabbat itself is a brightly lit, fairly ornate affair, complete with marquee, altar, and goat sacrifice (time for some Hammer blood). Luckily for Rex there's also a phone box nearby. It takes the Duc no time at all to turn up, and he hands Rex phials of salt and mercury, the results of his morning's research at the British Museum. Meanwhile the sabbat is in full swing, with an orgy that's about as Bacchanalian as it was possible to get in a British film in 1968. The celebrations, presided over by Mocata, culminate in a manifestation of the Goat of Mendes—"The Devil himself," as Richleau says. In fact, it's actually Hammer stuntman and frequent Christopher Lee double Eddie Powell.

Rex and the Duc literally crash Simon's baptism in their car, with Rex standing on the running board so he can throw a crucifix at the devil. The satanists scatter and Simon and Tanith are rescued—for now.

We're back at Richard and Marie's house, which boasts some beautifully designed Bernard Robinson interiors. Tanith is sent off to bed with Rex to watch over her. Despite playing the "young lovers," Leon Greene and Niké Arrighi don't really have a lot of chemistry in *The Devil Rides Out* and their budding relationship is perhaps the only thing in the film that lacks integrity.

Meanwhile the Duc has got Richard and Marie up to speed in his new hosts' enormous drawing room. He gives them some precise instructions as regards eating and drinking, and then leaves. But who's that hiding around the corner?

Mocata takes advantage of the opportunity to call. With Richard indisposed keeping Simon company and Rex with Tanith, it's up to Marie to deal with our urbane black magician. We then get a splendid scene where Mocata tries to bend Marie to his will, starting off with a long shot to emphasise the (safe you would think) distance between them, cutting to a couple of two shots from different angles where they

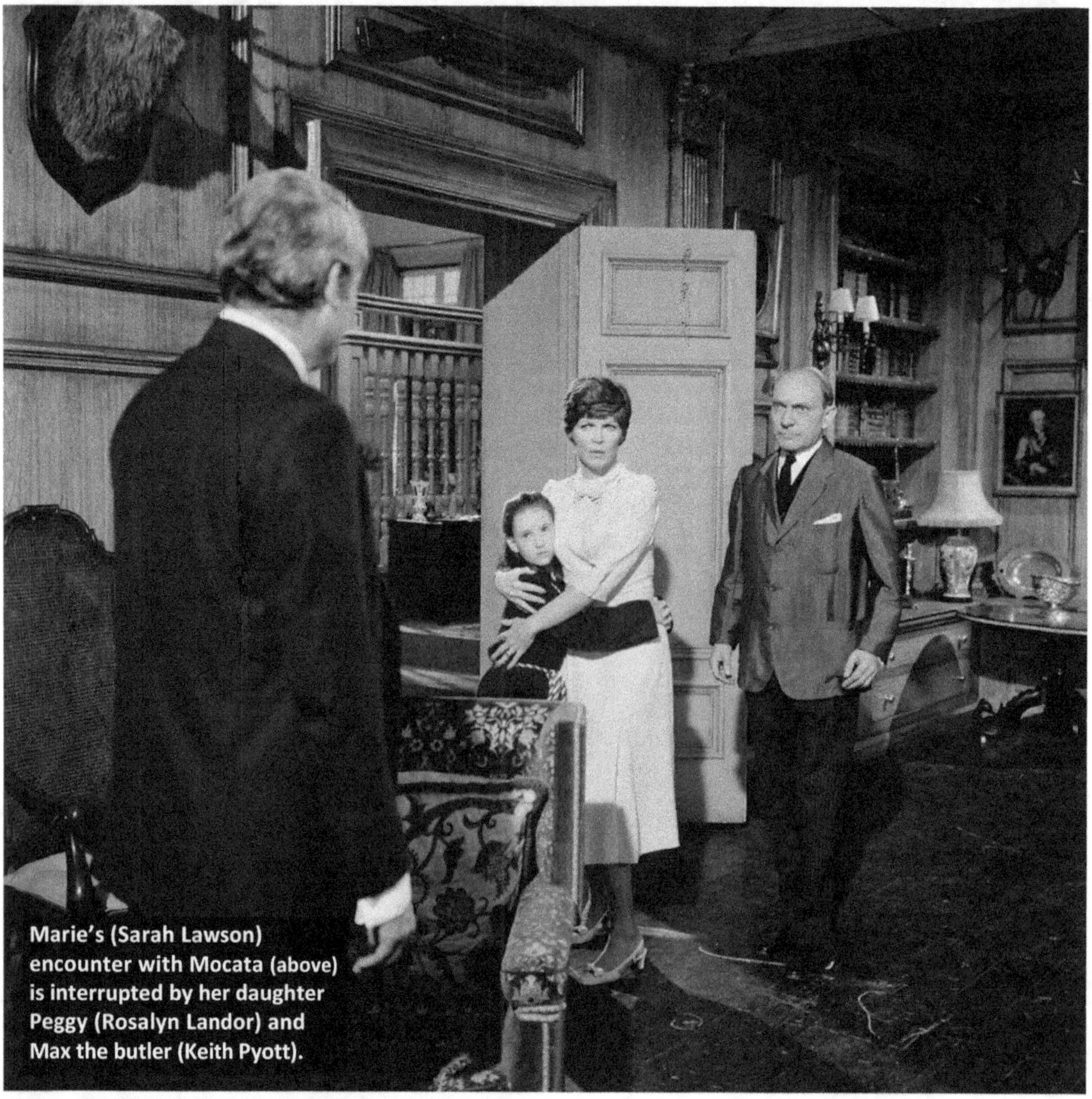

Marie's (Sarah Lawson) encounter with Mocata (above) is interrupted by her daughter Peggy (Rosalyn Landor) and Max the butler (Keith Pyott).

seem closer together, followed by closer shots still of first Mocata and then Marie as she tries to leave and he prevents her with just a few words. The camera stays fixed on Charles Gray, the one in control, whereas with Sarah Lawson we get a very slow zoom in to emphasise his increasing effect on her.

Upstairs, Rex has fallen asleep, giving Tanith, now under Mocata's control, the chance to take down one of the numerous swords this bedroom for some reason has on display. Next door, Simon tries to strangle Richard. Peggy saves the day by entering the drawing room and breaking the spell. Marie demands that Mocata leave, leading to perhaps this film's most quoted line. "I shall not be back, but something will. Tonight." Tanith escapes and Rex gives chase. She claims Mocata works through her, and they resolve to spend the night in a barn with her tied up so she can't harm anyone.

TETRAGRAMMATON AGYOS OTHEOS

NOMINE PA + TRIS
LII ET SPIRITUS + SANCTI
ELOHYM SOTHER + EMMANUEL + SABAOTH
TETRAGRAMMATON + AGYOS + OTHEOS + ISCHIROS

The Duc is back, and Marie explains what happened. Malin the butler (character actor Russell Waters, who would go on to appear in 1973's *The Wicker Man*) has had the unenviable job of clearing all the furniture and rugs out of the drawing room, but he seems to have managed it. Now it's time for the Duc to put his plan into action. The four of them—the Duc, Simon, Richard, and Marie, within the circle of protection the Duc has drawn—is as iconic an image as any from this film.

Mocata begins his efforts to take Simon. Richard is cynical, Simon is thirsty, and the Duc is afraid. The lights dim. Is that Rex at the door? Probably not, but that definitely looks like quite a big spider, one that gets to menace an imaginary Peggy before being vanquished by what we assume must be Holy water. Simon can't stop himself leaving the circle, so once again the Duc knocks him out. It turns out there's only one way to fight back and that's with the last two lines of something called the Susamma Ritual, which has the potential to alter time and space. It's thought that Dennis Wheatley may have got the idea for calling it that from William Hope Hodgson's Carnacki story "The Whistling Room," where the occult detective has to perform the "Saaamaaa Ritual." The words Christopher Lee will speak in a bit are not made up, by the way. They're from an ancient volume called *The Grimoire of Armadel* and are actually part of a ritual to trap a spirit in a bottle of water.

The sound of horses' hooves heralds the imminent arrival of the Angel of Death, sent to claim Simon's soul. He arrives on winged horseback and reveals his skull of a face (which our heroes must not look upon)

against a background that was supposed to be filled in with special effects but wasn't. Michael Stainer-Hutchins was the man responsible for both the Angel of Death and spider effects, and he also shot the entire opening title sequence. The effects have been criticised for being sub-par, but the fact is that Hammer ran out of money and didn't want to spend any more to allow Stainer-Hutchins to finish the effects the way he intended. The effects aren't actually that bad as they stand, and they certainly appear at a point in the film where the viewer is being swept along by plot and dialogue anyway. Nevertheless, in 2012 Studio Canal released a Blu-ray of the film with enhanced CGI effects, which do improve things for those who feel the film needs it.

The Duc says the words and the Angel vanishes. "It's all over," he says, but we know it isn't. Tanith is dead, as the Angel of Death cannot return empty handed, and Peggy is gone. Simon gives chase. The Duc says it would be suicide to follow, and instead summons Tanith's soul into Marie's body so she can reveal to them that Mocata is currently at the house with that handsome gate mount we remarked upon earlier.

Simon enters the house, which appears to have a purpose-built crypt for satanists to get up to their shenanigans. And they're

all there. Mocata plans to sacrifice Peggy. Our heroes arrive but it doesn't seem as if there's much they can do. Not until, that is, Tanith's soul takes possession of Marie once

CONTINUED ON PAGE 74

Peter Swanwick
frowns at the interlopers.

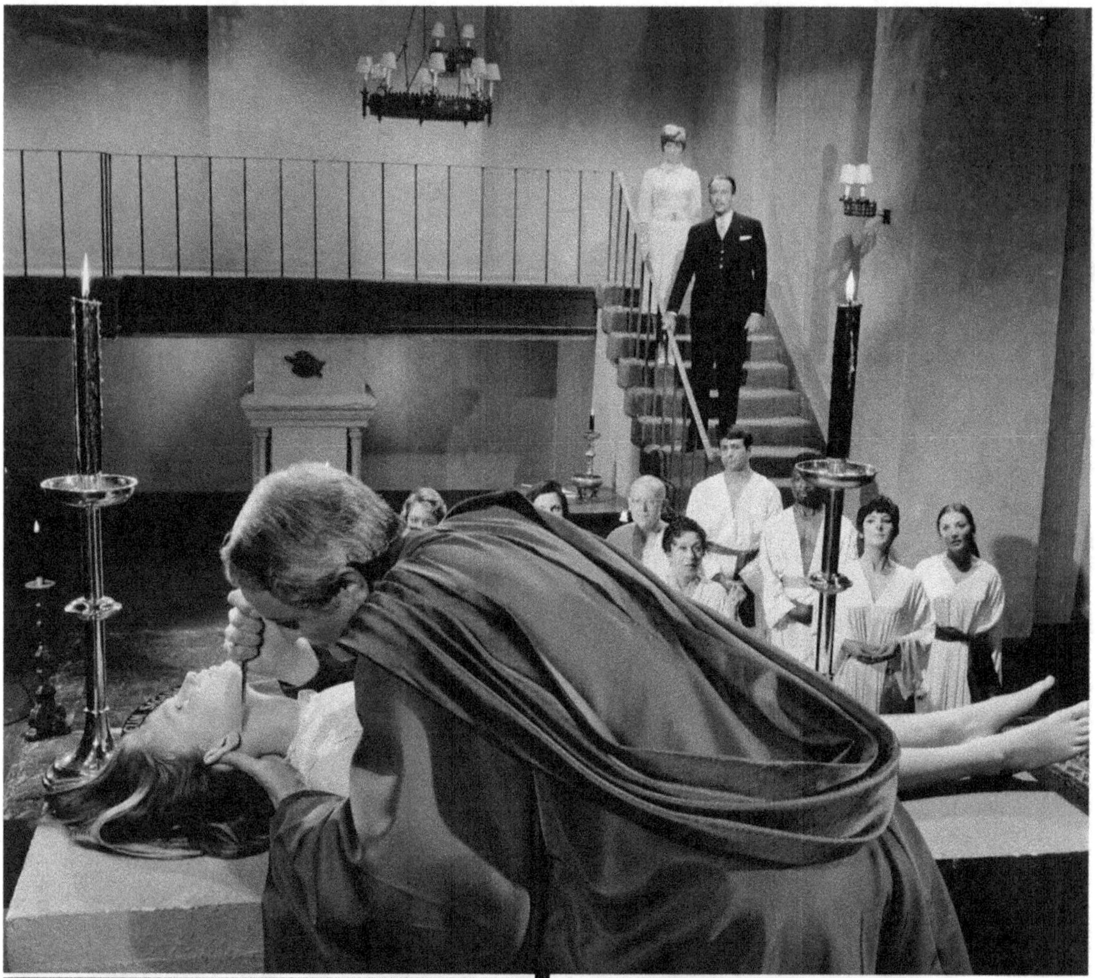

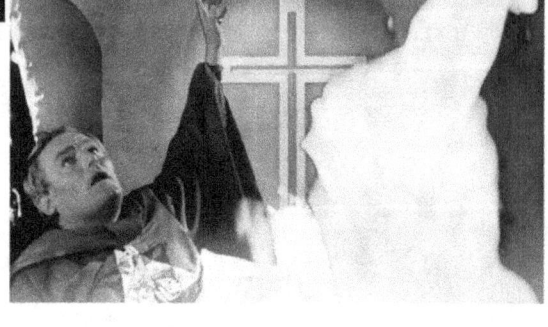

more and gets Peggy to repeat the words of the Susamma ritual, which causes everything to burst into flames. Michael Stainer-Hutchins was supposed to supply a lightning bolt that would hit the altar, but Hammer decided not to pay for it.

The survivors are transported back to the circle of protection at Richard and Marie's house. This time it really is all over. Even Tanith is alive again. It's up to Christopher Lee to clear everything up and explain what happened, both in general and concerning

Mocata specifically (apparently the Angel of Death took him instead of Tanith this time around). Otherwise they have been granted that plot device beloved of some writers—a complete reset.

Terence Fisher was always Hammer's first choice to direct *The Devil Rides Out*, as was Richard Matheson to write the screenplay. Matheson's association with the company went back as far as the plan to adapt his novel *I Am Legend* as *Night Creatures*, a project abandoned for reasons that have now

The Angel of Death.

Below:
A cross revealed by fire.

entered the realms of legend. Some say it was due to the British Board of Films Censors saying it would be banned if they made it, but others think it likely Hammer didn't have the money to do the project justice. Either way, aside from being a well-respected writer, having worked for Roger Corman several times meant Matheson was likely both cheap and fast, both factors that would have made Hammer executives happy.

The cast was a slightly different matter. First choice for playing the Duc de Richleau was Charles Boyer, with Gert Fröbe (who played *Goldfinger*'s eponymous villain) as Mocata, but he proved too expensive. Nevertheless, it seems Mocata was destined to be played by someone with a James Bond connection. Apparently Twentieth Century Fox wanted Linda Evans (of *Dynasty* fame and at the time a star in a show called *The*

All's well that ends well.

Big Valley) to play Tanith.

The film was released in July 1968 in the UK, double-billed with Michael Carreras' *Slave Girls* (US title *Prehistoric Women*). It was released in the US five months later in December with the same accompanying feature but with a different title—*The Devil's Bride*—because, according to at least one source, someone in the US distributor's office thought the public would interpret the original title to be a western. Presumably Mr. Wheatley was not the bestselling author in the US that he was in the rest of the world. However, another reason for the title change (and actually a more believable one) is that Roman Polanski's *Rosemary's Baby* had just come out, and an allusion to other members of the devil's "family" may have been thought

to be more profitable. Either way, it wasn't, and the film didn't do anywhere near as well stateside as it did in the UK.

Looking at it now in the context of other movies being released at the time, *The Devil Rides Out* feels very much like something from an earlier period of cinema. Not just in terms of its setting but in the fact that it would have been up against movies like *Rosemary's Baby* from the US and angrier, gorier British pictures like Michael Reeves' *The Sorcerers* or *Witchfinder General*, which was released just two months before *The Devil Rides Out* came out in the UK. Terence Fisher would end up directing only two more films, splendidly rounding off the Frankenstein saga that would be his lasting legacy to horror cinema, but even those, and especially 1973's *Frankenstein and the Monster from Hell*, would feel out of step with the rest of current cinema trends. Meanwhile Hammer would try Wheatley again in 1976 with *To the Devil a Daughter*, updating it to a modern setting and with a more modern approach. The result was likely a film that ended up in a version no one intended it to, but at least Hammer was able to mount one Dennis Wheatley adaptation that showed the studio at the height of its powers, and for that we can be very grateful.

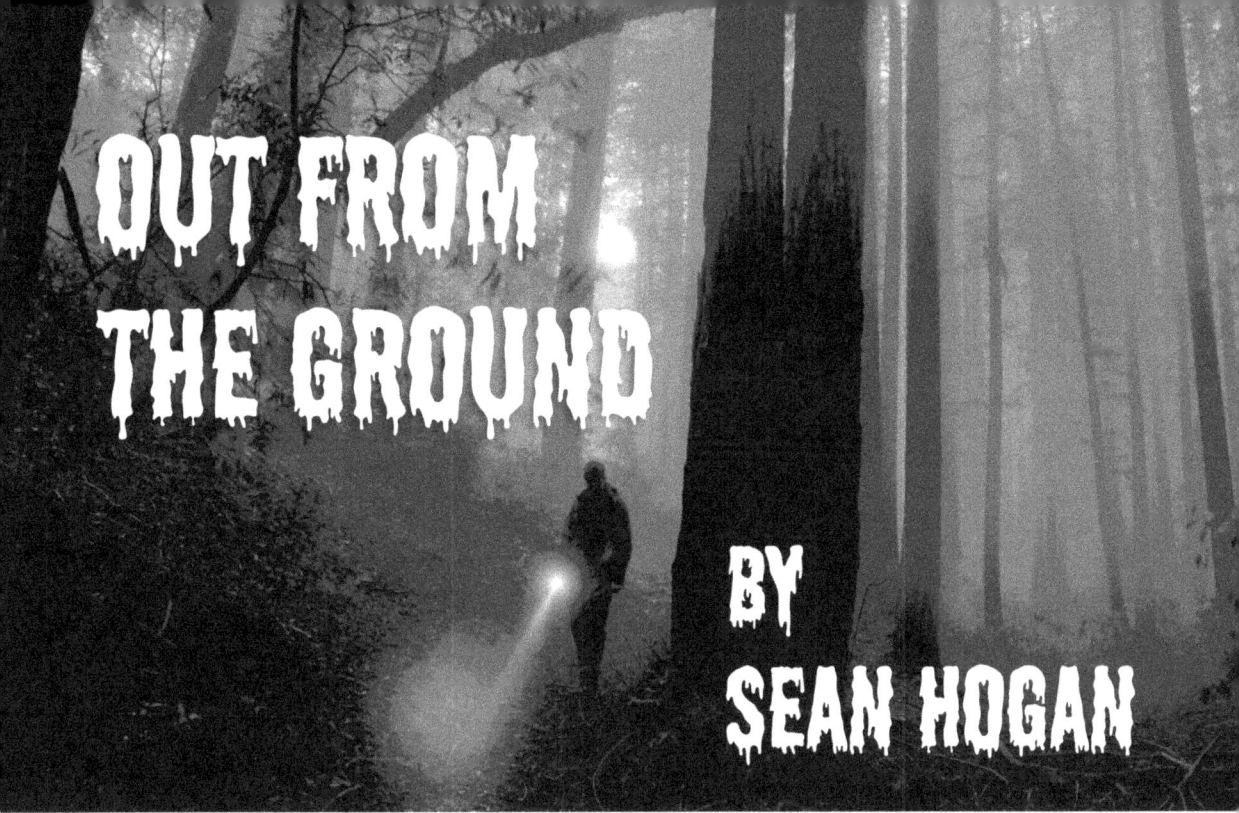

OUT FROM THE GROUND

BY SEAN HOGAN

EVERYONE KNOWS ME AROUND HERE. LIVED IN THIS TOWN ALL MY LIFE, NEVER SAW THE SENSE IN MOVING AWAY. Why would you even want to? You can keep your big cities. This is the best of the country right here. When people picture England in their mind, this is what they think of. Fields so green and vivid they look like someone's impression of a field, a painting on a canvas, as though you could just reach out and smear the wet pigment with your fingertips. A pint of ale in front of a crackling log fire, the taste of woodsmoke mingling with the hops and barley on your tongue. And when you finish your pint, the landlord already has a fresh one waiting for you, because he knows your drink as well as he knows your face, because everyone here knows each other, looks out for each other. My little sister Alex moved to the city, and when I visited her there it put me in mind of the biggest aquarium you'd ever seen. Thousands of glassy-eyed fish packed into this one space, not seeing anything or anyone, the grey air of the streets like stagnant water; breathe it too long and you'll wind up floating on the surface, where they'll scoop you up and flush you down the toilet without so much as a second thought. I tried to get her to come home but she wouldn't. It killed her in the end.

If she'd come back home I would have looked after her, just like I did when she was a kid. You know how it is, big brother and all that. Bit embarrassing, really. But that's what we do here, take care of each other. That's what we fight so hard to hold onto, an honest and decent way of life that the rest of the country is fast forgetting. That's why I became a copper. Not because of the uniform or because I watched too many detective shows as a kid or any of that crap. No, I joined the force because the rest of the world is getting bigger all the time and our place in it is getting smaller and smaller and someone needs to try and protect what we have. With what little power this badge and this uniform gives me, I do what I can to hold back the tidal wave of shit that threatens to sweep in and wipe all of this goodness away.

Which is why I'm sitting here now, a cup of milky tea in my hand, listening to Carl and Hazel Rawdon talk about their daughter

Edda. I've known the Rawdons all my life; their family has lived in the town even longer than mine, going back hundreds of years. Carl and I were at school together; I went to the pub with him to wet the baby's head on the night Edda was born. The Rawdons know me, and I know them. So my task is to offer trust, and reassurance. They need to gaze into my eyes and believe that I'm going to do all I can to find Edda, have faith that I can return their daughter to them safe and unharmed.

Hazel is speaking now, telling me how Edda works in The Quiet Lady, the pub just outside of town. It's about a twenty-minute walk from here, and when Edda finishes an evening shift, she'll normally leave the pub at around 11:45pm and be home just after midnight. But a couple of nights ago, she never came home. The Rawdons have tried calling Edda countless times since then, but she's not answering her mobile.

Her mother thinks she probably got a minicab home that evening, given how bad the weather was. I give her a small nod of agreement—I was out on a call that same night and remember how the rain was coming down, hard enough to wash all your sins away—and tell her I'll check with all the local firms.

Hazel's face looks somehow unreal, stony and immobile, like it's a barricade she's erected to hold back the flood of emotion roiling behind her eyes. Normally she's the one dealing with the grief and the tears, and I wonder how this feels to her, the shoe suddenly being on the other foot. Hazel has a bit of a reputation, you see. I don't know what she would call herself—a fortune teller, a psychic?—but in the town, people just say that *Hazel knows things*. Don't get me wrong, she doesn't sit here in her Gypsy Lee get-up talking a load of crystal bollocks or anything like that. But if you're having a bad time of it or have recently lost someone close to you, they reckon she might be able to help put your mind at ease. Hazel insists she doesn't charge money or anything like that, but people always leave her a few quid all the same, supposedly more as a thank you rather than payment. They say it runs in the family. I remember my mum telling me

that Hazel's mother Pearl was a witch, how they were all deathly scared of her as kids, but that didn't stop Mum running straight to Hazel's door after Alex killed herself. To tell you the truth, I always resented Hazel for that, milking our family's grief for a bit of beer money. I know it helped comfort Mum so I didn't say anything, but it didn't sit well with me.

But that's personal, and this is the job. And anyway, Carl's an old mate, and god knows they haven't had an easy time of it with Edda. She was always a wild kid, running around with boys and all that, and rumour has it she's got herself into a bit of trouble on more than one occasion; the sort of trouble Pearl taught Hazel how to deal with behind closed doors, or that's what people in town say, anyway. Still, the Rawdons always keep their own business private, strictly between themselves. Carl would never say a word about his family to anyone, even after he'd had a few in the pub on a Friday evening, but there were times when I asked him how Edda was and I could see something spark in his eyes. He'd look away hurriedly, like a stone skittering across the surface of a lake, and shrug. *Ah, she's all right. You know how young girls are.*

Clearing my throat, I ask, "Is Edda seeing anyone right now?"

There's a pause, and the Rawdons exchange glances, like I've just asked something shameful instead of a perfectly straightforward question. "I don't mean anything by it," I add quietly, even though we all secretly know what Edda is like. "I just need to get all the relevant details."

Hazel's eyes meet mine. "No," she says firmly. "There's no one. Edda's settled down now that she's working in the pub. She doesn't have time for any of that."

Her features are tight and pale, her eyes two frozen pools in the barren landscape of her face. I tell myself that her obvious umbrage at my query was merely heightened by her panic over their missing daughter, but I know that isn't it at all. Deep down, Hazel despises the sort of young woman Edda is becoming, and worries that I might be right, that she's gone and followed some boy off to god knows where. That maybe something bad's happened to her as a result. And she knows that I know this, because it's my job to know all that's hidden and shameful about this town, and right now she hates me for it.

Hazel leans over and whispers something fierce to Carl, who says nothing, just gazes fixedly at the floor. We all sit in silence for a few moments, before Hazel begins to roll a cigarette, her pallid fingers trembling like the strands of a cobweb. Both of the Rawdons have been chain-smoking ever since I arrived. I wait patiently for her to finish, saying nothing.

When the cigarette is fully rolled, she places it in her mouth and reaches for a nearby lighter, a cheap plastic disposable that refuses to ignite. Hazel swears under her breath.

"Here," I say, producing my Zippo and handing it to her.

She nods her thanks and lights the cigarette, inhaling deeply. Hazel's fingers gently caress the Zippo, as though I've just handed her a good-luck charm, and I notice her eyes starting to drift away, leaving this room and our conversation far behind.

I take that as my cue to wrap things up. After running through a final couple of details with Carl, I promise to keep the Rawdons updated on any progress, and climb to my feet. Hazel doesn't say anything, just slumps back in her armchair and begins to gnaw anxiously at her thumbnail, her teeth making a wet snapping sound against the keratin. The noise is very loud in the quiet of the room. I feel a sudden anger at her, and part of me wants to ask why she doesn't know where Edda is, the way she claims to know so many other things. If this was someone else's daughter, I think, you'd be first in line to offer tea and sympathy, telling her worried parents whatever you thought they wanted to hear. And afterwards, when you were offered a few quid for your trouble, you'd make a big show of refusing it, before finally accepting the money and furtively tucking it away in your purse, like a sordid little secret.

But I know I still resent her over Mum, over Alex, and so I push the thought away. Instead, I let Carl show me out to the hallway. He opens the front door, then turns to face me.

"You'll find Edda, won't you, Alan?" he says, and on this occasion the mention of his daughter's name does not cause his gaze to flit away into empty space. His eyes are piercing, staring steadily into mine. I'm suddenly conscious of just how much bigger Carl is than me. He always was, even back when we were young kids. No one ever messed with Carl at school.

I take his hand and grip it firmly. "She'll turn up soon, Carl," I tell him, as confidently as I can manage. "There's no doubt whatsoever in my mind about that."

LATER THAT NIGHT, I'm sat in my local, nursing a pint and thinking. None of my subsequent enquiries went anywhere. The barman in The Quiet Lady told me that Edda left alone after they'd closed up for the night, that she'd tried to book a minicab, but when she was told it was a thirty-minute wait she decided to brave the wet weather and walk. The Rawdons had given me the names of a few of Edda's girlfriends in town, but she hadn't stayed over with any of them, and questioning any of the local men she'd been involved over the last year or two with hadn't turned up anything promising so far either.

"So where do you think she is?"

I glance up to see Jonno, the pub's landlord, staring back at me from the other side of the bar.

I shrug. "Probably with some bloke somewhere. Chances are they all had a blazing row and Carl and Hazel just don't want to admit it. You know what that Edda's like."

"No one's seen hide nor hair of her, or so they say."

"I've no reason to doubt them," I tell him, before raising my glass to my lips and draining my pint. "But people don't just disappear, not round here."

I say my goodbyes to Jonno, and make to exit the pub. On my way out, I catch the eyes of a couple of the regulars, who each give me a wordless nod. Their meaning is clear: *Find the girl*. They all trust me to do what needs to be done. No one really thinks anything bad has happened to Edda, not yet, but a lurking, nameless doubt remains all the same; a doubt that, if allowed to linger, will slowly begin to eat away at the foundations of the community. In a town where everyone knows everyone, we all want to think the best of our neighbours, believe that we're all looking out for one another. Because if the slightest element of mistrust is allowed to seep in, it's like rot infecting the roots of a tree. Sooner or later, the whole forest will come crashing down.

Outside, I reach into my pocket for my cigarettes. I'm trying to quit, but allow myself the odd one every now and then, whenever I feel the need to unwind a bit.

Then I realise: I never got my lighter back from Hazel. It strikes me as odd that she never returned it, but I suppose we all had other things on our minds.

Annoyed, I run back into the pub and buy a box of matches, then hurry outside to my car. Lighting a fag, I sit silently in the darkness for a moment. I meant what I said to Carl and Jonno. I do believe the odds are good that Edda will be found. It may take some time, but as the days go on, and the search intensifies, sooner or later someone will eventually find out where she is.

Unless she's very, very, well hidden.

I start the engine and pull out of the pub car park. But instead of heading back into town, I drive out into the darkness of the surrounding countryside, making for an isolated stretch of woodland some miles away from the nearest built-up area. Once I arrive there, I pull off the road, making sure to park the car well out of sight. Removing a torch from the glovebox, I climb out of the vehicle and circle around to the boot, from which I take out a canister of petrol, a tarpaulin, and a garden spade.

For a brief moment, I wonder if I will be able to find my way back to her in the dark, but I have walked this trail so many times, envisaging every detail of the coming encounter in my head, that I pick my way through the tightly clustered trees as easily as a fox returning to its den.

I belong here, I think to myself, here in these dark woods alongside all the other watchful, cunning hunters. Part of a natural, ageless order of things. We are not greedy, or vicious. We hunters only ever take a little for ourselves, then give the rest back to the earth from whence it came.

When I first reach the clearing, I do not see her anywhere, and for an instant I almost believe that I have made a terrible mistake. That, as impossible as it seems, she was still breathing when I left her and has since managed to escape the woods. But then I flash my torch beam around and find her, lying motionless in the shadows, her greying, sunken flesh lifeless as clay. As I kneel down beside her, the night creatures exploring her body's hidden places react to the sudden glare of the torch and scuttle away into the undergrowth, and Edda is mine once more.

It wasn't meant to be her, not originally. At first I thought I would take a girl from another nearby town or village, someone completely unknown to me. It would be simple enough, I decided—find a girl walking alone at night, show her my warrant card, get her into the car under pretence of having broken some regulation or other. But the more I thought about it, the more I wanted them to recognise my face: the last face they would ever see. I wanted my victim to understand that someone they'd known all their life was about to wrest that life away from them, and that in actual fact, they'd never really known me at all. That dull, dependable Alan Hickey, who everyone says really ought to settle down and find himself a nice girl to marry, never actually existed. That the deadliest hunters hide in plain sight.

When it started to rain so heavily the other evening, I heard something calling to me, a sibilant whisper concealed underneath the busy crackle of the rainfall. It called me out into the night, coaxing me forth like an impatient lover. I got into my car and drove around for a time, unsure of where to go next. The streets were completely deserted, as if the sudden deluge had swept away the entire population of the town. Only I remained.

But I knew she was out here somewhere; the voice had promised me that much.

So when I drove past The Quiet Lady

and saw Edda emerging into the heavy rain, cowering beneath the makeshift carapace of her flimsy coat, I knew immediately that it was meant to be her all along. I had helped celebrate her entrance into the world; watched her grow into a young woman; observed her promiscuous cruelties from afar. It had only ever been a matter of time before our lives intertwined, like a bramble choking a rose.

I waited until she'd walked a short distance away from the pub, then pulled up beside her and lowered my window, shouting to be heard over the downpour. "Edda, it's Alan, Alan Hickey. You need a lift somewhere?"

She stopped in her tracks and squinted over at me, trying to discern my face through the streaking blur of the rain. "Alan the copper?" she said.

"None other."

Edda didn't hesitate, just ran around to the passenger side and climbed in. "Bloody hell," she said. "Pub's been like a morgue all night, and then I have to walk out into this. You're a lifesaver."

I smiled. "That's why I got into this job, to help people," I said.

She smirked. I suppose young people think such sentiments are corny and old-fashioned. Until the day finally arrives when they suddenly realise that *they* need help, and there's no one who cares enough to come to their aid.

My eyes moved over to the windscreen, gazing out at the road ahead. In all that rain and all that lightless gloom, I couldn't see more than a few feet in front of the car. It was as though the road into town, the same road I'd driven along countless times before, had been wiped away completely. All that remained was uncharted darkness.

I eased the car back out onto the road. "Now, shall I drop you home, or somewhere else?"

"Home is fine, thanks."

As we drove, I asked Edda how her folks were, and she started telling me about what a pain in the arse Carl was being, always getting up in her business and wanting to know where she was going and who she was seeing. And wasn't I old mates with him and

couldn't I have a quiet word? Of course, I did my best to encourage her to keep talking, and before long, she got so wrapped up in her complaining that it took a while for her to notice that I'd taken a wrong turning somewhere along the way and was now heading in the exact opposite direction from town.

Sitting upright in her seat, she peered intently out into the surrounding darkness, as though she had suddenly realised that darkness was all the future held for her.

"Where are we going?" she said quietly, not meeting my eye.

"Oh, I thought we'd drive around for a bit," I replied. "To give you a chance to talk."

"I'm fine," she said. "I'd really just like to get home, please."

I nodded calmly. "No problem. But I can't turn around here, so we'll have to keep on going for a bit before we can go back."

She said nothing for a moment. I kept my eyes fixed on the road. Then I heard the abrupt pop of her seatbelt. "You know what, Alan? Just let me out here."

"I can't do that, Edda. You'll get soaked."

Her hand flew to the door handle. "You let me out now or I'm jumping out."

"All right, all right," I told her, motioning for her to calm down. "You're really making a fuss over nothing, love."

She didn't reply. I pulled over to the side of the road, and as soon as the car was stationary, she made to open the door and leap out. Instantly, my left hand snapped out and grabbed her by the hair, dragging her backwards. Edda let out a startled shriek, which was quickly cut short as I brought my right hand up and punched her square in the face. Dazed, she could do nothing to prevent me from hauling her back inside the car and closing the door.

Taking out a pair of handcuffs from my glovebox, I cuffed her hands behind her back and set back out on the road, heading towards these very woods, which was of course where I'd planned to take her all along.

By the time Edda came around fully, we were alone together in this clearing. At first she cursed and screamed, but very quickly realised that wasn't going to get her anywhere. So then we had to go through the desperate promises and blandishments, followed by the begging and the pleading and finally, the helpless crying.

The rest of it I think I'll keep to myself. I don't believe that what happens between two people in private is really anyone else's business.

When it was all over, I lit a cigarette and stood there quietly smoking for a couple of minutes, enjoying the silence that had rushed in to fill the void left by Edda's passing. Standing there in the middle of the darkened forest, I began to think about the lies we all tell ourselves. I thought about my old mate Carl, and wondered whether, once all the grief and the anguish had eventually faded, he'd ever be able to admit to himself that his and Hazel's lives would be vastly easier with their troublesome daughter safely out of the way.

Finishing my cigarette, I removed the pair of knickers I'd shoved into Edda's mouth and quickly gathered up the rest of her clothes. I left her lying where she was, gazing up into the heavens. The rain clouds had passed and the moon and stars were perfect and precise in the night sky. Their cool light seemed to bathe Edda's face, washing away all the ugliness that had appeared there during her last few moments of life.

She looked beautiful then, as the last vestiges of life slowly ebbed from her features. But death is cruel in so many ways, and Edda now looks more like a grim parody of the girl I once knew, wearing a child's clumsy *papier maché* imitation of a face. I sit and gaze at her for a short while, but when I can't bear the sight of her sallow, misshapen grimace anymore, I get to my feet and reach for the canister of petrol.

Her body takes quite some time to burn. I stand well clear of the smoke, not wanting my clothes to become suffused with the smell of petrol fumes and cooking meat. When the flames finally die out, I begin to dig a pit. The soil of the forest floor is still damp from the recent rainfall and the work goes relatively quickly. Once the hole is a few feet deep, I unfurl the tarpaulin and use the spade to shovel Edda's remains into

its centre. To think that this twisted, blackened snarl of meat and bone was once a person; a pretty, frivolous girl who careened through life without the slightest care, never minding who she might bruise or hurt on her way. Did she ever imagine it might come to this? That one day, one of the countless men that she so blithely teased and taunted might simply snap and say, *Enough.*

Perhaps she thought that such things would never happen in a little town like ours, but in truth, they have always happened here. Hazel likes to tell the story of how one of her ancestors was hanged as a witch, and although we don't believe in such superstitions now, little has really changed otherwise. Men will always be men, and women will always be women. Some people like to believe the future is a straight line, moving constantly forward, but in truth the world just spins immovably in place, cyclical and endless.

Wrapping up the tarpaulin around Edda's body, I gather it up in my arms and place it carefully into the makeshift grave. I make short work of filling the hole back in, and as I flatten the piled earth with my shovel, I start to wonder if they will ever find her.

Far better that she should be left to lie undisturbed. It's a tranquil, restful spot, a perfect place for the dead to sleep and dream. And I should like to come back and visit Edda, when the mood takes me. I have so few people I can properly talk to, and we shared so very much, in the brief moments that we were together.

Collecting up my things, I return to the car and set out for home. The roads are deserted at this hour, and gazing out through my windscreen at the shadowed hills and fields, I am filled with a burgeoning sense of secret knowledge. I alone am privy to what has transpired out here tonight, and while there is a certain dreadful loneliness in that, there is also an undeniable feeling of power.

No one knows who you really are, I think.

When I arrive back in town, I park in the small residential parking area located behind my block of flats. As I climb out of the car, I am suddenly cognisant of the fact that my hands and clothes are filthy with dirt, and carry a lingering odour of petroleum. I know that I am unlikely to bump into any of my neighbours at this hour, but quicken my pace and hurry around to my building's front entrance, eager to be back in my own home.

I get as far as inserting my key into the lock when I suddenly hear the voice from behind me. "Evening, Alan."

Startled, I spin around to see Carl and Hazel Rawdon approaching from the shadows. As surprised as I am to see them, I'm careful not to let anything register on my face. It's possible that they've remembered some other small detail they believe might be pertinent to Edda's disappearance, and came to tell me in person. These are the drawbacks of living in a small town where everyone knows each other, or believes they do.

I nod. "Hello, Carl. Hazel."

Carl gestures towards my clothes. "What happened to you?"

I glance over at Hazel. She says nothing, her face unreadable. Looking back at Carl, I let out an embarrassed chuckle. "Had one too many beers. Needed to piss on the way home, so stopped in a field and slipped over in the mud."

"You're in a right state," he says.

"Yeah, I feel a proper tit," I reply. "I was actually going to go straight upstairs and jump in the shower."

"We just wanted a quick word, Alan."

"Can it wait until tomorrow? I don't have any news for you yet, I'm afraid."

Alan takes a step closer. Reaching into his jacket pocket, he produces a hunting knife and unsheathes it. The weapon is old, probably a hand-me-down from his father and his father before him, but it has been well cared for over the years, and the blade gleams wickedly in the electric light of the building's entrance hallway.

"No, it can't," he says quietly.

I look between their faces, emotionless as graven churchyard angels. "What's all this about?" I say. "What the bloody hell do you think you're playing at, Carl?"

"Let's all go inside," he replies.

"If you both turn around and go straight home, I'll say no more about this."

An insinuating wave of the knife. "*Inside.*"

There is nothing more to be said. We turn and go inside the building. My flat is on the first floor, and there is plenty of opportunity for me to shout out for help, to hammer on the doors of my neighbours and raise the alarm. But I do nothing. If the police are summoned, I don't know what the Rawdons will tell them, what they might think they know, and I can't afford any scrutiny right now. Not with my clothes encrusted with grave dirt and a muddy shovel tossed in the boot of my car.

I unlock the door to my flat and lead Carl and Hazel inside. Hazel closes the door behind us and fastens the security chain. Carl gestures with his knife, motioning for me to turn right into the kitchen. Once inside, he has me pull out a chair and sit down. Hazel, meanwhile, produces a length of washing line and begins to tie my hands behind my back.

I gaze over at Carl, keeping my voice low and even. I don't want anyone to get overexcited. "You're making a big mistake, Carl," I say.

He considers this for a moment, then glances across at Hazel. "Are we, love?"

She finishes tying my hands in place, then moves to rejoin Carl. "No," she says flatly. "No, we're not."

In the cold, merciless glare of the kitchen fluorescents I can clearly see the loathing etched upon Hazel's features. "I knew something was wrong the moment you walked in the house this morning," she tells me. "I just didn't know what it was. But when you handed me this"—she produces my Zippo lighter from the pocket of her jeans—"I held it in my hand and I saw you with Edda." Grief burns in her eyes, corrosive as acid. "I saw you standing over her. Smoking a cigarette without a care in the world, while my poor little girl lay there naked and dead at your feet."

I force myself not to scoff, choking back my derision. Instead, I say, "Hazel, I'm sure you believe in your gift, or whatever it is you call it. But not everyone will. Certainly not the police. And when they find out that you've held an officer hostage because of some *vision* you think you had, well. You don't need me to tell you how serious that will be."

All at once, Hazel is in my face shrieking, her features contorted with hatred. For a moment, she reminds me of one of those distorted faces people claim to see in the trunks of trees, howling lost souls trapped within the wood. *"What have you done with her?"* she screams.

Then Carl pulls her away. Putting his arms around Hazel, he speaks to her softly, and without another glance at me, she turns and leaves the room.

Carl exhales heavily. Unlike his wife, there is no anger in his eyes, only a fathomless despair. "You need to tell me where Edda is, Alan," he says. "Don't make this any harder than it already is."

"Carl, mate," I reply, reminding him that we're friends, that we've been friends for almost as long as we can both remember. "I don't know where she is. I want to find Edda, and I swear to you I will, but you need to stop this before things go too far."

He edges closer, raising his knife until it's level with my eyes. "If you don't tell me, I'm going to have to start cutting you."

I tell myself that I can resist anything he will do to me, that I *must* resist, because if I don't, the consequences will be so much worse for me than anything Carl has in mind.

He severs three of the fingers on my left hand before I finally break down and confess everything. I tell myself I am only sobbing because of the pain, but part of me wonders whether I'm crying with relief now that the world will finally know what I am.

THE FIRST THING I feel when I come to is the furious throbbing in the places where my fingers used to be. The second is the sensation of damp earth underneath my cheek, the taste of mulch and grit on my tongue.

I open my eyes to find myself back in the clearing where I buried Edda. I am naked, stretched out on the forest floor, my hands

and feet hogtied behind my back. Raising my head to look around, I see not only Hazel and Carl, but other faces I recognise from the town: Jonno, some of Edda's girlfriends, various people I see in and around the local streets and shops every day. Seeing that I am awake, they begin to close in around me, forming an unbroken circle as tight as a hangman's noose.

I cough and spit, trying to clear the dirt from my mouth so that I might speak clearly.

"All of you here need to listen to me!" I shout. 'Whatever you think you're doing, whatever the Rawdons have told you, you're accessories to the abduction and assault of a police officer." I writhe on the ground, suddenly humiliated by my nakedness, my utter helplessness. "Carl tortured me. That means anything I told him is inadmissible as evidence. So no matter what you might find here, it won't hold up in court. That means I'll go free and the rest of you will be looking at serious prison time."

No one says anything. Then their ranks part, and a small, stooped figure steps forward from the shadows.

Hazel's mother Pearl.

Wincing at the discomfort in her knees, she slowly kneels down beside me. As I gaze up at the old woman's impassive face, heavily lined with the inexorable passing of time and the weight of the dreadful knowledge she has used that time to accrue, my mind immediately flashes back to the stories Mum used to tell me about Pearl.

And as much as I always scoffed at those old wives' tales, I suddenly find that I am very afraid.

"This isn't about your *law*, Alan," Pearl tells me softly. "Men like you always think you can subjugate us with your rules and your threats, but there are laws far older than the petty regulations you hide behind. You put my granddaughter in the earth before her time, in defiance of the seasons of living and dying that we all must observe. And there is a price to be paid for that."

Rising stiffly to her feet, she turns and nods towards the others. Carl, Jonno, and a couple of the other men move forward and gather around me. Attaching a length of rope to the bonds fastened around my ankles, they loop the other end around a low-hanging tree branch and slowly haul me into the air. Once I am suspended a foot or so over the ground, my skull pounding with the sudden rush of blood to my head, they knot the rope in place. I swing gently back and forth like a carcass suspended from a butcher's hook, my soft belly and genitals exposed and defenceless.

It is then that I start to shout and curse, rapidly shrieking myself hoarse. But Pearl and the others pay my threats no mind. I chose my killing ground very well, and no one will ever hear my cries out all the way out here.

Wordlessly, Pearl holds her hand out. Carl passes her his hunting knife, then moves back to his wife's side. I stare across at Hazel. The rage I glimpsed in her eyes earlier this evening has now dissipated, to be replaced by a calm, beatific acceptance.

Stepping towards me, Pearl examines Carl's hunting knife thoughtfully, turning it slowly in the air as though it were a divining rod, an instrument to bring forth life rather than extinguish it.

My throat feels like it's filled with sand. "What good…will killing me do?" I finally manage to croak.

The old woman takes the blade and holds it to the meat of my breast. I can feel it pressing hungrily against my skin, sharp and cold and eager to warm itself in that which runs through my veins.

"You spill blood wantonly without ever understanding the true nature of its power," Pearl whispers. "But it is the oldest magic there is. Blood calls to blood. The women in my family have always known that. Edda knew it too. And now with your blood, I will call to her."

The knife slices into my chest, and I gasp. But Pearl's handiwork is fastidious and precise—she is very careful not to cut too deep. As my blood starts to blossom forth, I feel the warm liquid slowly coursing over my throat and face, splattering down onto the soil below.

Pearl is not finished, however. Her blade continues to trace a winding path across my chest, an interlocking series of delicate lines and curves. Is she toying with me? Vengefully drawing out my final moments before she at last administers the killing blow?

And then I finally understand: there is a deliberate *pattern* to the old woman's cutting.

Pearl is placing a mark upon me. An ancient symbol, something dark and unholy.

Behind her, the townspeople begin to chant in unison. I realise I don't understand the words they are saying. They might be some lost, arcane language or, for all I know, could just be complete gibberish. At the head of the group, Carl and Hazel break into some kind of weird, spastic dance, writhing awkwardly against each other like two mating insects. The very sight of it repels me, and I begin to berate and mock them all, laughing at their idiot superstitions.

All these years I believed that I was the only one with something to hide. Was there a reason they never approached me to join their group, to be one of them? Did they always know what I was, perhaps even before I understood it myself? Just as my sister knew; the awful, unbearable knowledge that drove Alex away to the city, that finally sent her fleeing to her bed with a lethal nightcap of vodka and sleeping pills, forever drowning out the vile memory of what I had done to her.

It is then that I hear it: a long hollow sigh reverberating throughout the soil, as though the very ground itself could no longer bear the weight of the long centuries of atrocities it had witnessed, the sheer amount of violence that it was expected to absorb and conceal, simply so that man's cycle of bloodshed might continue uninterrupted.

The townspeople suddenly fall silent, and in the nocturnal hush of the clearing, I hear the earth speak my name.

Alan, my love.

I begin to scream, and when her arms erupt from the soil and pull me to her, two lost lovers reunited, I am still screaming, even as Edda presses her seared and bloodless lips to mine and drags me down into the depths of the earth.

And as my mouth fills with mud and I can no longer make a sound, my mind is still filled to bursting with the sound of my own screams and will be so forever, down here in the dank eternal darkness where we forgotten dead things lie.

Sean Hogan is a writer and filmmaker based in the UK. He has published several books of cinema metafiction, including England's Screaming *and its sequel* Twilight's Last Screaming *(each named as one of the five best genre novels of their year by* The Financial Times*)*, Three Mothers, One Father, *and* That Fatal Shore. *His feature film credits include* The Devil's Business, The Borderlands, *the documentary* Future Shock! The Story of 2000AD, *and most recently, the critically acclaimed folk horror* To Fire You Come at Last. *He is currently in pre-production on his next film,* Scenes From A Young Girl's Disappearance, *and his new novel* The Corpse Road *will be published in late 2024.*

Accompanied Pipes

By Gary Fry

IT HAD BEEN JUST ANOTHER BOX OF PHOTOGRAPHS, NOTHING SPECIAL, HE'D THOUGHT: THE PAST CAUGHT AND EXPOSED. Why this particular image trapped his eye, Neil couldn't immediately say. After all, he'd been through so many of late. Despite a bereavement, when you imagined your hunger for every moment of a lost one's life would go unabated, banality in its many forms could leave you spent and indifferent to the years gone by. But there was something about this image that bit into him. Tentatively, he showed the picture he'd unearthed to Vanessa.

She raised her eyebrow and did her best not to sound judgemental. "Looks like your mum had yet another fella on the go after your dad flitted. How many's that—five? Six?"

"Maybe. This one's different, though." The photograph showed a gaunt, dark-eyed man with his arms around Neil's mother. "They couldn't have been together long. I'd remember more about him."

"Depends how old you were."

"She can't have been more than thirty here. So I'd be six, seven."

"Probably the third bloke she'd had it away with by then."

Mindful of Vanessa's condition, Neil didn't say anything to that. Vanessa and his mother's relationship hadn't been easy; they'd held fundamentally different outlooks on life. Dismissing her comment, he frowned at the picture. Though he couldn't say why,

Neil had the faintest inkling he knew something about this guy.

THAT EVENING he set at the piano, trying to summon ideas for a piece he'd agreed to write for the reopening of the village hall. In his fifties and living on royalties from a couple of hit songs, he liked to remain active, and contributing to the local community gave him a sense of belonging.

As he played, he reflected on how they'd moved here several years earlier, charmed by the village. It was different from the smoggy city where they'd grown up. Vanessa had been adamant about relocation; too career-minded to want children, she'd stockpiled her savings to secure early retirement somewhere bucolic. She was forty-eight but claimed her headmistress role had aged her.

Neil's fingers slipped on the keys, and what might have been a nascent melody evaporated as he worried about her. Menopause could be challenging, though without acknowledging its onset, what could be done to help? Perhaps she was in denial about her decline in fertility or maybe the recent deaths of several of their older family members had left her feeling vulnerable. Whatever the truth was, the last few months hadn't been easy, for either of them.

Neil struck a lifeless chord and then picked out a soulless string of notes and then stopped. He simply wasn't in the mood to compose; something he couldn't articulate was troubling him.

The photograph? The pale man with the dark eyes? Maybe. But if so, why?

He paused as he closed the lounge curtains against the encroaching night, his mind roaming free. Outside, Vanessa had stripped the weeds that had found a home over winter. The new season, a promise of a fresh start, went some way to raising Neil's spirits, and with the house locked up, he went through to the bedroom where he found Vanessa reading.

"Any luck?" she asked, glancing up as he undressed.

"Bit of a disaster, I'm afraid. Not even a hummable bar."

Watching as he tugged on pyjamas and then climbed into bed, she said, "They'll understand if it's a bit late."

He responded to her unexpected cuddle with awkwardness. "It's an *orchestral* movement, Ness. I need to get it written quickly. It'll take some rehearsing."

"But you've suffered a bereavement. In the great scheme of things, some music for the village hall's not *that* important."

"Just the same, I agreed to help."

Although her arms were inviting, he turned away, claiming tiredness. She seemed to understand. But he wondered whether he did himself. For some reason, he was confused, disturbed. As he tried to sleep, he thought perhaps dreams would reveal what was truly on his mind.

WHEN HE AWOKE the following morning— there'd been no dreams he could remember —he had music in his head. It wasn't so much a tune as a snippet, something that accompanied a theme in opera or identified a character in a film.

Hurrying out of bed before Vanessa began her slow ascent of the day, he went straight to the piano.

He couldn't decide which key would best serve the phrase's mood, so he began in C-major. He could modify it later if necessary. After attempting several variations— a semi-tone was involved, making it tricky— he transcribed the music to manuscript:

C-D-C-A-G-G#-A

Neil lacked perfect-pitch but he'd always been able to convert ideas into playable notes. The main issue here was where this latest one had come from. Was it original? Paul McCartney had apparently dreamt the melody to "Yesterday"—so why couldn't Neil with a shorter piece? The problem was that this interpretation felt wrong. He believed he'd *heard* the notes in the past—in this arrangement and with the same rhythm.

Leaving the piano, he went to the window, stared out. He whistled the fragment of tune, watching as a breeze unsettled the shrubs Vanessa had clipped yesterday; they twisted and cavorted as if dancing. Something about their movement disturbed him and his breath failed, the whistled tune standing empty on the air. All of a sudden, he knew to whom it related.

In the dining room he riffled through his mother's keepsakes and memorabilia, the ones he'd sorted out the day before. Amid jewellery and ornaments and plenty of age-yellowed paper, he found the photograph featuring the gaunt, dark-eyed man whose arms encircled his mother.

"It's my signature tune," said the man in the photograph, his voice coming from the deepest recesses of Neil's psyche. "Just whistle it, any time you like, and I'll come to you, my boy."

Before considering the wisdom of doing so, Neil brought together his lips and blew. In response, he heard only the wind around the bungalow's exterior, causing what little vegetation had survived Vanessa's cull to whisper in a language he couldn't understand.

HE SPENT THAT DAY in the throes of composition. Impulse rather than reason persuaded him to use the new melodic phrase as his main theme. By lunchtime he'd sketched most of the piece, a single movement for a small orchestra. The phrase would recur in different contexts, sometimes playful, other times tragic, and on further occasions another mood entirely, until whatever it represented had been explored in all its complexity.

But what exactly was he attempting to evoke?

Neil couldn't help but picture certain images, each perhaps facilitated by Vanessa's activities in the garden.

With the warmer weather, she'd left the patio doors open, and the aroma of the flowers she'd bought earlier that week, elusive yet pungent, combined with the music, suggesting something rushing through woodland, barging aside foliage, ripping fruit from low hanging trees, and kicking up dirt underfoot...or perhaps, Neil thought, under *hoof*. The creature deep in his mind appeared equine in form. He could almost see it...

"Are you ready to eat yet? Neil? Neil, I asked you a question."

He looked up as he tumbled back into the prosaic world, his ears suddenly ringing.

"Sorry, I was...miles away," he replied, and wondered how true this was. His imaginary forest had been unlike any in the decidedly unexotic UK.

After the meal he was eager to return to his composition, but Vanessa's body language persuaded him it would be politic to sit with her in the lounge watching TV. As she snuggled close to him, he swiped his phone to life and texted his late mother's sister. She still lived in her own home, despite being in her eighties, and all her faculties were functioning.

In response to an opening question about her wellbeing, Claire messaged back within seconds: *"Still beating them off with a stick—one of the walking variety these days, but the effect is much the same: dampened ardours."*

Neil laughed, causing Vanessa, now laying in his arms and smelling strongly of flowers, to glance up.

"Who's that?"

"Aunty Claire."

"Oh." Quietly satisfied, she returned her attention to the TV.

Following a few more playful texts, Neil asked: *"If I send you a photo I found among my mother's affects, do you think you could identify the man alongside her?"*

"The old trollop! I'll certainly have a go!"

Still smiling, if a little uneasily, Neil attached a jpeg of the photo. Before sending it, he hesitated, staring at the man gazing back at him across time. Even though the image was black and white, the man's eyes appeared uncommonly dark, a negation of the pale skin around them. Their intensity emphasised his other features: unsmiling lips, cropped black hair, wiry body. Had a fault occurred during the photo's reproduction? Surely nobody had ever possessed such an angular forehead, as if the bone beneath aspired to protuberances on each side...

Neil glanced away, queasy as the remembered phrase returned to him: "It's my signature tune... Just whistle it...any time... I'll come to you, my boy."

Resisting the temptation to put his lips to reissue the musical phrase, he sent the picture and awaited a reply.

But on this occasion Aunt Claire failed to respond. No message was delivered electronically across the hundred miles separating her home in Derbyshire to this one in Yorkshire.

Edgy again, Neil told himself that his aunt must have nodded off in an armchair, the advancing hour taking its toll on her. It was getting late, after all. He watched more TV, causing Vanessa to stir in his lap as he shuffled impatiently on the couch.

Finally, Neil's phone beeped.

"I have no idea who he is. Knowing my sister, probably just another one-night stand."

But the guy couldn't have been a brief acquaintance of his mother's; Neil recollections of him were becoming too vivid.

LATER, UNDRESSING FOR BED, frustrated, he whistled the musical phrase again.

"What *is* that?" asked Vanessa. Rather than being tired of hearing him rework it all day, she seemed bewitched by the melody.

"Something from years back. Do you like it?"

Vanessa thought for a moment, embracing him as soon as he climbed under the sheets. "It's…I don't know…*edgier* than your usual stuff. It sounds…well, *dangerous*, somehow."

He turned in bed, taking her in the same places she'd taken hold of him. There was no doubt about what would happen next. Vanessa's libido had been suppressed the last few years—understandably so, given midlife fluctuations in hormones—but was she beyond that now? He also was uncommonly aroused; maybe today's creative work had induced similar desire in him.

"So I'm *dangerous*, am I?" he asked, pushing his hands up her nightshirt to her breasts. "I'm not sure how I feel about that."

"Oh, I am."

Her dirt-lined fingernails dug into his shoulders as he entered her. She was as wet as she'd been when they'd married, and he every bit as hard.

They enjoyed themselves, combining in what had lately been an unprecedented way. It was as if they danced to music, a piece they heard in the absence of sound, animating them from within. It was magnificent, and once they were done, they lay in a tangle, with a heady floral scent drifting in through the window.

THE FOLLOWING DAY, Neil strolled to the village, heading for the Ivy pub to meet one of the musicians from the band. On his way, he passed the hall and observed how well the building had been renovated, its façade sandblasted and pointed, the roof boasting fresh tiles and guttering. Once the unkempt land around it had also been attended to, it would look splendid. Maybe Vanessa could transform the barren earth to each side of the entrance path.

"How's it coming along?" asked Barry Hughes, once both men were sat with pints. Barry was a retired solicitor who'd played violin since childhood.

"Rather well," said Neil, loath to say too much in case he compromised his inspiration. "Hope to have it finished in a day or two. Then we can start rehearsing."

"Ah, yeah, about that…" Barry took a quick slurp of beer. "Sorry to drop a fly in the ointment, old boy, but we have a problem."

"A problem?"

Neil had known it: his latest creative endeavours, Vanessa feeling better, the amazing sex last night… Life was never this good. He was fifty-three, and the standard refrain at his age was "bad stuff happens."

For some reason, right then he associated "bad stuff happens" with the photograph he'd found and his aunt's delay in replying about the man featured in it… But he pushed aside such nonsense and spoke again.

"What's the issue?"

"Stella Marsh."

Neil knew the woman: a retired GP who played the flute surprisingly well. "What's wrong with her?"

"Laryngitis. Could take a week to clear."

"Just before the performance, then."

"Yes." Barry glanced over their damaged pints. "Have you scored much for the old pipe?"

Neil suddenly visualised several pipes bound together and played by a single musician. Had this image arisen from a dream?

A bulky animal clip-clopped beyond the pub window, causing him to glance up anxiously. But it was only a youngster trotting through the village on horseback. Exhaling, he switched his attention back to Barry.

"The finale involves the sodding flute."

"Bugger." Barry leaned forward. "I don't suppose you could alter that? Stick James in with the clarinet?"

"Not really. It's to do with the aesthetics. By that stage, the flute best conveys the… well, the main theme."

"Better pray for a miracle, then." Barry took another swig of his drink. "You know, if Stella doesn't recover, we could always ask someone to whistle the ending."

WHEN HE RETURNED to the bungalow, the garden was full of flowers. Neil was surprised. He hadn't thought Vanessa had planned to buy any more; the borders were already bursting.

"Looking good," he told her. She was crouched in a corner using a trowel. "You've made terrific progress."

If gardening helped her feel more like her former self, Neil should encourage it.

"I'm surprised you didn't notice earlier," Vanessa said, standing and holding her garden tool like an impromptu weapon. "I woke and found all this waiting for me."

Neil was confused. Had the new growth sprouted overnight? He sounded distant even to himself as he said, "No. I went out the back way and headed for the village through the fields."

He looked again at the colourful garden, which only days earlier was choking with weeds. Little of it made sense. Despite the seasonal warmth, he was trembling.

"Well, keep up the good work," he said, forcing affection into his tone.

The look Vanessa gave him bore more than a little lust.

BY LATE AFTERNOON he'd only the orchestration to tackle, transferring notes he'd etched onto manuscript paper into separate lines for instruments.

It's my signature tune, he heard a voice say deep in his head, especially whenever he considered the musical phrase that dominated the piece. *Just whistle it, at any time, and I'll come to you, my boy.*

Why did the phrase "at any time" trouble him so? Had this man once acted as Neil's protector...or was something malevolent at work here?

Unable to figure it out, Neil was awhirl with speculation.

Once he added the final notes to his piece—a piercing cry from a flute, mimicking some animal tearing through the woods—it was late, night had fallen. He was glad to set the music aside and step into the bedroom.

Vanessa greeted him, her voice breath: "I need more."

She smelled of flowers. Of earth. Of unquenchable fertility.

HE DREAMED of rushing through a forest.

He was on the charge and not some equine animal. He panted and snorted, head down as vegetation whipped his flanks and his bone-thin legs. The race was wild, and he reached a clearing in which others dwelt, each displaying their exposed genitalia and, quite unlike himself, boasting only two lower limbs. As he threw back his long neck to howl at a full moon lurking amid tatters of cloud, his adherents—countless naked people wearing masks that sprouted curved horns—fell on all fours and began to copulate, whinnying and grunting, slathering and drooling. The creature he'd become was so pleased by the sight that, enhancing the orgy, it played a familiar phrase on an instrument composed of multiple pipes...

HE WOKE SHARPLY, trying to distance himself from the nightmare. Breathless, struggling not to disturb Vanessa, he headed for the bathroom. He felt his forehead for any newly developed protuberances.

But nothing was there, just his familiar wrinkling flesh. The mirror confirmed it was true.

He went back to bed, lying awake until dawn came and he got up again.

ANXIETY AHEAD of the first rehearsal crept in. After dressing and bidding goodbye to Vanessa—who looked under strain, perhaps following all her hard work in the garden lately—he left the bungalow, striving not to notice how much more the garden had grown overnight. It appeared only as a vastly blossoming display to each side as he headed down the path. He kept his head forward, clutching the copies of his composition.

When he arrived at the village hall, he learned Stella's condition had settled. In a matter of days she'd be able to perform in public.

"But the premiere's in forty-eight hours."

"Don't worry," said George, a cellist with thick fingers. "Stella's sight-reading's excellent. Give us a copy of the score. I'll pass it on for her to study at home."

Neil handed over the pages, even though it felt dangerous, like letting an animal off a leash.

But once the performers—eight on

strings, three on brass, two on woodwind, and one playing percussion—started to perform his work, his concerns faded. The piece was a success. He'd appreciated only a suggestion of its power on the piano. With a small orchestra dramatising it, its qualities were apparent. If the quieter early sections hinted at a mystical woodland, the later, louder ones thoroughly evoked one, a rhythmic surge through otherworldly forestation.

The more the music unfolded, the deeper Neil seemed to plunge. At one stage, intoxicated by the weird harmonies, the auditorium seemed to vanish and be replaced by a vast plane crammed with unrecognisable creatures, odd chimerical *man-beasts*...

"Neil?"

The word pierced him like an arrow fired by an archer, standing among trees.

"*Neil?*"

A second strike. His eyes snapped open, searching for assassins.

"You were miles away!" said Barry, smiling. "You been working too hard?"

Somehow Neil readjusted to his location, his bewilderment receding. The musicians stared his way, their eyes similarly glazed with transfixion. It was Barry, the most prosaic among them, who snapped his fingers several times, prompting everyone to refocus. "All right, folks."

"Do you...like it?" asked Neil.

"I feel quite...peculiar," said George the cellist, his hands falling seemingly idle across his lap, as had the other men's. The women shone with what looked like desire.

"It'll be better still when Stella joins us at the end," said one of them. "Orgasmic, perhaps."

No one laughed.

DURING THE NEXT few days, between several more rehearsals, Neil attended closely to Vanessa, who'd become unwell again. She was sick in the mornings and ravenously hungry in the afternoons.

Secretly Neil was relieved her libido had again lapsed; it meant he could focus his preoccupation. With his composition finished, he deliberately failed to whistle its theme, and whenever he'd stepped into the garden he noticed the flowers, lately growing

so rampantly, had faltered in their colourful conquest.

"Just a coincidence," he told himself, though deep in his mind he wondered whether that snatch of melody had induced magical transformations in his life. And did the brooding man in the photograph stand at the root of this phenomenon?

If Neil could remember his name he might be able to seek out someone who'd known him.

"It's my signature tune," Neil said, but he didn't add the other words he recalled, at least not yet. A half-insight drove him to his piano.

He'd originally transcribed the phrase in C-major. Now, Neil took a pen and wrote letters beneath each note: C-D-C-A-G-G#-A. There was nothing noteworthy here...but what if he changed the key? He tried several common variations—D-minor, F-major, B-flat-minor—trying at last G-major, the way his orchestral piece ended, where a flautist would reiterate that phrase with sky-piercing majesty.

He looked at the pencilled notes:

G-A-G-E-D-D#-E.

What to make of that?
One option was a man's name:

Gage D D Sharpe.

Trembling, Neil headed for the computer on its desk in one lounge corner. Following an unpleasant minute, during which nothing seemed to work quickly enough for him, he was online and searching for the name across the web.

The internet, with all its spooky omniscience, soon told him all he needed to know.

BY THE EVENING of the premiere, Stella Marsh had recovered and was confident she could contribute to the performance. In other circumstances, Neil would have been relieved, but now he wasn't so sure.

As he greeted attending villagers, he wondered whether he was experiencing a breakdown, whether the death of his mother, his wife's health, and so many nebulous recollections of the past had pitched his mind into troubling territory. Whatever the truth, as more people—almost all middle-aged—filled the hall, he realised he could hardly put a stop to the performance without coming across as some crazy artist who'd let his imagination consume him.

At least the dreams he'd been suffering made sense. Once everyone had settled in the small auditorium, he slipped backstage and reread the material he'd printed up about *Gage Damian Dafid Sharpe*.

The man had been a mystic from Wales who'd travelled the British Isles without ever setting down roots. That was why his relationship with Neil's mother had been short-lived. Sharpe had specialised in "conjuring manifestations of mythical figures." Preeminent among those was a figure half-man, half-goat, endowed with horns and a phallus, a player of pipes, and instiller of fertility: the *great god pan*.

Too much of this made sense of Neil's recent experiences, but might it have further implications for what might follow? With the audience seated and the performance about to start, he had one final opportunity to cancel it. But as the musicians gathered, slapping him on the back, grinning and winking, and in the case of one woman, licking her moist lips, he found himself with no choice but to lead them out to modest applause.

About fifty people had turned up, a fitting celebration of the grand old building. At the front, despite her indispositions, sat radiant Vanessa, her face flushed with an inner fervour.

Neil refused to reflect upon the possibilities her newly fertile appearance brought to mind, and so, after bowing to the crowd and turning to his fellow artistes, he set the piece he'd composed into motion.

A trumpet blared, violins soared, the combination suggesting arrival at a destination he'd trusted to listeners' imaginations. But *he* knew where they were about to be transported. Upon first iteration of *that* melodic phrase—the prompt for the mystical figure of his nightmares—the music plunged into a frantic landscape of lashing strings and piping woodwinds. Cellos underscored the frenetic movement, like earth shifting underfoot, while percussion kept savage pace with the headlong charge.

The piece settled down, horns depicting a mellower place in which birdsong trilled via clarinet, and cats summoned by violas prowled dense undergrowth. A little later, the hunt returned, strings shrieking, and timpani marking every manic surge. Then came Stella's flute recital of that imperious refrain.

The phrase soared like the leap of something otherworldly. The final two notes, a whole octave apart, depicted its subject's grandeur, the way it occupied a wildly alternative environment with such threatening force.

It was then that the village hall around Neil seemed to vanish in a hiss of fragmenting bricks, dissolving fabrics, and de-atomised people.

He stood again in that woodland plane occupied by so many naked others. Blindly conducting his music, he'd become a tyrannical master, an uncivilising harbinger of lust and chaos. Newer Gods held no sway here. He was the impish corruptor, great emancipator, father of fertility, inducer of amnesia.

He was *pan*. The great horned one. Behold his pipes, behold his tumescence.

Just whistle it, at any time, and I'll come to you, my boy.

Neil had done that at home: bountiful nature had responded, his garden exploding with colours. Now he pushed that fragment of melody into many more heads than his, and here was the result.

Once his composition thundered to its end, Neil turned to his audience.

Everyone had slid off their chairs to rut en masse on the village hall's floor. Even Vanessa was involved, despite her obvious pregnancy.

As Neil left the stage to pass among them like some fiendish deity, everyone screwed. Gasping, moaning, tearing off each other's garments. They conjoined with savage bliss.

Laughing hysterically, Neil stepped outside the hall to find the once barren plot of land around the building awash with fat-headed flowers, multi-stalked plant life, vicious tangles and creepers, flitting birds, prowling felines, fragrant scents, a fruitful wind, a tropical sky lurking above, and more, more, more.

As he'd anticipated, Neil now detected a rumbling from underground.

The website had claimed that Sharpe had died twenty years ago, but the researchers had failed to appreciate his command of the elements, including magical transformations of time and matter.

Neil had indeed whistled for the man, long after first being invited to do so, when his mother had enjoyed a fling with him. And now, bursting from the soil, here he came at last, his body more bone than flesh, and yet still sporting, amid what was little left of a face, an intense expression, along with twin horns jutting from such a prominent brow.

"*My boy,*" said the figure clawing its way up from the earth, its voice a death-raddled grunt. Moments later, the dirty, skeletal thing was on all galloping fours. "*It's been too long.*"

Suddenly Neil felt oh so young again.

Gary Fry is a semi-retired academic who lives in coastal countryside in the northeast of England. He has had published around 100 short stories, a bunch of novellas, and several novels. He was the first author in PS Publishing's Showcase range, and none other than Ramsey Campbell has described him as a "master of philosophical horror." He plays piano, loves dogs, and reads a frightening number of books each year. Visit him at: https://garyfrytalks.blogspot.com ■■■

HERE ARE TALES THAT WILL USHER YOU INTO

THE HAUNT OF
FEAR

FEAR

AN ENTERTAINING EC COMIC

NO. 4
JULY-AUG.

AUTHORIZED A.C.M.F

CONFORMS TO THE COMICS CODE

10¢

IN FOUR COLORS

FEATURING...

THE OLD WITCH

THE VAULT-KEEPER

TO— THOMAS ENGLISH EDITOR

THE HIDEOUS HISTORY OF AMERICAN HORROR COMICS

BY JOHN M. NAVROTH

JOHN M. NAVROTH'S FEAR IN FOUR COLORS

THE HIDEOUS HISTORY OF AMERICAN HORROR COMICS

#4- THE GHOULUNATICS!

"In our culture the perversion of children has become an industry."
—Gershon Legman, *Love and Death: A Study in Censorship*

WELL, WE'VE MADE IT ACROSS THE RICKETY OLD BRIDGE OVER DEADMAN'S SWAMP AND HAVE LUCKILY PASSED OVER THE LAST OF THOSE DECAYED and bloated bodies floating by. Ugh! Now let's slog further along in this noisesome and slimy undergrowth. Wait! What's this up ahead? Why, it's an old, dilapidated shack, surrounded by a—gulp!—graveyard!

Shall we take a peek inside? Gads! It's piled high with comics—and not just any comics—they're all EC Comics! Well, let's see here—Oops!—gotta watch out for this deadfall in a hole in the floor; those spikes at the bottom look awfully sharp.

Ahh, there we go. These comics look like they're still in amazing shape; must not be any leaks in the roof.

Don'tcha just wonder how all these great comics were made? Let's take a looksee, shall we, and find out!

THERE IS NO DISPUTING that in the 1950's EC Comics produced the most celebrated horror comics of the Pre-Code era. Indeed, they have achieved current-day legendary status among a multitude of worldwide fans and collectors, and for good reason. The key to their success is due in large part because of the incredibly talented writers and artists who wanted to turn out the most entertaining stories that a dime could buy.

It's hard to believe that the same comics that became roundly criticized for their violence and gore had their beginnings as illustrated stories from the Bible! When William Maxwell "Bill" Gaines assumed the duties of his late father Max's publishing company (Max was killed in a recreational boating accident on Lake Placid in 1947),

EC's initials stood for Educational Comics, and as the name implied, the brand published *Picture Stories from the Bible*, *Picture Stories from American History*, as well as comics on other wholesome topics, including titles intended for children. Now that he was sole owner, Bill wanted to alter the editorial policy to reflect more mature and daring themes. However, he found himself in relatively uncharted territory and initially had reservations that his ideas and limited abilities would keep his company above the waterline. Even his father had nagged at him, saying he'd "never amount to anything."

Max had left the Gaines family financially well-off, and son Bill really wasn't a big fan of comics at the time; instead, he

had aims to become a chemistry teacher. In later years, Sheldon Mayer, who was the editor of DC Comics during EC's heyday, remembered: "I got the feeling that Bill went into the business as a joke, to see if he could screw up things, change them for his private amusement, and still manage to make money doing it…" True or not, it was that attitude that enabled Gaines to eventually create what would become an institution without artistic restrictions and without worrying about a cost-conscious publisher lording over what should or shouldn't be published. The result was a firebrand, the likes of which had not yet been seen in the comic book industry. During just five short years, Gaines and his staff of sharp writers and highly talented artists lay bare and exploited such topics as bigotry, racism, and a host of other "uncomfortable" social conditions and psychological dilemmas that were collectively thought by conventional standards to be best left in the shadows. That these subjects were even considered as stories for the lowly comic book is an anomaly and the importance of the matters that were

covered—subtly or not—cannot be understated. That they would soon be singled out as a gateway to juvenile delinquency is at once both laughable and tragic compared to the instructive lessons that could have been learned otherwise.

It is interesting to note that the legend of EC Comics essentially began with a friendship. After he hired Al Feldstein, Gaines soon realized he had his creative lynchpin to move forward. While Gaines was the "guiding light" of the enterprise, Feldstein already had years of experience in the industry which must have been incredibly valuable to Gaines, whose own inexperience at running a comic book company at this point was untenable at best. Another significant factor is the two hit it off almost immediately.

Albert Bernard Feldstein was born in Brooklyn, New York, the son of Russian Jewish parents Max and Beatrice. He had a talent for drawing, and at the age of 15, he entered a poster contest for the 1939 New York World's Fair and won. Bolstered by his success, he took classes at the High School of Music and Art in Manhattan with the idea of eventually becoming an art teacher. In the meantime, he needed a job to pay for his transportation and other needs. After hearing how comic book artists earned a "lot of money," he put together a portfolio of his work, saying he had never seen a comic book up until this point! After pounding the pavements of New York he met with no success.

Fortuitously, one of the editors who rejected his work suggested he try a place that created and packaged comics for publishers. As fate would have it, he was hired on at the Eisner & Iger shop (aka Syndicated Features Corporation) erasing inked comic pages, as well as performing duties as an all-around office assistant. Working his way up, he eventually got the go-ahead to draw his own comic pages. In a 2003 interview, he explained: "[At the Iger shop] I began to learn to do Comic Book Art [sic]…first, by inking backgrounds…then penciling and inking backgrounds…then inking figures penciled by others…then penciling and inking figures …and finally doing whole pages from beginning to end." One of his earliest background assignments was for Fiction House's *Sheena, Queen of the Jungle*. There was plenty of

other talent around for him to learn from during this time: Matt Baker, Nick Cardy, future EC artist Jack Kamen, Joe Kubert and many others were among the artists churning out comic book pages on the Iger "assembly line." Still setting his sights on a teaching career, he continued attending classes at Brooklyn College and the Art Students League in Manhattan.

During World War II, Feldstein enlisted in the Army Air Force in early 1944 at the age of 17, avoiding combat after he told his officer in charge he was an artist. While serving Stateside, he found opportunities to continue drawing, which included posters, sign-painting and a comic strip. Once out of the service, he went back to work for Iger.

In September 1944, Feldstein married his high school and college sweetheart, and the subsequent pressure of raising a family suddenly loomed as a concern; the simple truth was that he needed to increase his wages in order to better provide the things that a spouse and children required. At some point, Feldstein realized that if he freelanced, he could make considerably more per page than he was getting at Iger, who was taking a large percentage off the top. With that in

mind he solicited his work and began finding jobs with other publishers. At Fox Feature Syndicate he focused on teen humor comics, scripting and illustrating stories for *Meet Corliss Archer*, *Junior*, and *Sunny* between September 1947 and July 1948. Drawing these stories also allowed Feldstein to show off his considerable ability to draw "Good Girl" art. (He might have learned a few tricks from Matt Baker and Jack Kamen—two brilliant Good Girl artists in their own right—while working with them at the Iger shop.)

Providing the lettering for many of Feldstein's stories for Fox was Jim Wroten. It was likely sometime in late 1947 or early 1948, when Wroten approached Feldstein and told him that Victor Fox was on financial shaky ground. Armed with that knowledge, they decided to flee the henhouse and find work elsewhere.

At this time, Bill Gaines had only been at the helm of EC for about seven months and he was on the lookout to shore up his staff with new and emerging talent. Then Feldstein came knocking with his professional portfolio, complete with generous examples of his Good Girl art. Gaines immediately put him to work creating EC's own teen humor comic, *Going Steady with Peggy*. When the story and art was completed, Gaines decided to shelve the project when he learned that the teen comic market was faltering. Consequently, the strip was never published.

"I was going to do a magazine for them [EC] called 'Going Steady with Peggy'," Feldstein recalled in a later interview, "then the sales on the teenage market were showing weakness. It was an industry of a few innovators and a lot of followers. So I said to Bill, 'Well, let's tear up the contract.' I'll work for you on other things and we'll be friends. That's what we did and I guess it kind of sealed our friendship."

In the meantime, Feldstein was working away on *Crime Patrol*, *Gunfighter*, *Saddle Justice*, and *War Against Crime*, illustrating stories written by Gardner F. Fox and others. It was not long until he went to Gaines and asked if he could both write and draw his own stories. Bill gave him the green light, a clear indication that he had become very aware of Feldstein's abilities.

While the story varies, on one particular occasion, Feldstein and Gaines had a discussion on what was next for EC. "I came to him one day and said, 'Look, Bill, why are we following these idiots, and when the trend dies, getting caught? Why don't we innovate, and why don't we have people follow US?' Bill was a science-fiction and horror fan, and I was a horror movie fan, and I said, 'Why don't we try horror?'"

The two of them were also fans of mystery radio shows such as Arch Obler's *Light's Out* and *The Witch's Tale*, the latter which featured an ancient old Salem witch named Nancy who introduced each episode. Aware that some publishers had already experimented with horror titles, Feldstein convinced Gaines to give it a try.

"He [Gaines] really didn't want to innovate," Feldstein later said. "He was cautious as a publisher for a long time. So, I came up with two titles, *The Crypt of Terror*, hosted by the Crypt Keeper and *The Vault of Horror*, hosted by the Vault Keeper."

"Complete in this issue! An illustrated terror tale from The Crypt of Terror!" read the text box on the cover of the December 1949-January 1950 issue of *Crime Patrol* #15.

With an on-sale date of 8 August 1949, Al Feldstein's "Return from the Grave" was the first story of what would soon become regular fare in their soon-to-be horror titles. Johnny Craig provided the cover art that was devoid of anything related to crime except the title and replaced it with an image show-casing Feldstein's horror story.

Following close behind *Crime Patrol*, *War Against Crime* #10 (Dec. 1949-January 1950; on-sale date 20 September 1949) carried a similar announcement: "Complete in this issue! An illustrated terror tale from The Vault of Horror!" This time Feldstein's "Buried Alive" was the lead story behind a Johnny Craig cover.

Crime Patrol #16 and *War Against Crime* #11 (both cover-dated February-March 1950) continued with two more stories by Feld-stein: "The Spectre of the Castle" in *Crime Patrol* and "The Mummy's Curse in *War Against Crime.*

Yet, these were not the first horror stories published by EC. Pre-dating what would become the "New Trend" titles were two horror-themed stories that appeared in EC's short-lived superhero comic, *Moon Girl.* Generally regarded as EC's first horror

story "Zombie Terror!" appeared in *Moon Girl* #5 (Fall 1948), written by Dick Kraus and illustrated by Johnny Craig. However,

in issue #4 (Summer 1948) Moon Girl is menaced by the Undead in "Vampire of the Bayous." The villain is a vampire of the supernatural kind, not the human variety, which certainly qualifies it as a horror/suspense story. The script is by Dick Kraus with art by Sheldon Moldoff, who would create and sell his own package of horror comics (*This Magazine Is Haunted*, *Worlds of Fear*, etc.) to Fawcett in 1951 after his *Tales from the Supernatural* project was accepted—then dropped—by Bill Gaines. In addition, "The Werewolf's Curse," scripted by Dick Kraus and illustrated by Howard Larson appeared in *Crime Patrol* #11 (April-May 1949) and had all the signs of a horror story. No explanation is given of the wolf creature other than it appears as a result of a family curse, but the last panel describes the tale using the terms "horror" and "the supernatural."

Gaines and Feldstein were encouraged when the sales figures came back, indicating that Feldstein's horror stories were a big hit with readers. They went all in, and *Crime Patrol* became *The Crypt of Terror* with issue #17 (April-May 1950). Likewise, *War Against Crime* was re-titled *The Vault of Horror* with issue #12 (April-May 1950). The numbering was continued from the previous titles, in order to avoid additional second-class

postage permits. They completed their "unholy trinity" with *The Haunt of Fear* #15, re-titled from their languishing western comic, *Gunfighter*. A prototype of The Old Witch, the third of the horror hosts, beckoned readers to enter on the Johnny Craig cover, but her first appearance in a story wasn't until issue #16 (July-August 1950).

Under the heading "The Witch's Cauldron," she introduces "The Mummy's Return," written by Feldstein and illustrated by Jack Kamen. Feldstein would draw her in the next issue; in "Horror Beneath the Streets!" Feldstein writes himself and Bill Gaines into the clever story where they get chased into a sewer by The Old Witch after leaving the office for the night. There they are confronted by The Crypt Keeper and The Vault Keeper, who won't let them out until they sign a contract to publish their comics! It wouldn't be until issue #4 (Nov.-Dec. 1950) that readers would see the more familiar rendering of The Old Witch by Graham Ingels in the creepy little story, "The Hunchback," plotted by Gaines and Feldstein and scripted by Feldstein. The three hosts were collectively named "The Ghoulunatics" and they would be thrilling readers with their outrageous stories for a good while.

Officially announced as EC's "New Trend," issues rolled off the presses and—after a few fits and starts—became increasingly popular, eventually becoming among the most sought-after horror comics among the many titles available on spinner racks across the country. Each title had a letter column, and readers would sound off on their favorite stories or otherwise make wisecrack comments as only kids can. Even a national fan club was formed, complete with a welcome letter, membership card, certificate, cloth patch and bronze pin. Praise went to the art, but the stories themselves also drew attention for their wicked twist endings and other terrifying tales of murder, gore, and dismemberment. It was the latter that would get them into a boiling witch's cauldron a few years later with parents, religious groups and self-righteous morality crusaders.

FEATURING...

THE CRYPT-KEEPER

THE OLD WITCH

THE VAULT-KEEPER

When Gaines came around to an interest in writing, he and Feldstein developed a formula they called "springboardng" which they both found effective in turning out the overwhelming number of scripts needed to fill each issue. Outside of Johnny Craig, Jack Olek and a handful of others, they produced the largest quantity of text, not only because they were able to maintain creative control, but they loved the excitement in creating the stories as well.

"Bill got involved with a lot of reading," Feldstein explained in a 1997 interview. "He was always overweight and always taking some sort of diet pills. He was foolishly taking a decodrine [Dexedrine] pill around dinner time, when he shouldn't. So, he'd be up late at night, not being able to sleep. He thought he was an insomniac, but I think he was just reacting to the decodrine. He'd read and he'd come in in the morning and he'd have these springboard ideas. Pretty soon, we started plotting stories together."

Feldstein found himself doing less and less artwork, as he believed "stories were the thing." He later wrote: "These stories that Bill and I wrote were commercial ventures to produce a magazine that would entertain and SELL."

After plotting and scripting stories with Gaines, it was

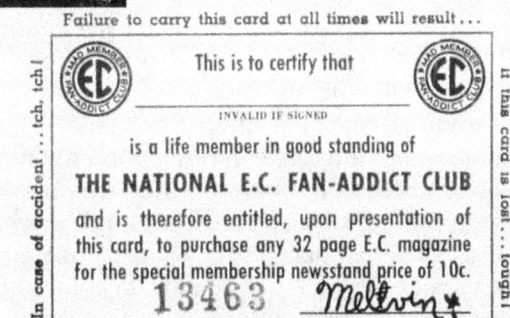

also Feldstein's job to design logos and breakdown the pages themselves before the artists ever put pencil to paper. "I wrote everything directly on the [illustration] board," Feldstein said. "The only downside of that was that I was actually doing the layout. The artist had no say in how big or how small a panel would be. I had a tendency to do rather regular panels. I stopped doing some of those crazy things that many of the comic books were doing with circles and elongated panels. They were confusing."

The prolific Feldstein wrote well over 500 scripts for EC at the rate of about four scripts a week for over four years. During that time he claimed he never wrote a script beforehand and always wrote it directly on the comic page so that he had easier control over the pace of the story and could better fit the dialogue and captions. This kind of workload kept him away from illustrating stories, but amazingly he still found the time do an occasional cover. Since this series focuses on horror comics, it should nevertheless be mentioned that EC also published a variety of New Trend comics on other subjects as well: *Weird Fantasy*, *Weird Science*, *Weird Science-Fantasy*, *Crime SuspenStories*, *Shock SuspenStories*, *Frontline Combat*, *Two-Fisted Tales*, *Piracy*, *Panic*, and of course, *Mad*, the ultimate counter-culture humor magazine that entertained and influenced millions.

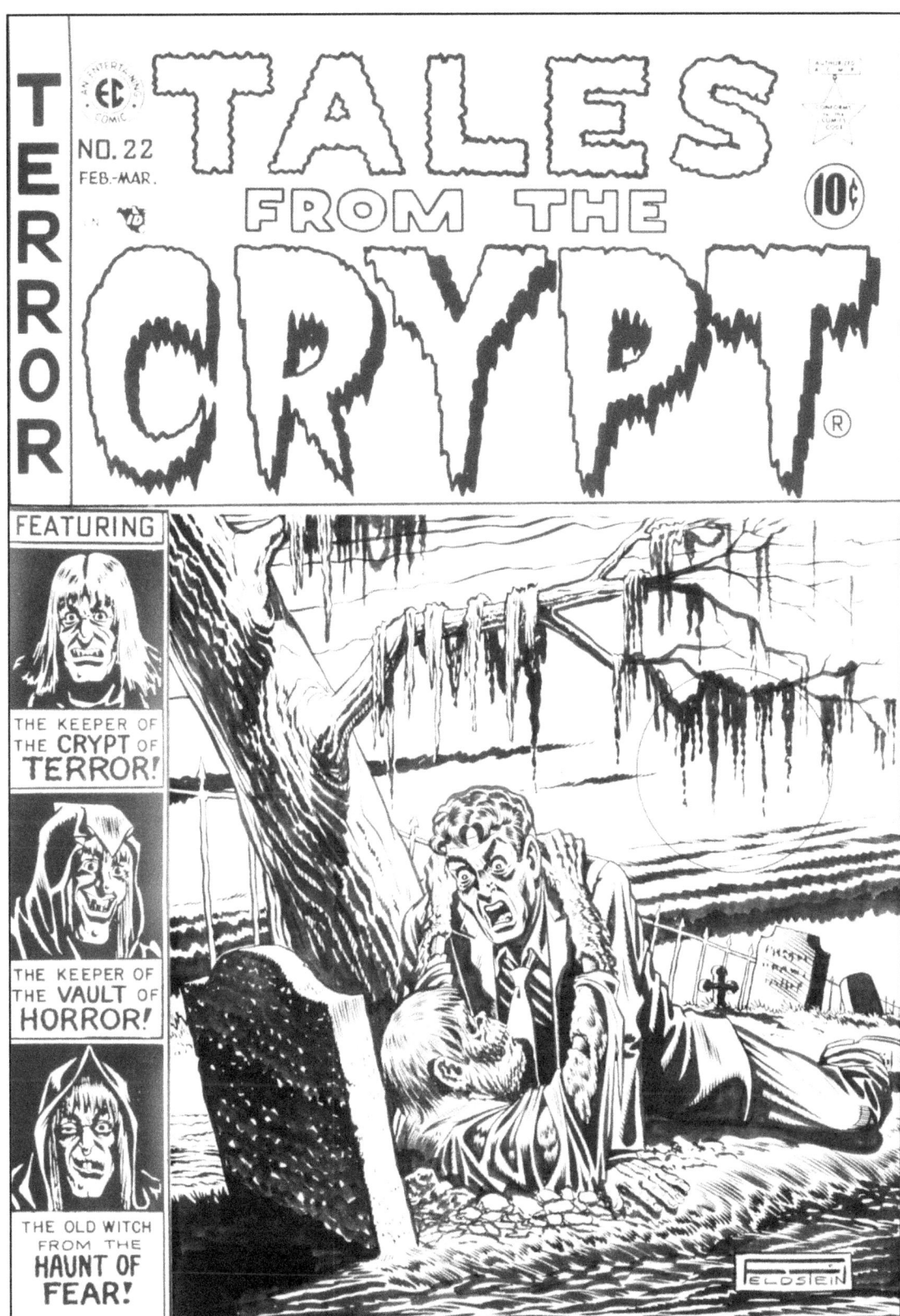

Despite the layout constraints, artists were lining up and knocking at the door of 225 Lafayette St., New York, after they learned that this EC Comics outfit paid upon completion of work and had another story ready to go at the same time! As a result, Gaines never had a problem bringing more talented artists to the fold. Feldstein also made sure stories were created with a particular artist in mind. In addition, he encouraged each artist to draw in their own unique style. It was not long before the EC offices were filled with the exclamations of artists admiring each other's work, in effect, creating their own "springboard" for them to outdo each other. The comradery between Gaines, Feldstein, and the rest of the staff became almost palpable.

There are no doubts that EC's horror comics and other titles were a class act, and although a lot of the more controversial stories are still discussed today, it is largely the art that people remember. Gaines and Feldstein managed to assemble the most gifted group of artists yet seen in the comics industry, and there wasn't one considered marginal in the bunch. With the exception

Graham Ingels (by Reed Crandall, from the fanzine Squa Tront #1)

Bottom: One of Ingel's "Ghastly" EC horror covers.

of Feldstein's page layout technique, they were unfettered by any strict conventions, and as a result, free to illustrate a story in any direction their talent would lead them.

The most revered of the EC's artists today is Graham Ingels. Hired by Feldstein in 1948, he was assigned to EC's western, war, and romance comics. Originally, Gaines wasn't too keen on Ingel's work. What he didn't know was that thus far in his career Ingels had been restricting his natural style in order to fit in with the types of comics publishers wanted him to draw. "When we started the Horror [sic] titles," Gaines once said, "we didn't use Graham because we thought he was good at it, we used him whenever an artist came into the fold, and we had to use him for something, so we just stuck Ingles into the Horror books and it didn't take us very long to realize what had happened…that Ingels was Mr. Horror himself." Ingels was dubbed with the nickname "Ghastly," and he began signing his art with it.

Jack Davis was another popular artist among fans. He had a "scratchy," cartoon-like style that fit perfectly with the outlandish stories he illustrated. He was also the fastest of the EC

artists and was capable of dashing off a 7- to 8-page story in 2 or 3 days. Harvey Kurtzman, New Trend war comic editor and creator of *Mad* magazine said of Davis: "His talents are as a craftsman, a stylist and a humorist all combined." Ironically, Davis

himself didn't particularly care about drawing horror comics!

Johnny Craig was a highly respected veteran at EC and the one artist that spent most of his working day at the office. Craig's work is distinguished by his very clean lines, influenced by the great newspaper cartoonist, Milton Caniff. Gaines commented that "[Craig's] beautiful clean, charming artwork and the dreadful things that eventually happened at the tip of his pen added to the effect." His only shortcoming was that he was a very slow artist, and Gaines and Feldstein had to plan his assignments accordingly.

The list of the other EC artists reads like a "Who's who" of comic art and illustration talent: Reed Crandall, Will Elder, George Evans, Frank Frazetta, Jack Kamen, Bernard Krigstein, Angelo Torres, Al Williamson, Wallace Wood, and more.

Brother of artist John Severin, Marie Severin joined EC as a colorist in 1949, working on war books and then the rest of the titles. In an interview she said: "What they liked is that I really studied which colors looked best and sharper next to one another, the subtleties of it. I would also

proofread the colors." She would later become even more well-known during her career at Marvel.

Here & previous page: Graham Ingels' "Ghastly" covers. Opposite: Three by Jack Davis.

Also on board was letterer Jim Wroten who had worked with Feldstein at Fox and had warned him about the publisher's financial troubles that led to them both working for EC. Wroten had been a salesman for Keuffel & Esser's Leroy pen, a mechanical device primarily used in the drafting trade that was fitted with a pen for use with a template to make clear and uniform letters. After leaving Leroy, Wroten and his wife, Margaret, formed Wroten Lettering along with other family members. One of their accounts was EC and it is their painstaking mechanical lettering that adds to the distinctive look of the EC line.

Headed by the three Ghoulunatics, EC's trio of horror comics kept on selling as well or better than any of the other Pre-Code horror titles. Although there were other covers that have become notorious over the years (see *Nightmare Abbey 6*), it was EC's superbly drawn, gloriously gory and frightening scenes depicted on covers by Feldstein, Craig, Ingels, et al, that really attracted readers to grab them off newsstands.

Overshadowing all the exhilaration was an early indication of what was to come for not only EC comics, but other horror comic

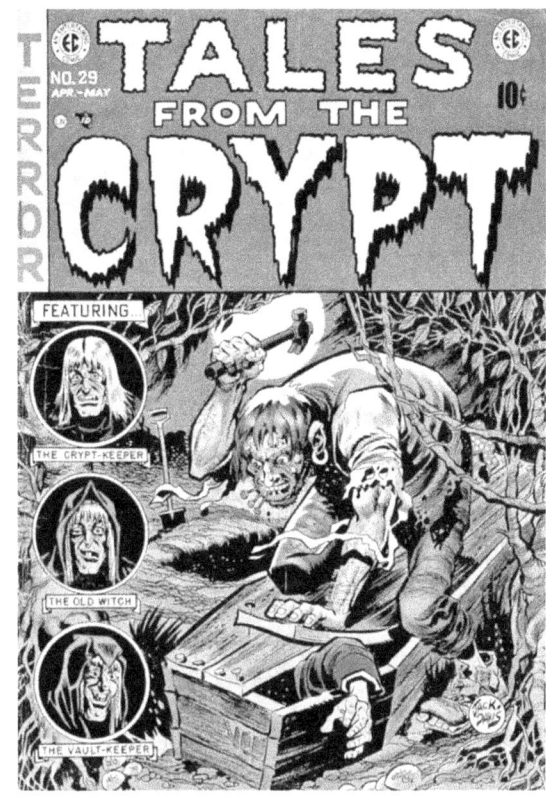

publishers as well; Gaines opted to change the title of *The Crypt of Terror* to *Tales from the Crypt* with issue #20 (Oct.-Nov. 1950)

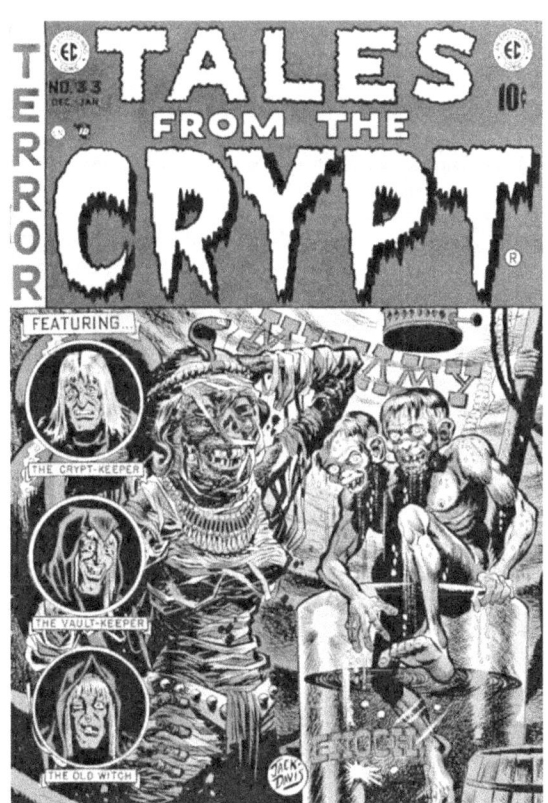

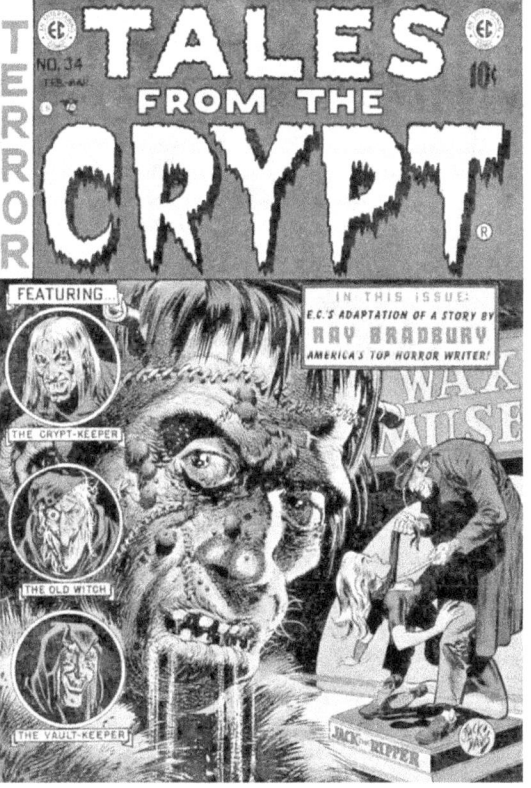

because "the wholesalers made some noise." This was a not-so-subtle sign that the supply chain—the life's blood of any publication— was suddenly cautious about the material they handled and was likely the result of a certain psychiatrist's inflammatory articles

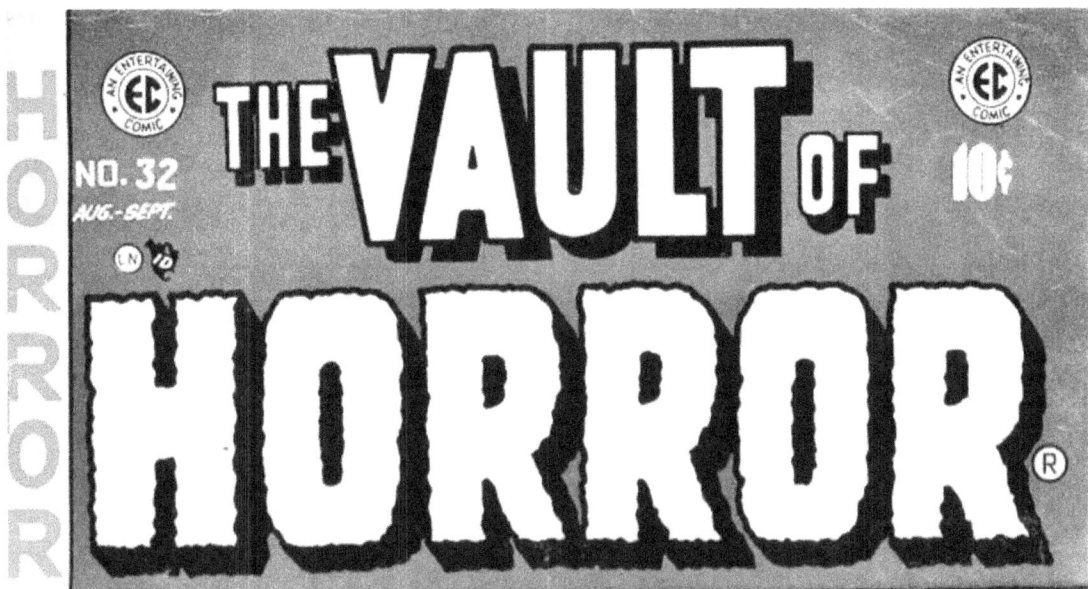

concerning comic books that were appearing in family magazines and getting parents to think about what just kind of "funny books" their kids were reading.

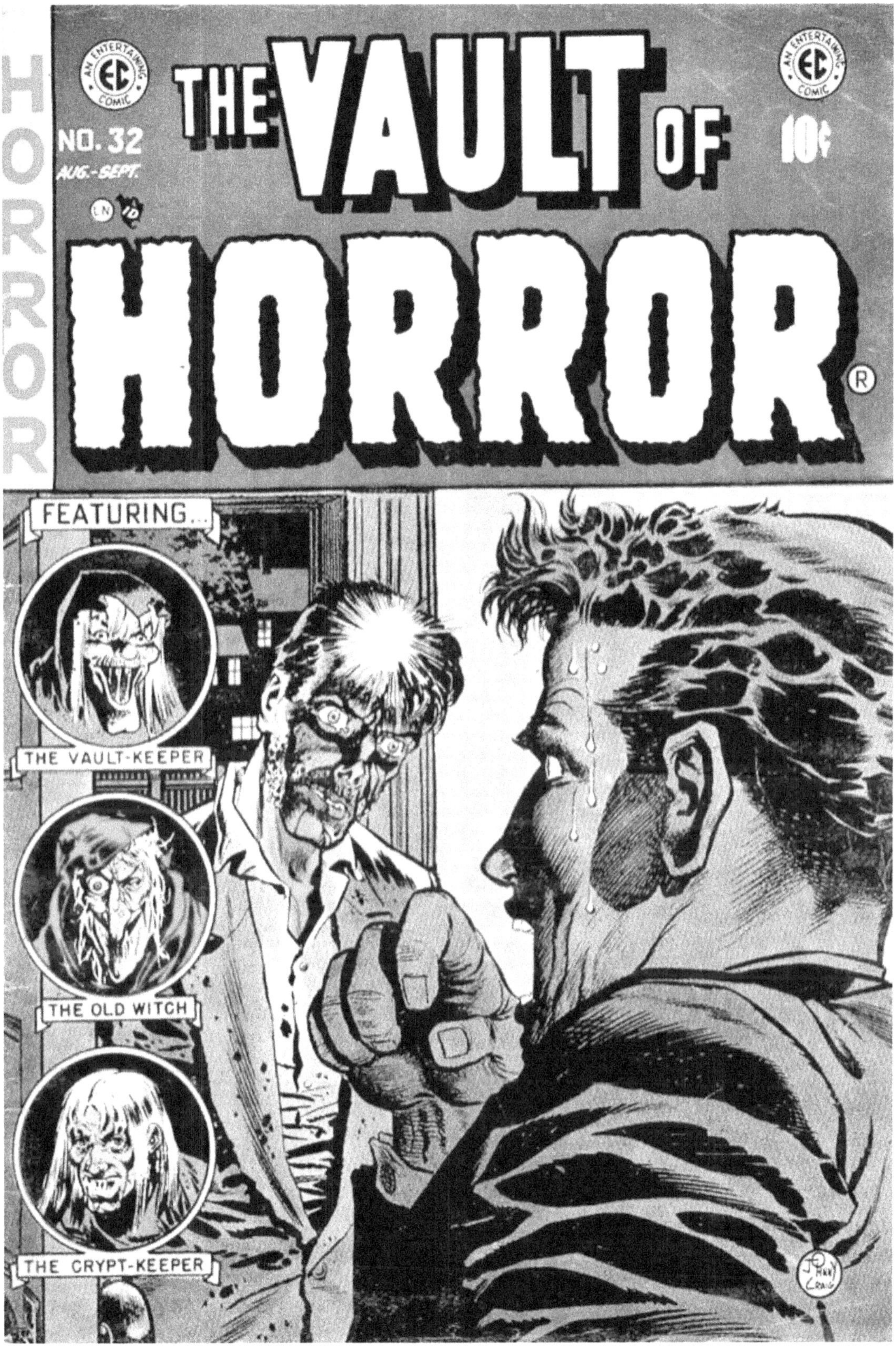

Combined with the first three issues of *The Crypt of Terror*, *Tales from the Crypt* ran

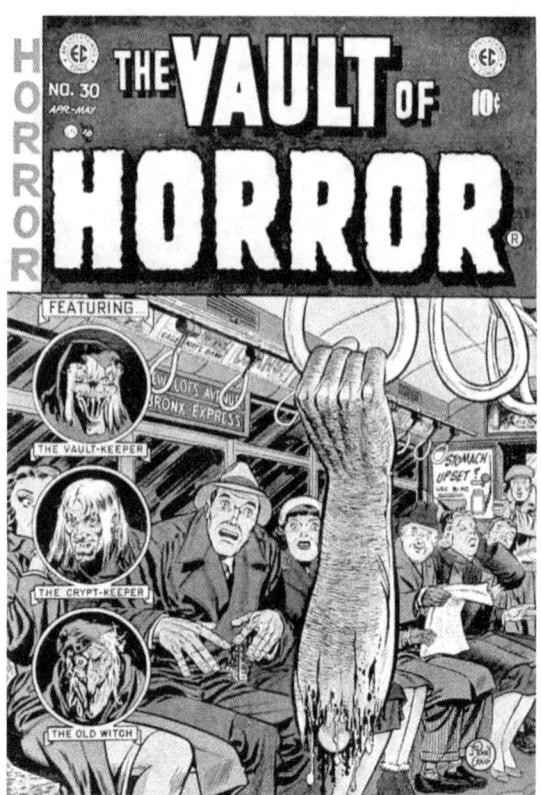

for 30 issues (April-May 1950 until Feb.-March 1955), *The Vault of Horror* ran for 29 issues (April-May 1950 until Dec. 1954-Jan. 1955) and *The Haunt of Fear* had 28 issues

(May-June 1950 until Nov.-Dec. 1954). *Tales of Terror* was an annual published from 1951 to 1953, each containing a selection of four remaindered comics from the previous year.

Masks and movies: EC Comics have spawned merchandise, such as these Ghoulunatics masks from Trick or Treat Studios, and film and television productions, including *Tales from the* Crypt, a 1972 British horror movie adapting five of the old EC Comics stories. Below, left: the paperback novelization of the film, by former EC writer Jack Oleck. Below, right: the secret to EC's neat, text-heavy word balloons. Bottom: a thick, 1951 EC Comics Annual.

They are now considered rare because they were distributed only to select cities. *Three-Dimensional Tales from the Crypt of Terror* was a selection of re-written and re-drawn stories published in Spring 1954 using the anaglyphic 3-D printing process.

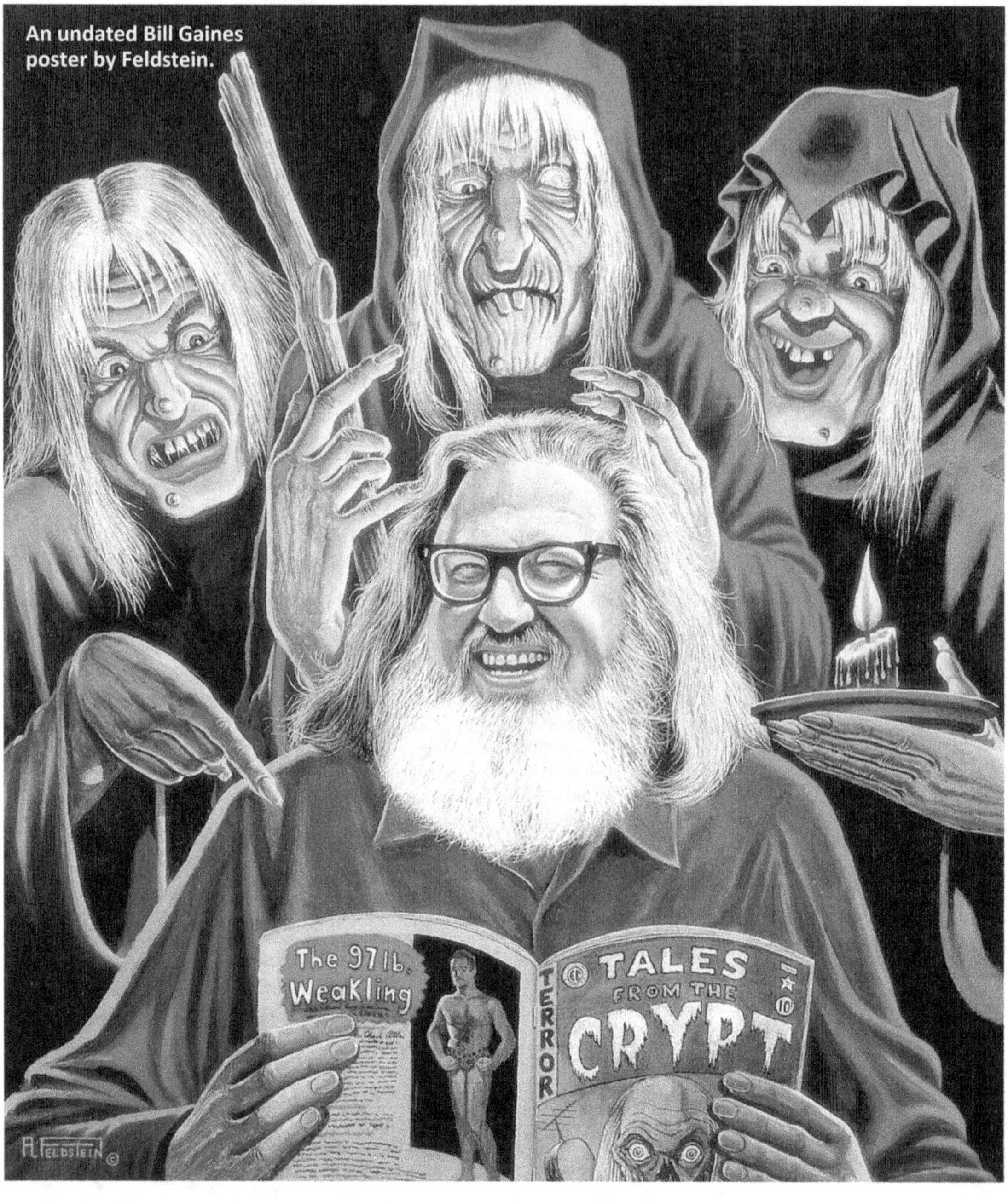

An undated Bill Gaines poster by Feldstein.

Just these few titles represent the pinnacle of horror comics during the Pre-Code era and have set the hangman's noose at a height few others have reached. While some occasionally came close, EC's combination of Gothic, atmospheric horror, and tense, true-to-life psychological terror went largely unmatched during those few short years.

It all hinged on the willingness of Bill Gaines to take a chance on launching his New Trend books which led to him catching that elusive and rare lightning in a bottle that fans are still talking about today. "The old EC stories were largely sick humor," he once said. "Almost every one of those horror stories was tongue-in-cheek. EC stories differed from a lot of stories in comics because 'virtue' did not have to triumph."

Next: "THE GREAT HORROR COMIC PURGE"

For readers interested in learning more about vintage horror comics, visit John's website at fearinfourcolors.blogspot.com

ONE WILL GROW TO EAT THE OTHER

BY MICHAEL KELLY

TRAUMA IS A GHOST THAT HAUNTS YOU. GRIEF ANOTHER.

DAD WAS DEAD. MOM GRIPPED IN A PALL OF ANGUISH. AND SOPHIE WOULDN'T SHUT UP.

"Ophelia," Sophie was saying, "we all perish in the end. Sometimes our end comes sooner than we'd like."

I stared at her. It was night. We were on the backyard patio. Candles on the table pushing back against the intruding darkness.

"Maybe he really is in a better place," Sophie said.

"Get bent." I folded my arms tight across my chest, looked down. "It's not like he was ill, Soph. He was *taken*." There was no proof of that. That's what I chose to believe. He was just gone one day. Missing. Until they found him. Part of him.

"'For in that sleep of death, what dreams may come.'"

I looked up. A strange smirk stretched pumpkin-like across Sophie's face. "C'mon," she said. "You should know that one." A sigh. "It's just projection, Ophelia. This thing you found in the cave. It's not our dear dead Dad. Have you heard of *Apophenia*?"

Always smarter than me. "No."

"It's connecting something to another thing when there truly is no relation. Random coincidence. You just don't want to believe Dad is really gone. He is. Trust me."

I'd found a cave. There was something in the cave. A body, perhaps. Dad, perhaps.

His embodiment, anyway. Sophie had scoffed at the idea.

"They found his remains, Ophelia. He's not missing anymore."

Technically, they still haven't found his body. Just his head.

"What is it then?" I asked. "What could it be?"

The candle flames guttered and Sophie's face flickered orange and black. "Hmm."

Sophie loved making up stories. Loved scaring me.

"Fifi," she said—and she only said my nickname when she was trying to wind me up, to scare me, to get my attention— "imagine this area hundreds of years ago. Before the parched land and contaminated creeks. Inhabited by the Cree. They fished the waters. Cultivated the land. And they found those caves. They didn't live in them— they'd already settled—but they mined them for quartz and other stone to make tools. And they were spiritual places to the Cree."

I looked up. Ancient stars glinted in the dark. The crescent moon cut a sharp grin against the fabric of the night.

Sophie continued: "A Cree elder had sons. Twins." And she smiled sharp and wicked like that moon. "He favored one over the other," she said. "One was good, he imagined. The other evil." She winked. "A tired trope, Fifi, I know. But stay with me. One twin was constructive. One was de-structive." Sophie paused, features serious. "Which are we, Fifi? Maybe we're both. Maybe we're the same."

"I'm not like you."

"The Elder disavowed the one son," Sophie said, "and sent him to live in the cave. Each day he would send the other son to the dark cave with a meager food offering. Half a cob of corn. A few bits of rabbit. A tiny scrap of whitefish. Unbeknownst to the Elder, the twins would swap places so that on alternate days the disowned son would come back from the cave, smiling and sweet. This went on for weeks and the Elder was none the wiser."

Sophie grew pensive. "Imagine not know-ing your own child, Fifi." She sighed. "But the Elder was poisoning the food. He meant to poison the 'evil' twin but was slowly poisoning them both. They took ill. And one morning the Elder found his son dead. Instead of grief, a great rage consumed him. How could his favored be dead? Why couldn't it be the other? So he carried the lifeless body of his son to the cave, vengeance on his mind, and found that the other son was also dead. Only then did he realize his mistake. His rage grew. Conspirators both! And he bound them together, made them one, and left them in the mouth of the cave."

A sudden wind pulled at me and I shud-dered. "That's not what's in the cave," I said.

Sophie just grinned.

TRAUMA IS A GHOST *that haunts you. Grief another. Terrible twins. One will grow to eat the other.*

That's what the thing in the cave told me.

I wrote it down when I got home from leaving the offering to the thing in the cave in the hills beyond the foul creek behind our suburban house. The pale moon and my cell phone's flashlight guided me down the hillside through the wild bracken and across the slippery moss-coated rocks protruding turtle-like from the black, sluggish water. Quickly over the back fence then around to the front. Extinguishing the light from my phone, easing the key into the recently oiled lock, then crossing the dark foyer and padding lightly up the stairs, trying not to wake Sophie—Mom already numbed asleep—to my silent room where I opened a Word document on the laptop and typed it out.

One will grow to eat the other. What did it mean?

The thing in the cave was a scarecrow. That's what Sophie said when I showed it to her the day before I secretly left the offering. And it *did* resemble a scarecrow. It was like a large cross or a canted X, made of wood or bone—I wasn't sure which—with muscly, twining sinews, and a nubby growth at the top like a malformed Jack-O-Lantern. Some sort of old sculpture, perhaps. Ancient, maybe. When I put Dad's old denim shirt on it, the offering, I briefly touched the thing and it felt like everything and nothing, smooth and rough, warm and cold, alive and dead.

I don't know why it wanted the shirt. But Dad was never coming back, and Mom hadn't cleaned out his closet, so I obliged. It was difficult to place the shirt on the thing's tilting frame, so I draped it over the strange lump, its "head," like a cowl. It hadn't said it was an "offering," but it felt like one. And it hadn't specifically asked for the shirt. *Bring me something of his*, it'd commanded. Dad was always wearing that shirt—the denim faded bone-white like a sky leeched of all its blue—unbuttoned with a tattered band T-shirt underneath. That's how I picture him still. It was like having him back.

"A scarecrow is all," Sophie said that day. But scarecrows don't talk. And this thing did. I didn't tell her it was speaking to me. I told her it most definitely was *not* a scarecrow. "What would be the point of putting a scarecrow in a cave?"

"To scare things away," Sophie said, smug. Sophie was 486 seconds older than me. Older and wiser.

"Things?" I asked.

"Animals," she said. "People. Us, probably."

"*Us?*"

And then she started in on one of her stories. That 8-minute age gap felt like 8-years, to me.

Sophie held her phone under her chin, flashlight on. Her face was a hooded corona, her eye sockets and mouth deep dark holes.

I shivered.

"Fifi," she said, "do you remember that girl, Jenny, who disappeared from school last year mid-term and never came back?"

"The one who moved?"

"Uh-uh," Sophie said, her dark mouth grim. "Didn't move away. She died. Was killed, actually. Murdered."

I laughed, but it wasn't a pleasant sound. "Another of your fictions, Soph."

Her voice grew quieter. "Everyone just assumes she moved. Kids suddenly vanish and we don't think anything of it. We don't question it."

"What other explanation is there?"

"Shhh," Sophie said. "Not so loud. He'll hear." Her voice was odd, echoey, as if coming from somewhere else in the cave.

I glanced at the thing. "Who will?"

"The killer," she whispered. Sophie leaned toward me, the phone still lighting her face in half shadow.

A scuttling, scraping sound. Something moving. She was pulling out all the stops. "Cut it out," I said.

"We'll get to that part." She paused. I heard another faint noise. Sophie cocked her head. "I heard this from a kid who knows Jenny's parents," she said. "Jenny was over in the next county, riding her bike down those red dirt roads, going to meet some guy. This guy, Dale, says Jenny never showed.

"Dale lived in this big old house with his big old man, with nothing but crows and cornfields as neighbors. Jenny's Dad found Facebook messages to Dale and went out to the house alone one night. He found a shed of bones, Ophelia. Human bones. Femurs, tibias. And skulls. A whole shed of skulls."

Daylight was disappearing, and the cave grew dimmer. Sophie's flashlight was dimming, too, that grin darkening.

"Jenny's Dad kills them both, Ophelia—Dale and his old man. What else could he do? They both had to be in on it. He found a big, hooked knife in the shed, went into the dark house and gutted them both while they slept. Ripped them wide open."

"Sickle," I said.

"Whu—?"

"The big knife. The hook. It's called a sickle. Or a scythe." For once I felt smarter than Sophie.

"That's not the point," she said. "Jenny's Dad drags the bodies to the corn field behind the house. Tears out their intestines. Stuffs straw and dried corn husks into the bloody cavities. Makes crosses out of old fence planks. Nails them to the crosses and plants them in the field."

"I—um, that's ridiculous. I would have heard about it."

"Nah," Sophie said. "Took ages to find them. The house was big. The stalks high. Cops did a 'wellness' check when Dale went missing. Found them in the field. Crows had got to them. Ironic. Wasn't much left. Cops somehow traced Dale to Jenny, which led to her dad, via tire treads, mud, what have you."

"It would have been on the news, my socials."

A small chuckle from Sophie. "Cops and media are in on it. Sheesh, Ophelia, you know you can't trust either. A. C. A. B."

"In on what?"

"Cover up," she said. "Turns out Dale and Pops took a kid every autumn at harvest time. Some sort of bounty to ensure abundant crops every year. There was that kid, Mark, year before last. *Moved* away."

In the near-dark I sensed Sophie smirking. "Good one," I said, a slight tremor to my voice.

A soft wheeze, then a scratching sound. "You can stop now, Soph."

"I'm not doing anything," she said.

I sighed. "Okay." Then, "You said the killer might hear us. But he's dead now, right?"

"Oh, there's always another killer," Sophie said. "That's how it works. Do you want to know what happens next?"

My voice was whisper soft. "Sure?"

"This."

And she turned out the light, leaving me in the dark with the dad-thing. I sensed it there in the quiet and the dark. Waiting.

I supposed it was better than not having any dad. *Trauma is a ghost that haunts you,* it'd said. *Grief another.* Like something Dad would have said. It was a smart dad-thing.

I knew all about trauma and grief now. Mom, too. Sophie acted as if nothing had happened. Mom said that's how Sophie deals with things. Ignores them. I knew better. She just didn't care about anything. Not Mom, not me. Certainly not about Dad. She only cared about herself. And her stories.

THE WORLD IS FULL of smiling monsters.

I wrote that one down, too. I wrote them all down. It's true, I thought. A smile is disarming. Here's someone who is happy, it says. Someone you can trust. A smile is like that sickle, curved and cutting. It can decapitate you.

When we first moved to this house, with our own rooms, before I found the thing in the cave, and before the creek completely smelled of ammonia or sulphur, before it choked and moved like cold molasses,

Sophie and I would follow it home from school. We'd watch the tiny brown fish darting, and race twigs or bottlecaps in the faster moving areas. In the lazy summer silence of the ravine, we'd whittle branches into pointy killing sticks with one of Dad's penknives. Hunt for frogs with those very sticks—stabbing them in the back and pinning them to the ground to flail and spasm in the hot sun.

One such day, on the muddy bank of the creek, we found a two-headed turtle, languid and still in the early summer heat. Sophie put aside her pocketknife and the stick she was whittling, plucked the turtle up, nestled it into her palm. The tiny heads cast about, eyes searching, mouths opening, closing.

"Imagine," Sophie said, holding the tiny turtle up to me, "this could have been us."

I sensed one of her stories coming.

"Two-headed twins," she said.

"That would never happen," I said.

"You're probably right," she said. "We're lucky. We both made it out. One of us didn't die."

"Made it *out*?"

Sophie smirked. "The womb, silly girl. We made it out of the womb. Not all twins do. Sometimes…there's the vanishing twin. Here today, gone tomorrow. Turns out one twin simply absorbs the other. Kills it."

"Why?"

Sophie flashed her monstrous smile. "It's what we always do in the end, isn't it?"

She stroked each of the tiny turtle heads in turn, her face placid, a faraway look in her eyes as if daydreaming. "There once lived a two-headed girl. Girls, I should say, as each was an individual. They just shared a body. They had a doting, loving mother. 'Two heads are better than one,' she'd say. But the father refused to accept it. Being a father doesn't automatically make you a good person, does it, Ophelia? The girls are loving, attentive, content and happy and considerate. Everything a parent dreams of. Perfect. Except for the one thing. Two, actually. Their shared heads. The father is ashamed. Takes them to all the doctors and specialists. There's nothing to be done. The girls are healthy and vibrant and intelligent. Beautiful. But the father can't see their beauty. They are an abomination. A cruelty inflicted upon him." Sophie glances at the fidgeting turtle, looks back to me. "There's nothing quite so fragile and frightening as the male ego, is there?

"One scorching day while their mother is at work, the father bundles the girls into his pickup. 'A picnic,' he says, whiskey on his breath. 'Just us!' A fever in his eyes. He drives far out into the country, along roads of hard-packed dirt that hadn't seen rain or even another vehicle in many a month. The girls look this way and that, puzzling about their surroundings. Worry etches their faces. A knot grows in their stomach. In the bed of the truck, under a tarp, is a bone-saw. A shovel. And, if needed, an axe. He's a mad surgeon.

"Down another dirt road wedged in by tall pines, then onto a tiny tract barely wide enough for the truck, and into a small clearing. The girls are beyond worried. They grab for the door handle, but their father pulls them from the truck, drags them to the back, unlatches the gate and reaches under the tarp for the bone-saw."

Sophie's hand is wrapped around the turtle's body. It's just two searching heads, sensing, assessing for threats.

"And," I say, not able to help myself, "what happens next?"

"Much later that day the girls were found limping down a country road, dishevelled and dirty. There was blood on their clothes. They said they were out walking, got lost, cut themselves on brambles and thorns. And later still, when their father never returned from work, calls were made. He hadn't shown for work. No one had seen him. And no one ever saw him again."

Sophie placed the turtle down. It slowly inched toward the water. She picked up her knife, eyed the blade. "You see, Fifi, they never checked the blood on the girls' clothes. It wasn't their blood. Their will to survive was stronger than their father. Just another weak man." She watched the turtle, creeping forward. "Would it have worked?" She reached for the small creature, flipped it over. It's arms and legs floundered in the stagnant soup of the summer air. "I wonder," she said, as she rested the knife-edge on one exposed neck. "Would it change anything?"

With the knife pressed to the turtle's neck, Sophie waited. The turtle stilled, as if playing dead. The heat was so thick it seemed even the world waited. But I didn't. I got up and left.

I knew it wouldn't change a thing.

Sophie's text read: *Meet me at the cave. 8pm.*

And that's where I found her, inside the darkening cave mouth, as the early autumn pumpkin-sun dripped beyond the far horizon like a runny watercolor.

She stood beside the dad-twin-thing, a backpack at her feet, phone in hand, its glow the only light in the cave. "My dear, Fifi. My dear, Ophelia. What dreams may come."

Sophie looked up at the thing—the light from her phone illuminating a small, sardonic smile on her face. She lifted a corner of the shirt, let it drop, then looked back to me. "What a lovely, personal touch." Her voice as cold as her dead-penny eyes.

Sophie turned her phone screen toward me. "I found something of yours. Your little writings."

She'd been in my room, then. "Stole, you mean."

"He always liked you more." She squinted at her phone. "Such wisdoms, Ophelia. 'Trauma is a ghost that haunts you.' Truly profound. And this one. 'We enter this world with nothing, and so leave it with nothing.' Brilliant." Sophie smiled. "This one is classic. 'The world is full of smiling monsters.'" Her own smile widened. Her finger scrolled along the screen. "But my favorite—'One will grow to eat the other.' Truly apt."

"What of it?" I said. "What do you want? Why did you ask me here?"

"This is the next part of our story, Fifi. Don't you want to know what happens next?"

"No."

Sophie bent, unzipped the backpack, pulled something out. It briefly glinted in the glow of her phone. Dimly, I could just make out its long curve.

"Fifi?"

"What?"

"Are you afraid of the dark?"

"No."

"You should be." She dropped the phone.

The world went dark. Movement, as if a shuffling forward. And I sensed it there in the sudden gloom. Waiting.

THE OFFERING fit neatly in the backpack. I'd have to figure out what to do with the rest. The sickle would help.

And now? Now I wait. I wait for it to speak to me. I wait for it to tell me what to do.

Michael Kelly is the former Series Editor for The Year's Best Weird Fiction. *He's a World Fantasy Award, Shirley Jackson Award, and British Fantasy Award-winning editor. His fiction has appeared in a number of journals and anthologies, including* Best New Horror, Black Static, Nightmare Magazine, The Dark, Year's Best Dark Fantasy & Horror; *and has been previously collected in* Scratching the Surface, Undertow & Other Laments, *and* All the Things We Never See. *He is the owner and Editor-in-Chief of Undertow Publications, and editor of the magazine* Weird Horror. *Michael is fond of beer and bourbon, and has spent most of his adult life vainly attempting to play guitar.*

FIVE TYPES OF ITCHING

BY STEVE DUFFY

WHARTON HAD BEEN AT THE ROOMING-HOUSE FOR NEARLY A MONTH BEFORE HE MET THE COUPLE WHO LIVED IN THE NEXT-DOOR APARTMENT. It was summer, and the streets of New Orleans were an ordeal by fire; three floors up, there was at least the suggestion of a breeze off of Pontchartrain, albeit malodorous and weak. Wharton kept the French windows wedged open and lived as much as he could on the balcony, which had the sun first thing and shade by the hottest part of the day.

It was the man he saw first, or his legs at least, over on the adjacent balcony one July afternoon. The legs were visible from the thighs down, showcased by a pair of Bermuda shorts and resting on a sun-lounger. They were unlovely things, kneecaps sunk in dimpled flab, as if their owner hardly exercised, possibly never left the apartment. Above all, though, there was the rash. Every inch of exposed skin was crawling in a raw and angry-looking eruption. What was going on beneath the shorts, Wharton didn't like to think. Up till this point, he'd been moderately curious about his neighbours; one glance at the balcony made him resolve to postpone any rendezvous.

This resolution lasted a little under a week, until Wharton was climbing the stairs back to his apartment after his evening trip to the liquor store. Reaching the top floor, he saw that the door next to his was ajar. A woman in a wrap was kneeling in the doorway making *ps-ps-ps* noises to the house cat, a nondescript rusty tom that hung around the stairwell and the hallways. The cat, which had a different name on each landing and answered to none, ignored her. She straightened to her full height of a little over five feet as Wharton mounted the last step.

"Cat never comes when I call it," she said, her voice thin and dolorous.

"I don't think it belongs to anyone in particular," he said.

She shrugged. Now, you need to know that Wharton was socially awkward and prone to gawking at the ladies instead of making conversation, which went a long way towards explaining why his relations with them had been perfunctory at best. Generally, though, it was the lookers that set him to gawk, the hotsy-totsies and red-hot mamas. This woman ticked none of those boxes: an unthinking man, or someone in more of a hurry than Wharton, might have marked her down as "dowdy" and moved along. On this occasion, however, he found himself lingering; found himself wanting to prolong the encounter, even, which was so unlike him as to render him even more tongue-tied.

Why was this? What was going on? Nothing he could put into words, but he was getting something from this woman. Some aspect of her presentation, or lack of it, didn't so much enrapture him as perplex him, left him with questions that were at the same time niggling and captivating. She was like a puzzle in a magazine that ought to be the work of a minute to figure out, but which could leave a man tearing his hair out indefinitely, no nearer an answer yet determined not to give it up. And after all, he reminded himself, when it came to priorities, his time was his own to waste: there were no outside demands on it, he could spend it as he chose. So instead of retreating to his own apartment, he swallowed and said, "Hot, isn't it?"

Again the shrug. It shifted the wrap a little from her shoulder, so that Wharton was confronted with the unblemished whiteness of her skin beneath it. "You got some wine in that sack?" She could see the shape of the bottle through the brown paper, he supposed. "You put wine in the icebox, it's coolin'."

"I guess," he said, trying to keep up. Had that been an observation, or an invitation? He decided not to risk it. In different circumstances, and given suitable encouragement, Wharton might not have been averse to sharing his wine, but he'd only bought one bottle, and splitting it three ways would hardly satisfy anybody—because, of course, there was the owner of those legs on the balcony to consider. So instead, he raised his hat, feeling clumsy and self-conscious. "Nice talking to you."

"Meow-meow," the woman called forlornly, as the cat tipped its liquid length down the stairs with a parting hiss. If it had been able to speak, thought Wharton, the cat would probably have sounded like this woman, a plaintive, diffident mewing for attention.

Safe in his apartment, Wharton sipped his wine, slowly at first, then too fast, while night oozed through the streets below. Still the woman next door was on his mind. His standards of feminine attractiveness were frankly unrealistic (which again helped to explain why he was unattached and dismally virginal at the age of twenty-eight), but there was something about the plain neighbour lady that was digging into him like a hook in the gulping mouth of a catfish, something that tugged and tugged and gave him no rest. Maybe it was in her gaze, the artless play of intentness and indifference in it, or in the loose, unselfconscious manner in which she inhabited her body, careless of whatever effect it might produce in the onlooker. It felt, he reflected unoriginally, very much as if she'd gotten under his skin.

The next evening, there she was, waiting at the door of the apartment. Again, he was on his way back from the liquor store, and this time he'd bought three bottles of the sweet Zinfandel, for reasons best known to himself. "Hello again," he said.

"You been to the corner," she said, not really as a question.

"I have."

"Melvin said I was to ax you in, come visit with us," she said. "We got ice, glasses—my daddy's old wine glasses. Heirlooms."

"Melvin?"

"That's my man," she said, "he's inside. You can call me Dora."

"Her birth name," came a plethoric voice from inside the apartment, "is Adorestine."

"That's right," she confirmed, not looking round.

He swallowed, and proffered the paper sack, one hand supporting its weight. "Best put these in the icebox then, I guess." She took the clinking load to her bosom with both arms wrapped around it, brushing up against him in the process, close enough for him to get a whiff of her scent. Musky, with a base-note that was weirdly but not unpleasingly sour; was it perfume, or could it be the natural odour of her skin? With her bare foot she pushed the door wide open. It was dark inside, and his eyes needed a moment to adjust even from the dim light of the hallway.

So far as the floorplan went, the apartment was a mirror image of his own, but that was where the similarity ended. Whereas Wharton's rooms were furnished sparsely with a few basic sticks of stuff that didn't belong to him, this place was crammed with a wild assortment of bric-a-brac, keepsakes and curios too disparate to itemize. It looked, he thought, as if someone had tried to fit the contents of an entire house—one that was much older, much fancier and much larger—into a single apartment.

"So, Adorestine, that's an unusual name," Wharton hoping this would pass for conversation.

"Not in my parish," Dora contradicted him. "They's always been Adorestines."

"It's a family tradition," added the voice, presumably that of Melvin. It sounded at once orotund and hollowed-out, like the spiky case that protects the horse-chestnut. At first Wharton couldn't locate its owner in the all-over gloom. "There's one in every generation, isn't that right, dear?"

"It certainly is," Dora said, as if Wharton was about to argue the point.

"Whim of the paterfamilias." Wharton had caught sight of the speaker now, out on the unlit balcony. A silhouette on a sun-lounger, that was about all he could make out in the backwash of streetlight from three floors below. "Your daddy, whatever his shortcomings, and they were many, was a stickler for tradition."

Wharton introduced himself. "We don't have any passed-down names in my family," he said apologetically.

"Names is about all Dora's family got left to pass down, isn't it, honey? Names and customs and the big brown eyes that hypnotize." He chuckled. Wharton, unreceptive to repartee, didn't know if he meant it for a joke. "My name is Melvin Inkpen, a combination that crops up nowhere else in my own, somewhat more variegated, family tree. I won't get up, if it's all the same to you."

"So, Melvin and Dora Inkpen?" Wharton was trying to get everything straight in his mind.

"Dora Inkpen? Heavens no!" A rich burst of laughter, punctuated by painful coughing. "Dora and I are living in what you might call sin—certainly what my family calls sin, I won't presume to speak for hers. Her family name is Guilloret, but just Dora will suffice. Has our new friend brought refreshments, my beloved?"

"Got wine in this sack," Dora said. "Three bottles."

"A friend indeed." The shape made as if to lift its bulk from the sun-lounger, grunted, and collapsed back on it. The tubular aluminum frame grated under its weight. "Well, they belong in the icebox, darlin'—see to it, why don't you? That couch to your left is mighty yielding, Wharton, take a seat. It's close enough to carry on a conversation." But not close enough for Wharton to get a glimpse of his host.

On a dresser alongside the couch stood a Tiffany lamp with a red chiffon scarf draped across the shade. It provided the only illumination, barely enough for Wharton to make out more than shapes and shadows in the corners of the room. Light showed briefly from the kitchen as Dora opened, then closed the door of the refrigerator; more junk was all it lit upon.

"Here," Dora said, handing him his drink. Wharton held it up to the lamplight. The glassware was embossed, old-looking, of a smoky purpled hue, the colour of wild poppies that grow from scorched seeds.

"We got out the fine glasses just for you."

"You've been expecting me," Wharton said, making a pleasantry of it.

"That we have," Melvin said from the balcony, as Dora set the wine on a card-table at his side. She hunkered down on a miniature hassock at Wharton's feet, from which she stared at him with a fixity he found disconcerting at first, then after the second or third glass, beguiling.

"Tell us your life story, Wharton," Melvin prompted. Wharton's life story was a Reader's Digest Condensed Book at best, but he took a shot at it. He began with his sheltered upbringing in Florida, his neurasthenic mama and his absent, never-mentioned pa; skipped quickly through his spell in the Army—he'd passed the entire war at Camp Blanding as a clerk, never even left his home state; went on to explain how he'd come to New Orleans after reading Kate Chopin's *The Awakening*, mentioned his night classes in art and semantics, and thus came neatly to the end of himself.

"Tell me a little about yourselves," he suggested. It was Melvin who took up the offer: not a peep out of Dora, though her eyes never left Wharton's damp and sweating face. She reminded him of a broke-down terrier, the pet of a long-ago neighbour back in Boca Grande, that never barked or chased or wagged its tail, just sat on the stoop and fixed the passers-by with a melancholy stare.

They'd met four years ago, said Melvin. "Back when I was engaged in anthropological studies, down in Terrebénie Parish. You ever been in that part of the country, Wharton? Well, it's not to everybody's taste. The marshes and the swamps and the old sacred groves of bald cypress and flowering dogwood, the dripping heat and the constant stench of decay, the scandalous customs of degenerate families. They don't get too many day-trippers, you follow me? Still, someone must have reckoned it blessed earth once upon a time, as per the name. Turned out a blessing for me, anyway, because 'twas there I met my queen, my Evangeline, my Creole darlin' Dora, the apple of her daddy's eye until I plucked her."

It turned out that Melvin always talked this way, relentlessly affected, overripe as an old ham actor. Wharton did his best to find it quaint, but in practice it was never less than tiresome. For her part, Dora seemed to pay it no mind, saying little, not shifting from her hassock except to refill their glasses.

Once, when the kitchen door swung all the way open, the shaft of light stretched out as far as the balcony. There it lit on Melvin, caught in the act of stripping the cellophane from a fresh pack of cigarettes. "Off," he roared, "off, you slattern," but not before Wharton had seen.

It was worse than he'd thought. The rash was not confined to Melvin's legs, but ran the length of his entire torso, as seen through his unbuttoned shirt. There were big disfiguring plaques of it across his face, extending back over his forehead and his hairless scalp. No wonder, thought Wharton with horror, he hides from the light. Thumbing his Zippo, Melvin lit a cigarette. In the close cupped glow, Wharton saw his host's eyes dart in his direction.

"I thank you, my sweet," Melvin said, as Dora set his drink down beside him. "And could I prevail on you to bring me an unsullied towel?" He handed her a white cotton hand towel that had been lying across his lap. Wharton saw that it was spotted all over with blood, an effect his art tutor might have described as "pointillist abstract".

"And keep that damned light off, would you please?" Melvin called after her. "Unfiltered light at this time of the evening is anathema to me," he added for Wharton's benefit. "As I'm sure it must be for you, in the circumstances."

Had he been staring? It was the thing with girls all over again, only in this context it was doubly embarrassing. Hastily, Wharton redirected his attention towards the kitchen, where the light was on again. Dora's kitten voice came from within, a plaintive meow, "I got to look for a fresh towel, don't I?"

"Turn it off," Melvin bellowed, "turn the damn thing off. Can't you manage by touch?" A click, and the kitchen light was extinguished. "You should know that Dora is possessed of the most exquisitely delicate touch," Melvin explained. He seemed calmer now the light was out. "Aren't you, my precious one? At times such as these, when my affliction is at its most burdensome, I can stand no manipulation but hers."

"Here's a towel from out the icebox," Dora said, dropping it into his lap. "You want anything else?"

"Only your presence, my sweet," Melvin said with contentment. "Only to breathe the very air you exhale. And afterwards, you might apply the unguent, but only when our guest has departed."

Wharton choked down almost the whole glass in one swallow. "I guess it's about time I should be making tracks," he said, once the wine had cleared his airways.

"Really? Why, the night is young. We're not driving you away?"

Wharton denied it, tripping over his words in the process. "You're sure? Well, another time, another time. It has been a pleasure to make your acquaintance, Wharton. And a pleasure to sample your *vin ordinaire*, which goes without saying."

Dora accompanied Wharton to the door. Thank you for a very interesting evening," he said, wondering if he ought to have said "pleasant."

"He wants me to cream him," Dora said in a low voice that probably wouldn't carry to the balcony. "He likes for me to cream him when it's bad."

"Is it—does it—it looks very aggravating," Wharton managed.

"He suffers from it somethin' fierce," Dora said. "You see how he been scratchin' at it, all that blood on the towels? Some nights it drive him crazy."

"I'm sure," Wharton said. She was standing very close to him, and the wrap had shifted from her shoulder again. If he wasn't careful, he could see a lot of the way down her front.

"That's how come I got to cream him, all over," Dora said, and without a shift in her tone, "well, g'night." And the door was closed and Wharton was left on the landing with a bellyful of booze and a head full of imaginings. *The voice of the sea is seductive*, Miss Chopin had written, *never ceasing, whispering, clamoring, murmuring, inviting the soul to wander in abysses of solitude.* But it was

Dora's mournful voice that went shooting through his head in the hours before sleep. Why? Because. Because there was no why.

HAD THERE just been the garrulous Mr. Inkpen to consider, Wharton might well have let things cool with the neighbours at this early stage of their acquaintance. Conversation with Melvin was like courtroom cross-examination by a drunken old Southern caricature of a prosecutor, and Wharton wasn't sure that he needed much more of it. There was, however, the matter of Dora.

Maybe if I spend more time around her, he temporised, *I'll get to the bottom of it*, whatever *it* might be. That at least was what he told himself. Really, he just wanted to see more of her, see all there was to see if possible (that slip, the way it fell open and she didn't seem to know it). For the first time in his life, he was finding out what it was like to spend time with a woman who wasn't his mama. Accordingly, he got into the habit of visiting the next-door apartment most evenings when he wasn't at classes.

July became August, and there was no let-up in the weather until one sweltering night of constant rumbling from the coal-black clouds piled up above the city. Dora was serving the drinks when a crack of lightning brought on the rain, hammering on the concrete balcony, conjuring a rich petrichor that brought to Wharton's mind that elusive base-note of Dora's perfume.

Melvin lumbered to his feet, almost tipping over the sun-lounger. "Dora," he yelled, and she ran to help him into the room, fitting into his armpit like a crutch. "Tláloc, bringer of thunder and lightning, damn his old damp bones."

Wharton was gripped with a sudden unease lest Melvin take a seat alongside him on the couch. To his relief, Dora guided her man to an armchair across the room, into which he flopped his considerable bulk. "Fetch my drink, stormbringer, it'll be three parts rainwater unless you rescue it. My reference, Wharton, was to the ancient Aztec god of the rains. Have you taken any classes on comparative religion at your little night school?"

Wharton shook his head. For the first time, he was able to get a really sustained look at his host. Melvin was monstrous in every dimension: a round bald head with a thick neck, like a medicine ball resting on a horse-collar of fat, a big sack of belly that flopped over the waistband of his shorts like knocked-back dough. The scabbing was still the first thing you noticed, the thing to which you always came back, however reluctantly, with a mixture of pity and horror. Melvin's epidermis was like the bleeding hide of a wounded crocodile, thrashing around in a ditch filled with broken glass. He was really not a sight to gaze upon, and Wharton did his best to look elsewhere. But there was nowhere else to look: Melvin commanded all the attention in the room.

He'd asked him a question, Wharton remembered, something about comparative religion. "Is that your field, Melvin?" he temporised.

"It was, in the days before I became incapacitated. By love—" he bestowed an affectionate squeeze upon Dora as she passed him his wineglass—"by love, and by this damnable affliction. Two sides of the same coin."

Wharton mumbled sympathetically. He'd never seen Melvin's eyes properly before, only stray piggy glints in the darkness. They were buried in the swollen angry flesh that pressed upon his sockets, but they were as knowing and as penetrating as Dora's were bland and unknowable. Between the two of them, Wharton felt himself trapped in the panopticon, and blushed horribly.

"No need to be mortified by my unsightly condition, Wharton. I apologize for confronting you so directly with it. You see now why I prefer the shadows on the balcony."

"I guess it's good to get some air to it," Wharton faltered. "To the, um, I mean, to the affected..."

"Air! Indeed." Melvin sipped his wine, and spat it back into the glass. "I don't think this timorous little vintage can stand any more watering. Freshen it, Dora, if you please. That's right, stir those little legs I love so well. Look at her go! Like one of those frisky black squirrels that used to sport among the eaves of her old family home back on the bayou. Ah, that's better. Your health, Wharton, in lieu of mine." He threw

back half the glass in one swallow.

"Air... there isn't really any fresh air in the city, is there? It's all been breathed in and out a hundred thousand times, stale with the stink of spicy food and wrecked digestions. Though god knows there was little enough air in that fetid ancestral swamp where first I met my honey-lamb—how long ago was that, now?"

"Four year," Dora supplied monosyllabically. She was back on the hassock, legs wrapped around her knees, with eyes only for Wharton.

"Four year," mimicked Melvin. "But it was love at first sight, was it not? Have you ever read Immanuel Velikovsky, Wharton? How rapidly the planets are knocked out of their settled courses. How swiftly catastrophe follows on the coattails of harmony and bliss." Another copious gulp.

Melvin's Hawaiian shirt was unbuttoned as usual, and his fingers were unconsciously scratching at the exposed portion of his belly. Wharton did his best not to stare. "How did you two come to meet, exactly? You never said."

"Why, I engineered an invitation to the family home, didn't I, chickadee? In the furtherance of my researches. I was desperate to gain access to the old man's library, but very soon I became more desperate to gain access to his daughter." Melvin chuckled, in a way that was not pleasant on any level. "In both cases, I was successful, though it's only fair to say that in both cases knowledge came at a cost, and the dear sweet Jesus knows I paid it."

Good lord, thought Wharton. Did anyone *really* talk like this, even in the Quarter? Apparently so; for surely no one could keep up such an extravagant pretence. All the while, Melvin's nails were digging at his stomach, opening barely-healed scabs, littering the lap of his Bermuda shorts with flakes of dead skin, drawing streaks of fresh blood across his belly.

"Was it worth it? It's a question I ask myself many a time, as I sit out on that balcony and watch my flesh mortify without hope of sanctification. And the answer is always, always, yes. Sunk costs, Wharton, sunk costs. Here we are, and here I am, as you see me. And here is my Adorestine, light of my life, soother of my cruelly flayed hide, fetcher of life's little necessities." He tapped a fingernail on his empty wineglass. "In your own sweet time, dear. Wharton, you are scarlet. Have you caught the sun today? Would you like Dora to apply some of my special preparation?"

"I can cream you, if you want," Dora said matter-of-factly. Wharton blushed more deeply, if such a thing was possible.

"That's all right," he said. "I guess I might have gotten a little sunburn out there."

"Touch of the sun," Melvin said expansively. "All the more reason. It's an unwelcome side-effect of cosmic disturbance. Planets crashing out of alignment, orbits plunging ever closer to the sun," illustrating with his empty glass. "Well, Dora, if Wharton doesn't require your ministrations, you might see about a refill for me, and perhaps a fresh towel? Ah, if only what ails me could be cured with a simple dab of calamine!

"There are four types of itching, Wharton," he resumed, glass topped up by the dutiful Dora, "that's what the specialists say. They classify them thus: the neurogenic, the psychogenic, the neuropathic, and the *pruritoceptive*," over-enunciating the unfamiliar word for emphasis. "That is to say, the products of—" Melvin ticked them off on his pudgy chitlin fingers—"a disordered central nervous system; psychological disorder; neuronal pathology; and those processes involving the skin itself. I flatter myself on having discovered a fifth. How 'bout that? Inkpen's Syndrome. Someone should write a paper on me."

Wharton waited for him to explain this new kind of itch, but Melvin didn't pursue the matter further. Instead, he drank off the rest of the wine in record time, lapsing afterwards into slurred semi-responsiveness. But for the constant scrabbling at his belly, a person might think he'd dozed off— or did he continue to scratch in his sleep, all unconscious? From time to time, like a sleeper ridden hard by the nightmare, he'd yell: sometimes it was just yapping, like a dog with a trodden-on tail, sometimes words and phrases. "Hot baby damn," that was one that stood out; another was "creepin' Jesus";

still another began "High holy" and ended with something that sounded like a person hiccupping while trying to pronounce "Cotulla" (which Wharton took to be a reference to the town in Texas). With each of these eructations, Melvin would slap at his belly, as if tormented by mosquitoes from hell, then subside into uneasy slumber. It was an education, to put it mildly. *He certainly puts on a show*, thought Melvin dismally as he sat sipping his drink.

And yet later that night, after he'd torn himself away, Wharton could think of nothing apart from Dora, her hands slick with some gentle soothing lotion, stroking the burning surface of his cheeks, caressing him all over, pausing only to brush the hair away from her soulful chestnut eyes. *I can cream you*, she'd said. *If you want.*

HE WAS ROUSED from his sleep by an insistent knocking at his door. When he went to answer it, bed-robe thrown about him, who should it be but Dora, the girl of his dreams. "Melvin's awful bad," she informed him, without so much as a hello. "Ambulance come at dawn, took him to the sanatorium."

"That's terrible!" Wharton was shocked. "Are you going to visit him? Do you want me to come with you?"

"He axed for you," Dora said. "Tell Wharton to come see me, he said, so I passed it on."

"I'll go this afternoon," Wharton said.

"He said to tell you come at once." Her eyes round, a child retelling a fairytale perfectly remembered yet only half understood. "Said there might not be time."

"I'll go right away," Wharton said. "Will you be coming?"

"No, you're to go on your own," Dora said. "I got the *ad*-dress." She handed him a slip of paper. Wharton waited for her to go back to her apartment so he could get dressed. In the end he had to say, "Excuse me," and retreat to the bedroom. Tugging on last night's tobacco-smelling clothes, he was unaccountably conscious of her presence in the next room, in that wrap that seemed to fit her at no place in particular.

The sanatorium was out at the end of the Canal streetcar line, a short walk off

Metairie Street. A large and dismal cemetery lay at its rear, all Spanish moss and white marble turning mildew green. A sign on the railings said "Folse Clinic", and there was a flight of steps leading up to the main building, a shabby Greek Revival mansion with double-height columns and a pedimented portico. Wharton signed in at reception, and was given directions to a room on the back second floor.

Melvin's voice came in answer to his knock: "Enter." Wharton opened the door, and almost jumped back into the corridor. The hospital bed was empty, but Melvin, looking redder and more unwholesomely swollen than ever, was wedged into a large zinc hip-bath in a tiled alcove alongside it. "Excuse me," Wharton fumbling for the doorknob, "I'll come back later—"

"Enter, I said," Melvin directed, and Wharton slunk back in. "Dora roused you, then?"

"She sure did," Wharton admitted, his eyes everywhere and anywhere except on the vision of his neighbour's naked and abraded body immersed in some sort of oily suspension.

"That girl," Melvin said fondly. "I really don't deserve her. Well, Wharton, it's quite the five-alarm fire here. I'm running a monstrous fever, my skin is sloughing like a filthy cottonmouth, and the doctor fears a general infection has set in." He wriggled in the hip-bath. "My organs, he says, may be compromised. Well, I could've told him that. Do you know, I think I've marinaded enough. Would you kindly ring the bell there, Wharton? I'm about as slippery as a mudcat."

The bell summoned two assistants in white coats, who took a grip beneath Melvin's armpits and hauled him from the bath with an audible plop. A wash of greasy overflow spread across the tiles. "Venus rising from the waves," Melvin noted. "Towel me." For a horrible second, Wharton thought he was talking to him.

Patted down by the assistants and hoisted back in bed, Melvin gestured for his cigarettes. "Quite an eyeful, isn't it, Wharton?"

It was awful. Not an inch of Melvin's hide seemed to be untouched by the horrible squamous rash. Everywhere there was inflammation, thick ugly scabs peeling away from the scaly crusted skin. In some places he appeared to have gouged his nails in deep, ploughing parallel rows of furrows into the flesh. There was a clear plastic cover over the mattress, and when Melvin squirmed in discomfort, which was often, it made a crackling sound. It put Wharton in mind of someone squeezing a cut of supermarket meat done up in cellophane.

"Dr. Folse will be along later," Melvin said. "He's fascinated by the deterioration in my condition—perhaps he's the man who'll write the definitive work on Inkpen's Syndrome. I've been consulting him for years now, since the days when my condition was merely unbearable. Have I been scratching myself, he wanted to know when I was admitted this morning. Have I?! Light me up a cigarette before he arrives, Wharton."

"You seem so much worse than last night, even," Wharton said, lighting two Camels and offering him one.

"No, no, in my mouth," Melvin directed. "I can't handle them with these." He lifted up his hands, which were swaddled in boxing gloves of bandage. "Precautionary." He sucked deeply on the cigarette, reducing it to half its length, then motioned for Wharton to remove it. He did so, taking exquisite care not to touch Melvin's lips.

"Dr. Folse is right about the scratching, though, even if his diagnosis leaves something to be desired. You see," his voice dropped, grew conspiratorial, so that Wharton had to lean, much against his will, across the bed, "last night, after you'd toddled off to your bachelor pad, the little woman and I partook of a little, let's call it quasi-conjugal bliss." He chuckled disagreeably. "That girl leaves her nails long, Wharton. Oh, it's spicy, but in my condition... well, in retrospect, it may not have been my wisest decision. And I have made some unwise ones, believe me, in my time."

Wharton didn't know where to put himself. The thought of Dora and Melvin conjoined was so fundamentally unattractive that it shut off his imagination with all the force of a cast-iron cover dropped over a manhole.

"Damn, but she's captivating, Wharton—I mean it in the truest, most unambiguous sense of the word. She claimed me, you know, my Adorestine, way back in Terrebénie Parish, her family's place on the bayou. The moment I clapped eyes on her, I knew I had to have her. You know I'm no Rudolph Valentino these days—I dare say you'll second that, won't you, Wharton?—but back then before my affliction came upon me I had women who were ten times more beautiful, a hundred, eating from the palm of my hand. And yet I ended up with her and her only: I gave it all away for a shot at Dora, and I never once looked back. I caught the itch." He glanced down at the scarified ruin of his body.

"How often have I asked myself the question, why her, why this one above all others? How often I've reminded myself *the answer just doesn't matter*. You know how it is, don't you, Wharton? I mean, you do see it? Useless to speculate on these matters. Once you have an itch, the only thing to do is scratch it. And if there's one thing I'm an expert on, it is after all the matter of scratching. Again, please."

Gingerly, Wharton held the cigarette to those cracked and bleeding lips. Melvin sucked deep and blew out a plume of smoke, an ancient scaly dragon whose fire has guttered and finally gone out.

"That place, though, Wharton! That old mansion, gone to seed and half collapsed into the swamp. I wish you could've seen it before the townsfolk burned it down. Her father, Daddy Guilloret, that old ogre. The family owned half the parish once, you know. Big, big people thereabouts. Now, they had nothing but the house, which was falling into pieces around them, and their history, which was the force of gravity that dragged it down. I went there in search of the history, you know, the books and the lore and the old traditions, and I found it all come to life in the form of little Dora.

"The circles I was moving in back then, they were hardly respectable, even by the laissez-faire standards obtaining in the Quarter. They were bound up in the un-mentionable, Wharton, so we shan't mention them more particularly, but suffice it to say that your mama wouldn't have approved. Unless she was an extremely broad-minded lady, or—ahem—not a lady at all, if you take my meaning. Ancient rituals, strange deeds done at dead of night, summonings and conjurations. That old cemetery," gesturing in the direction of the window, "it could tell some wild tales, son.

"It was in this dubious company that I first heard of the Guillorets, the grandees of Terrebénie Parish. A fine old family once, that some said had degenerated into something more like a cult, though others said that's really how they'd started out, right back from day one. They'd been settlers back in the days of d'Iberville, maybe even before that. The old man used to say they'd always been there, though what he meant by that I never could tell. 'Always'—it had a ring to it. Their bloodline was concentrated but not pure, that's the delicate way to put it: there was a taint about them that went beyond simple miscegenation, so went the whisper, and it had to do with wild things done in secret, out there in the swamps. Offerings and rewards, bounty in return for sacrifice; occult knowledge, and in those days I hungered after knowledge above all else. I wanted some of that magic, Wharton, and so I went after it.

"Civilisation, if you can call it that, ran out a long way short of the Guilloret mansion. I remember driving down that dirt track half weed and half ruts, mangrove swamp on either side, sweating like the pig that knows it's dinner. You'll know it when you see it, they'd told me; well, they got that right. Charles Addams could not have drawn it, Wharton. It was nightmare abbey, where memories went to die, and the living inhabitants were nothing but caretakers, waiting for the rightful owners to rise up from their graves and take up occupancy again. The stagnant, greasy creek had risen right up to the edge of the lawns—what had once been lawns—and in the tall grass I could see alligators lift their prehistoric heads and watch me climb the steps up to the front door.

"It was just Dora and her father by then, all the rest dead or otherwise unavailable. The old man didn't like me, but he surely loved to brag, and for that it helps to have an audience. I spent weeks in that filthy old wreck of a house, listening to him ramble on, and by the end of the first night I could tell his brains had gone to mush. I kept prodding at him, though, trying to get him to share his secrets, show me the library. If there was any knowledge left among the Guillorets, I figured, that was where I'd find it. But he was stubborn: I kept on asking, and he kept on dodging the question, putting it off. I'd have given it all up as a bad job, if it hadn't been for Dora.

"She used to sit and listen to us, Wharton, the way she sits and listens to you and me now: on the same hassock, if you can believe it. She rescued it from the house along with the rest of that junk that clutters up the apartment; got it out before the old place went up in flames. Torches and pitch-forks, Wharton, a lynch mob of the locals, scene from a black-and-white Boris Karloff horror. But I'm getting ahead of myself. Another cigarette would be nice." Mutely, Wharton lit him a fresh Lucky.

"Funny: Dora wasn't even a name to me before I came to the Guilloret place. Soon I wasn't conscious of anything else, not in the whole wide world and all the worlds beyond. From the very first night she came to me, slipped into my bed in the chittering, shrieking back-country night, I knew I had to possess her for all time, the same way I had to possess the inner secrets of that old Guilloret cult. It was all one thing in my head, braided together like the raven hair of night. And the obstacle that stood in the way of both those goals? The old man, damn him. He had to go, Wharton. There was no way around it.

"Well, we won't go into that sordid business. Suffice it to say that I got into the library at last, and found nothing but empty shelves, a handful of old books rotted into pulp in the constant humidity or else eaten up into crumbs by bugs. Everything was ruined, had probably been that way for generations. The place was as vacant as the old man's head had been when I stove it in— goaded beyond endurance, Wharton, I assure you—just minutes earlier. No honorable jury would convict. I remember the windows were open wide, and I remember standing there and howling my frustration into the night; I remember the high rotten smell of the swamp, like some monstrous bloody after-birth, and out there on the banks of the creek I swear I heard those alligators laughing at me through those idiot grinning jaws of theirs.

"But I had my Dora, and really that was all that mattered to me now. I brought her out of that hellhole, and I carried her back to New Orleans. We feasted on each other, Wharton, like you wouldn't believe. Day bled into night and back again a dozen times, a hundred times, and we hardly ever left the bedroom. She taught me more about the truth of this world than any old manuscript or grimoire ever could have. All the awful secrets of her line she carries within her, in the unplumbed depths of her gaze, in the dark between those flawless milk-white thighs. How they opened like the moon-flower, those thighs, how they'd yawn awake when midnight came around! You're blushing again, Wharton. Don't tell me you're not picturing it." Wharton, who could picture nothing else, said nothing.

"I thought as much," Melvin said, with another of his mirthless chuckles. "It's considered ungentlemanly, not to say coarse, to hold forth upon the physical charms of one's inamorata, but in this case, which is to say Dora's case, and yours in a way, I feel I can make an exception. That soft layer of puppy fat, that slackness of tone—why, it doesn't detract from her charms, far from it, it makes her all the more fascinating! Even the mouse-brown hair, so lank and lifeless, the thick springy tufts that nestle in her armpits, that fuzzy cloud where the good Lord—"

The good Lord alone knows where all this indelicacy might have ended up, but just then came a knock at the door. It heralded the arrival of Dr. Folse, proprietor of the clinic, with a clipboard tucked under his arm and two white-coated subordinates in tow.

"Saved by the bell, Wharton," Melvin sighed. "The good doctor's here to put me to sleep. You'd best get home, and fill in Dora." There was just enough ambiguity in his phrasing to keep Wharton in a fever of his own imaginings, all the way back into town.

• • •

"HOW'S MELVIN?" Dora wanted to know, letting him into the apartment. She had on the same wrap she always wore; Wharton wondered if it ever got washed. It smelled of her, that musky ambiguity, which he absolutely didn't mind: to him, it was more alluring than any scent of freshly laundered fabric. What had Melvin said about the stink of the Terrebénie swamp, earlier that afternoon?

"He seems in an awful way," Wharton said, and corrected himself lest she become upset: "I mean, he's having a pretty rough time of it."

He needn't have worried about causing her distress. "I hope they giving him his morphine," she said. "I told him 'take it with you,' but he said they'd probably give him all he wanted, he was payin' enough."

"He's on—he takes morphine?" Never before had Wharton knowingly come across a drug addict, as he now understood Melvin to be.

"It eases him," Dora said, "with the itchin' an' all."

"I guess it must. Um, I don't know— I guess they are."

"I told him take his own," she said. "His cream too. I make the cream special, it's a family thing, you got to mix it at certain phases of the moon. He said Doctor Folse wouldn't go for that. I guess it wouldn't be the same if it wasn't me creamin' him, anyway. My family knows 'bout itchin'."

"...I got these," Wharton said, his throat painfully constricted, proffering two bottles of their regular Zinfandel. Dora grasped them by the neck and stowed them in the frigidaire.

"Sit down," she said, "while it cools." Wharton sat on the couch, twisting his hat in his hands. A fan was oscillating on the adjacent table, pushing the air around rather than refreshing it. Its creaking back-and-forth movement reminded Wharton of a long-forgotten character from his hometown, a doddering old paretic who'd terrified him as a child, the way he'd sit all day on a bench down at the beach, head wagging senselessly back and forth.

As Dora passed by the fan on her way back from the kitchen, the breeze caught the fabric of her wrap, blowing it half open at the front. If this was provocative, what happened next was downright incapacitating. Instead of taking up her usual place on the hassock at his feet, she hopped on to the opposite end of the couch, curling her legs up beneath her and training her unblinking gaze on him from half the usual distance.

"So," she said, and her high small voice seemed to fill the room in Melvin's absence, "what did you boys talk about?"

What was he to say? "Oh, you know, we, uh, about his, er condition?" It was important above all to keep away from the actual content of Melvin's drugged soliloquy.

"Did he tell you how come he first started itchin'?" And here it was again, the stuff he dared not mention.

"Not really." Which was true, so far as it went. "I mean, he mentioned it..."

"He never had it when I first met him," she said, pushing her hair back behind her ear from where the fan had been ruffling it. *Mouse-brown*, wasn't that how Melvin had described it? Unwashed but not dirty, just lank and uncombed. He did his best to blank out Melvin's further discussion of the subject.

"So he said."

"Somethin' he caught back in the parish," she said, "They's lots of people round there come down with that itchin'. Only our family know how to fix it. Got a base of 'gator fat."

"Alligator...?"

She nodded. "Some of them swamp 'gators, they so fat you just wouldn't believe it. Been feedin' real good for a long time, you know? No knowin' how old they are. Gone stupid in they old age. Let you come right up to 'em, even if you got a cane chopper in your hand."

Wharton gulped. "Aren't you...weren't you afraid?"

"I grew up round those things," she said, "back when it was just Daddy Guilloret an' me. Before Melvin ever come along."

"Do you miss the old place?" he asked inanely. That anyone could miss such an existence seemed impossible to him.

"I like it fine here," Dora said, without detectable enthusiasm. "I got all my things from the old place, made Melvin hire a truck. This here is all mine," waving a hand at the junk strewn all around the room, "like Papa's dowry to me."

For Wharton, every conversational gambit was opening on to fresh embarrassment. All roads seemed to lead to Melvin's story about the wooing of Dora and the lengths to which he'd felt compelled to go. Best get back to the furniture, quickly, before something terrible happened. "It's pretty, though," he ventured. And then, something terrible happened. Out of nowhere, astonishing himself, he hadn't meant to say it but out his mouth it came, "And so are you."

"You think I'm pretty?" Dora asked, with no more vivacity than if he'd said "This couch sure is saggy."

"I'm sorry—I don't know why I said that, I apologise—"

"It's all right," Dora said in the same monotone. "I don't mind. You a nice man, Wharton. Got a pleasant manner."

"So do you," Wharton said, digging his hole ever deeper. Remember: he'd never learned caution at the hands of any woman, experience had never taught him when to jam on the brakes, and now it was already too late. Why was he behaving like this? He wasn't even drunk.

As if reading his mind, Dora said, "Stay there," and got to her feet, which were as ever bare. Did she even own stockings, let alone shoes? While Wharton loosened his collar and pulled at the knot of his tie, she disappeared into the kitchen and came back with the wine. It hadn't had time to chill properly, but Wharton took a deep draught of it anyway. She settled back on the couch, a little nearer to him now. "You think I'm pretty?" she repeated.

"Yes," he admitted helplessly.

The corners of her mouth moved up—you couldn't really call it a smile. "Melvin says all sorts of fancy things 'bout me, don't he?"

"Yes, he does." Almost inaudible, Wharton's assent.

"I guess I got one of those faces men find comely," she said, and pushed her hair back again. "Daddy used to say I was a vessel of concupiscence, ain't that pretty?"

"It certainly is," Wharton agreed, not knowing in the slightest what it meant.

"He was always comin' out with that fancy stuff, like out of books? Him an' Melvin, when they got together, why, it was wall-to-wall jawin', hours on end. Grimoire this, Azathoth that, Sebek, Sobek, till my head just would not stop from spinnin'. I couldn't follow not even the half of it. Here, I brung the bottle with me." She refilled his glass, which had somehow become empty in no time at all. "Words, words, words, non-stop, talkin', talkin', talkin'. I swear some nights I'd just leave 'em to that back-and-forth jabber o' theirs, Wharton. To hell with their stupid ol' Cthulhu." *That* had been the word. "Don't they say actions speak louder'n words, though?"

Her hand was resting on his own, the one not holding the wineglass. That other hand began to tremble, so much so that Wharton was obliged to set the glass down on the table at his side, lest he spill all over the both of them.

"Why, just look at my nail polish," she said, extending her fingers. "It's all chipped. I should put new on. Would you do it for me, Wharton?"

Wharton's hands were so unsteady, he knew this would be impossible. "Uh, maybe later?" he temporised. Dora shrugged and set her hand back to rest on Wharton's trembling paw.

"Melvin used to say that's foolishness an' woman's stuff," she remarked, "but I think it's right romantic. Why, he wouldn't even paint my toenails." She swung a foot up into Wharton's lap, dropping it at the very epicentre of his discomfort. "Will you do my toenails as well, Wharton? Paint those lil' piggies, make 'em all pretty?"

"I surely will," he managed hoarsely. Everything was cranked too fast, and simultaneously running in exquisite slow motion.

She lifted her foot away, stretched her legs to rest on the hassock, leaned back into the yielding creaking couch. "We got plenty of time," she said. "Melvin's in that clinic place for good, I think."

"Well, I guess they have to do some tests..."

"Oh, he ain't comin' out of there," she said flatly. "He's just all used up with that condition of his." She hitched over towards him, squeezed his jittering hand. "Will you take care of me, Wharton, now he's gone?"

"I—uh, you know, I'll do whatever I can…" Too fast, slow it down, slow it down—

"Gonna be quiet round here without him, though," she said, her hand on his arm now, stroking up and down his bicep. "Lord, how he could talk!"

"He, uh, he sure likes the sound of his own voice." Wharton felt like Judas in the garden. "But you know he'll be out of there before you can say—"

"You know sometimes he'd carry on so much, it'd just make my head ache," Dora said, ignoring him. "I swear I coulda dropped unconscious." As if to demonstrate, she flopped, all of a piece, against him, resting her head on the pillowy swell of his belly. *Stop, stop*, but he couldn't move a muscle: the whirlpool of panic and desire was just too powerful.

"I like a doer, Wharton, like the strong silent type? Man like you. My ancestors"— she pronounced it *incestors*—"my daddy's folk, they weren't blabbermouths, they done stuff. Real stuff, you know? Serious. I don't believe Melvin was a serious man at heart— he never understood us, understood our ways. You get right down to it, why he was just all talk. You're not like that, are you, Wharton? You know there's more to life than jabber."

Head still resting on his belly, she made little scratching motions with her fingertips on his chest. Gooseflesh tingled all across Wharton's body. Absent-mindedly almost, she began undoing the buttons of his shirt, from the neck on down. Even then, he didn't know what to do, so in the end she had to show him. "Let's not get in the bed," she whispered, her breath hot in his ear as she tugged at his belt, "I ain't changed the sheets from Melvin."

COME SUNDOWN they were sprawled on the couch still in a sticky tangled mass. Wharton, a great beached whale flabby with guilt like one of Michelangelo's damned, lay trapped beneath Dora, motionless, too scared to move, too scared to think. It seemed too much to hope that at some point he'd wake up from this extraordinary dream and be just regular Wharton once more, chaste and inexperienced, blissfully ignorant of sin. Dora was a dead weight across him, not moving, asleep he supposed, and the scent of her body was the only thing that made it seem halfway real.

"It's night," came her voice, out of darkness. She lifted herself partway off him. There was a soft wet smack where their sweaty flesh parted. "Where's that wine?" A glugging sound, and then the bottleneck was pressed against his own lips. He sucked at the tepid wine; it stung the mucous membrane in his mouth, pulling his lips into an involuntary pucker.

"We need some light here." She knee-walked across him, fumbled on the barley twist table alongside the couch. A scrape and a sulphurous whiff, and there was Dora, materialized out of night, putting a match to a candle. Even in the warm illumination of the flame her skin was creamy white and flawless. Wharton regarded it with reverence and terror, still not daring to touch it on his own initiative.

She fell back into him, and Wharton was returned to the muddy sucking wallow of his thoughts. When he'd been little, the thing that frightened him above all else was the concept of irreversibility—the notion that even the best-behaved boy in the world might accidentally do something so terrible that it could never be taken back, could never be apologized for or made right, not with all the desperate penitence in the world. His mother had played ruthlessly on this fear, leaving small Wharton a tearful heap at day's end as she held possession of the battlefield. Now here was grown-up Wharton feeling it all over again, but without knowing exactly what he'd done wrong, which only made it ten times worse.

Trying to empty his mind, he found himself gazing at the candle, pretty much the only thing he could gaze at in the darkness of the apartment. It was an oddly shaped thing, he thought, thick as a church candle, not smooth and cylindrical but irregular, whittled-at. Focussing more narrowly on it, he realised that it had been carved to represent a human figure, rough and streaked with grease. By now its head was melted half away where the flame had made a crater, so that any features it might have had were unrecognisable, but the general shape of the body reminded him unpleasantly of Melvin.

"What's that?" he said, his voice sounding like someone else's in his head.

Dora stirred in his lap. "What?"

"The candle. It's unusual."

"You like that?" A hand reached out into the candlelight, saliva glistening on its fingertips: it pinched out the flame with a sizzle, regifting the room to night. "It's called a poppet. It's a thing the women do in my family. Maybe I'll do one for you."

Time passed incalculably, and then the telephone was ringing. "Get that for me, Wharton," Dora told him, rolling off to his side so he could get up. He located the instrument by sound more than sight, fumbled it off its cradle, held the receiver to his ear.

Someone was asking for Dora. "She can't come to the phone right now," Wharton said, his tongue a wad of half-chewed meat between his teeth. "Can I take a message?"

"It's to do with Mr. Inkpen," said the voice, and Melvin straightened up.

When he replaced the receiver, he heard Dora yawning from across the room. "You best light that candle again," he told her. She did so, and propped herself up on one elbow

"That was the clinic," he said. He felt as if he was reciting some tragic poem from memory, and because it was all a bad dream, he was naked in front of the entire school. "Dora, they got some bad news about Melvin."

She yawned again. "Did he die?"

"I'm afraid so." Wharton was taken aback. He'd meant to break it to her gently. "Doctor Folse says he died just now. He thinks it was his heart, some sort of adverse reaction."

"Poor Melvin," she said, as if the cat who lived in the hallway had been found run over in the street. "That's a shame." She smoothed away the tangled hair from her face. "Will you see to the arrangements for me, Wharton?"

Wharton just stood there, not knowing what to say or do, unsure how to negotiate the next few seconds, or come to that the entire remainder of his life. He felt like one of Dora's poppets, melting away from the head down, wondering whether the dread that had settled on him would ever take a definite shape, or just leave him rendered down to a puddle of wax. He realised that he was scratching at his belly, where Dora's head had lain.

"Come over here," Dora said, and he did so, pathetically grateful for a straightforward instruction. Over by the sofa, the candlelight disclosed a little round plaque of roughened skin on his stomach, about the dimension of a lipstick print from a lover's kiss, and in that instant the exact contours of his fundamental fear stood revealed to him.

Steve Duffy lives and works in North Wales. His most recent collection of weird stories, These And Other Mysteries, *was published by Sarob Press in 2024; he's currently in the process of putting together his next. Steve was the winner of the International Horror Guild's award for Best Short Story 2000, and in 2015 he received the Shirley Jackson Award for Best Novelette.* ■■■■■■

THE THIRD FLOOR

By Jo Kaplan

MOST OF THE TIME, THE HOUSE WHERE KYLA LIVED HAD TWO FLOORS, BUT ON RARE OCCASIONS THERE APPEARED A THIRD. She could never anticipate when it would be there. The entrance, too, was never in the same place. Sometimes she would be bounding up the stairs to her bedroom after school, leaping over the fifth from the top, which bellowed with every touch, and find that though the stairs turned out onto the hallway of the second floor in the usual place, they also continued upward to a door that sat at the end of a dark alcove. The door was always closed. Other times, it appeared in peculiar places, like the time she opened the door to the bathroom and discovered to her astonishment a set of stairs on the other side of the bathtub where no sane architect would place them.

The first time she noticed the stairs to the third floor, Kyla ran back down to her mother and told her there was more house than they'd had previously. She'd heard her parents use that phrase before when discussing her as-yet-unrealized little brothers and sisters.

Theirs was a narrow house crowded in by equally narrow houses. It had just enough rooms as it could fit, and they were all small. The second floor held two bedrooms, Kyla's and her parents', and the bathroom they shared, and the closet at the end of the hall; the first floor was able to contain only the kitchen and living room. So Kyla understood that when her parents said they needed more house, they meant they needed more rooms to house the additional children they would have liked to add to their family.

It was with some eagerness, then, that Kyla took her mother's hand and pulled her up the stairs, thinking she had made a discovery that would solve their problem. When they arrived at the second floor, however, the additional stairs had vanished.

Kyla gaped. "They were right here."

"I'm sure they were," her mother said indulgently.

She looked for them always after that. Sometimes she went down to the first floor, stood with her back to the stairs, then turned and raced up to catch them before they went away.

The next time she saw them was in the hall closet. Instead of going to get her mother—for she knew they wouldn't be there when she returned—she climbed. The light from the hall behind her let her see the patterned wallpaper on either side, a wallpaper that did not appear anywhere else in the house. As she approached the top, however, her gait slowed. It was darker the higher she went. She made it four steps from the top when she stopped. What use would it be to open the door if she couldn't see anything? This was what she convinced herself was the problem, not that she was afraid of the door in its alcove.

Knowing it would likely not be there when she returned, Kyla hurried back down the steps to retrieve a light. If she had a light, she told herself, then she wouldn't be afraid to go all the way up this time. Just as she expected, when she came back, the closet was only a closet again, shelved with blankets and towels. She shined the flashlight inside to be sure there were no stairs hiding on the other side of the shelves, then closed the door.

After that, she carried a flashlight around the house even in broad daylight. Her mother assumed it was a game, and Kyla played into this belief by occasionally flattening herself against the floor and shining the light under the couch, shouting out when she spotted a stray penny or a spider lurking in its corner. Her father smiled and told her to let him know if she ever found some treasure under there. All she found were dust bunnies.

Kyla knew her house had only two floors, just as she knew she had ten fingers, but this didn't stop her from wanting to see the third floor, the one she knew did not exist.

It was in her bedroom closet she next found it. Her parents had already tucked her in and turned out the lamp. Having turned over in bed only to realize her favorite stuffed rabbit with a missing button eye was not at her side, Kyla threw off the covers and felt around for it in that strange empty space under the bed, where the dark seemed to press up more acutely. Not finding it there, she clicked on her flashlight and pulled open the closet.

There were the stairs.

An oval of light crossed the patterned wallpaper into the dark at the top. She went up, with every step glancing behind her to be sure her bedroom would remain where she'd left it. The air grew still and quiet the further she ascended, gaining a quality like an attic long stifled from ventilation. A dizzy ache muffled her ears the way it did on an airplane's ascent. She opened her jaw to ease the pressure.

Her heart was pounding as she reached the alcove. There seemed a weight here, and she had the distinct impression of some presence lurking nearby, just on the other side of the door. How she sensed this, she could not say, only that it reminded her of trick-or-treating, when she would raise her hand to knock on a door knowing innately, somehow, that its inhabitant stood just behind, waiting, bowl of candy in hand, frozen in time, ready to throw open the door.

The tarnished brass doorknob felt warm in her hand. It did not turn. She jiggled it left and right. A part of her was disappointed she had tried all this time to make it to the third floor only to be locked out. Another, perhaps greater, part of her was relieved, certain she did not want to step through this doorway.

And yet she could not give up quite so easily. Kyla raised her fist and knocked three times on the wood. The sound was dull, as if the door were a foot thick. She stepped back, satisfied she had done all she could and planning, in the back of her mind, never to seek out the third floor again. Before she could turn away, a line of light appeared along the crack beneath the door. This was attended by a pneumatic hiss as the knob began to turn.

Kyla rushed back into the darkness, running, for longer than she expected, down those stairs, past the endlessly repeating patterns of the wallpaper, while the hissing grew louder behind her. The dark of her bedroom was very far away. Even the air smelled different, stagnant. When at last she made it to the bottom and slammed the door behind her, Kyla backed away from the closet, clutching the flashlight to her chest, waiting for that thickening of the air, that sense of a presence just on the other side. She waited for a light to appear in the crack.

After some time, when she had gathered up her courage, Kyla opened the door and saw the shelving of her closet, the one-eyed rabbit staring back at her.

FOR YEARS, Kyla forgot about the third floor. She might even have come to believe that what she thought she'd experienced had been no more than a vivid dream, one which pursued her for a time and then sank into the froth of the unconscious. Other things occupied her mind—the growing rift between her parents that, she was sure, would have ended in divorce had her mother not died suddenly of a pulmonary embolism, the tedious jobs she worked to put herself through college, her marriage and subsequent purchase of a quaint two-story townhome.

It wasn't, indeed, until she began to think about growing her own family that she even remembered finding a staircase in her bedroom closet as a child. Her husband was waiting for her in bed, preparing to commence their first purposeful attempt at pregnancy. Kyla flipped off the bathroom light and swung open the door, expecting to see him with one knee cocked playfully up where he lay. Instead, she was confronted by darkness so absolute she palmed the switch again. It was not the master bedroom through the doorway but a staircase, lined by the very same wallpaper she'd glimpsed in her youth. If pressed, she would not have been able to recall the pattern well enough to draw it, but seeing it again, there was no mistake.

The bathroom's overhead lights glared on white tile. There were no windows. This had not bothered her upon purchasing the house, but now, with no egress from the tiny room except the stairway leading up, she felt the first prickling of claustrophobia.

She went up.

She expected the door to be locked when she reached for the handle, but it turned.

Surprise carried her through the open doorway, and then she was on the third floor.

Rather, she was in the hallway of the third floor. It extended left and right as far as she could see, lined with doors set at even increments. Between each door hung a sconce emitting a patient glow. The walls were papered with that same pattern that encased the stairs. A door across the hall revealed a staircase going up. She closed the door and moved to the next only to find yet another staircase. On and on she went down the hall. Behind every door was another staircase, each identical to the last. It made her dizzy to think about where she was right now. Nothing of this size could possibly exist in her house.

She decided to go up to the fourth floor, where she found more of the same: another door-lined hallway. The only difference was that several of the sconces had burnt out, leaving periodic pockets of shadow.

Surely, she thought, there had to be something other than halls and stairs. Surely they had to lead somewhere. But each time she opened a door, she found no rooms, no closets, no exits. Only staircases.

Foregoing the doors, she peered down the length of the hall, wondering how far it went. Each way tapered into muddy shadow after some indescribable distance. The soles of her bare feet scraped against rough carpet, which bore a different pattern from the walls, one which seemed an endless series of unfinished squares. The more she looked, the more she sensed someone moving far down the hall, far enough she could make out the shape of it only barely, but she became increasingly convinced there *was* someone there, very far down the hall, perhaps staring back at her and wondering about her. She raised an arm to wave, feeling foolish, not sure if what she saw in the distance was a person at all, but it seemed to lift something of itself at the same time. Thinking the person had waved back, she hurried forward, passing several dozen doors on the way, her speedwalk turning to a jog turning to a sprint—yet the person remained, it seemed, the same distance away as before. Indeed, it seemed the person was running away from her as she ran toward them.

When Kyla looked in the other direction, she thought she saw another figure at that end of the hall. At least, she imagined the person stood at the end of the hall, but neither did the hall seem to have an end either way.

She decided to go up to the fifth floor.

It was identical to the others, save where the wallpaper had begun to peel away from the wall behind it, bubbling up in loose spots. She wanted to press it back, but she stopped herself from touching it; the paper seemed too soft and spongy, as if there were something more behind it than an air pocket.

She went up again.

After some time, she lost track of what floor she was on. She worried the only direction she could go was up. Even when she turned around and tried to go back down the way she'd come, she found the stairs had changed directions. It was with great relief that she finally opened a door to discover a staircase that went down. She hesitated before it, still curious about the others, wondering where they went, if they would eventually reach some mysterious top floor, some place with actual rooms. Or, she wondered, did they simply continue upward, ad infinitum, the way the hallway seemed to extend infinitely to either side? She decided she would not find out. She took the stairway down.

After trying several doors on the next level, she discovered some half a dozen different descending stairways. Surely they all led to the same lower level, just as all the ascending stairways did—but *was* she sure of that? Did it matter which one she took? No, she was sure they would all lead to the same level. She took one at random and went down, losing track again of how many flights she had ascended and now descended, losing all track of where she could possibly be in relation to her bedroom, to her house, if she was anywhere at all in relation to her house anymore.

Her gut did not begin to twist sickly until she was quite sure she had descended more levels than she had ascended. It didn't seem possible, but she kept finding more and more and more staircases that led downward, each seemingly identical to the last. And so she went down, her ears pulsing with heavy stagnant air, wishing she had never gone up to the third floor in the first place, wondering, in the back of her mind, in a way she did not really allow herself to consciously wonder, whether she would ever leave this place.

And then she found it: a door at the bottom of a staircase, which deposited her into a dark room.

For a moment, she stood blinking to adjust her eyes. By degrees, dim shapes made themselves known, and she came to recognize her bedroom. On the bed lay a shape snuggled under the covers. Her husband must have gotten tired waiting for her to come out of the bathroom and gone to sleep. Why hadn't he come to check on her, though? It wasn't like him to fall asleep when he anticipated sex.

She did not close the door behind her when she stepped into the room, for she was sure when she did, reopening it would lead her back into the bathroom. Instead, she crept to the bed and crawled beneath the covers. Some hours later, the morning light would gradually reveal her husband's sleeping face, and she would lie beside him wondering if it was *her* husband. She would notice how the house was both familiar and strange, which she told herself was because they'd moved in only a few weeks before. Yet she could not convince herself nothing was wrong, that it did not smell wrong, that it was truly the house she had purchased. And she could never really be sure she had come out where she'd meant to, that she hadn't picked the wrong door.

Jo Kaplan is the Shirley Jackson Award-nominated author of It Will Just Be Us *and* When the Night Bells Ring. *Her short stories have appeared in* Fireside Quarterly, Black Static, Nightmare Magazine, Vastarien, Horror Library, Nightscript, *and many other places. In addition to writing, she teaches English and creative writing at Glendale Community College and is the co-chair of the Horror Writers Association's Los Angeles chapter. She also plays cello in both the Symphony of the Verdugos and the band Guerra/paz.*

GOYA'S SATURN DEVOURING HIS SON (1823)

The Last Gallery

by Gary McMahon

In art, there is no need for colour; I see only light and shade.
—Francisco Goya

I**T WAS FINALLY TIME FOR JACKSON TO ADMIT THAT HE HAD NO IDEA WHERE HE WAS.**

He'd come off the motorway over an hour ago, forced onto a slip road by the line of cones separating traffic from the roadworks. He'd followed the diversion signs until they'd simply stopped appearing, then continued driving in the same direction because he wasn't the kind of man who liked to turn back and retrace the way he'd come. The poorly lit country roads were narrow and confusing, taking long bends and climbing for miles to empty peaks before dropping away into tree-lined tunnels of darkness.

He glanced at the dashboard clock. It was after midnight. If Jenny hadn't left him three weeks ago, she'd be wondering where he was. He smiled but felt no humour—just a tug inside his chest, as if something had snagged there, perhaps on a rib. These site visits for work were part of the reason she'd always felt so neglected—and right now, he couldn't blame her.

The car headlights cut yellow slices through the darkness, showing only more of the road. On each side, high verges blocked his view of the fields.

"Come on," he whispered, either to himself or to the night. "Give me a break here."

The radio crackled—a sibilant hiss of static. It had stopped working half an hour ago, the signal cut off by the trees, the verges, the desolate location.

He glanced to his left, out of the side window. There was a drainage ditch running along the side of the road. It was pitch black; he couldn't make out how deep it was. For a moment, he thought he saw swift movement inside the ditch, as if something small were running along beside him, tracking him through the dark.

Reaching out with an unsteady hand, he turned the dial on the radio, but still there was no signal. Something like a mournful voice tried to make itself heard, and then there was more of that awful static. He switched it off. Stared straight ahead.

That was when he saw it. The faded, wavering light of a sign at the side of the road, perhaps a mile ahead of him. He couldn't make out what the sign said: it's light was too feeble, and it was flickering wildly.

Jackson pressed his foot down on the accelerator. Just a little. Not too fast. He didn't know these roads; they were dangerous in the dark.

Once he was closer, he began to make out the words on the defective sign:

Petrol
Snacks & Drinks

Relief rushed over him, a warm wind on a cold day. Now that there were signs of life, he could admit to himself that he had been afraid.

As he came abreast of the sign, he slowed and turned left onto a gravel forecourt. There were no other cars parked there, and beyond the empty car park, there sat a small, squat prefabricated building with a couple of old petrol pumps standing on concrete plinths outside.

He stopped the car and switched off the engine. Opened the door. The night pressed in, pushing up against him. Even from here, he could tell the petrol station was unmanned. Despite the sign being illuminated, it was clearly shut for business. In fact, now that he looked closely, the building looked abandoned, perhaps another victim of the recent lockdowns.

"Best check. Just to be sure." Talking to himself made him feel less alone. He'd started doing it after Jenny left, and the house seemed too large for his presence. All those empty rooms; so many drawers and wardrobes bereft of clothes.

His feet crunched in the gravel as he crossed the car park in the direction of the little building. As he got closer, he saw there was another, separate, building behind it. Was it a garage, or perhaps a café? There was no signage on the shoddily clad sides of the building to indicate its purpose so he couldn't be sure.

When he approached the petrol station, he noticed the windows were smeared with dirt. He tried to peer inside, but the glass was opaque with filth. He tried the door, rattling it, but of course it was locked. Feeling a little lost, he walked around the perimeter of the station until he came to the second building.

This one had no windows, just a wooden door. Instinctively, he reached out and turned the handle. The door opened. He stepped back, afraid, and watched as the door swung smoothly open onto a darkness that seemed to swim with agitated life.

He looked behind him, at his car sitting on its own on the gravel; then he looked back at the open door.

"Hello?"

There was no response. This building was also empty.

He almost turned back, walked to his car, started the engine, and drove back the way he'd come. But that same stubborn instinct that had led him here kicked in and instead he took a step forward, towards the open door. He watched as his hand reached out and pushed it all the way open to the wall, and he stepped inside.

His eyes adjusted to the darkness almost instantly. Inside the building there was a reception desk. The wooden floor was solid but covered in grime. The desk itself looked neat and tidy, although when he stepped towards it and touched it with the tips of his fingers, they came away coated in dust.

Upon the desk was a sheaf of papers. He fanned them outwards, like playing cards, and realised they were badly photocopied advertising flyers for some kind of art show. He picked one up.

Enough ambient light—although of a monotonously flickering kind—came through the doorway to enable him to read the flyer. It was for an exhibition called "Summoning the Vision." Beneath the crude, blocky font, there were a couple of faint photographs of framed paintings. Their subjects were too difficult to make out in the meagre light, even when he brought the flyer closer to his face. The name of the artist wasn't listed.

Long ago, when he was young and not yet broken by life's demands, he'd fancied himself an artist—nothing much, just the occasional watercolour for his family and friends, but deep down, he suspected that he possessed no real talent and eventually gave it up as a bad idea. Jenny hated art and literature. She had no time for creative endeavours. She only ever looked at photographs that depicted real life events and read nothing but self-help books and confidence-building manuals.

He replaced the flyer on the desk and slowly turned to his right. There was another door, this one already open. Beyond, he could just about make out a series of black rectangles on a blacker wall—surely these were the framed pictures that made up the exhibition.

Whenever this place had closed, the owners had obviously moved out in such a hurry that they'd left everything behind. They were probably saddled with debt and hadn't seen the point in salvaging a bunch of amateur art.

Jackson didn't think about what he was doing, he simply walked towards the door to the gallery, too intrigued by what might be in there to register trepidation. There was nothing here to be frightened of, not unless you were creeped out by old paintings.

Some of this stuff might be worth money.

As soon as he stepped across the threshold, a subtle illumination lit up along the base of the walls, obviously triggered by some kind of sensor hidden in the door frame. He wondered how long a building needed to be untenanted before the power company cut off the electricity.

By the swampy, low-level lighting, he could make out that the large room had been blocked off into a series of viewing compartments—floor-to-ceiling black drapes formed narrow corridors, in which were presumably housed the paintings.

Walking past a series of teasingly empty picture frames, he followed the route to the first painting. Moving along the black-curtained chamber, he was directed to a point at the far end, where a painting hung on a free-standing frame, its tripod legs splayed and secured to the wooden floor.

Jackson had to get close to see the painting properly. It depicted in smeary oils a small, slender man in a brown suit. He was standing in an empty room with no windows. The walls were made of either rock or mud. Brown was the dominant colour. The man seemed to be staring at a point near the umber ceiling, at something which sat just out of the frame, but seemed to possess a weight that had cracked the walls. The subject's face was impassive, and his eyes betrayed a look of something that was not quite fear but something similar—awe, perhaps?

"Not very good, is it?" Jackson turned away from the painting and started to feel his way along the curtain, looking for the entrance to the next gallery. After a few minutes of blind groping, his hands found a seam, and he pulled the curtains apart, then stepped briskly through into the next section.

This time, there was no frame or easel. The artwork had been daubed directly onto the dark wall of the building. It showed the same little man, but this time he was lying flat on his stomach, prostrate before something that loomed high above him, at the apex of wall and ceiling—something more than a shadow yet not quite solid enough to be a solid form. This time it seemed that the shape was emerging through the cracks in the walls. The man had his hands clasped over the back of his head in a protective gesture.

"Oh, how crass." Jackson wasn't sure why his reaction to the piece was so strong, or so negative, but he was appalled. "Crude and obvious: cheap little horrors. No wonder you went out of business."

Jenny would have hated this. It was the kind of place he always dragged her into on holidays—weird roadside attractions and grubby little backstreet galleries. Looking for a bargain, another sucker to cheat out of something they didn't realise was valuable.

At this point, he became aware that he had a choice to make. Either continue along the galleries, viewing the rest of the art, or turn back and return to his car. Again, he was averse to retreat: his urge to keep moving forward took over, as it usually did in such moments.

He found the gap in the curtain and pressed on.

The third painting was something altogether different. It put him in mind of Francisco Goya's infamous "Black Paintings."

Much better, he thought.

The large canvas was suspended by thin strands of fishing line from the unseen rafters. The floor-level lighting cast it in a hellish aspect. The painting depicted the same man as the other two pieces, but this time he was naked and his rawboned, yellowish body was covered in what appeared to be dark brown sores. His eyes were wide; his toothless mouth gaped wider than should be humanly possible; his head had been shaved and strange symbols were carved into the flaking, brownish skin of his scalp.

Behind the man, the shadow had solidified into something approaching a figure. It had a bulbous body and far too many dark, sketchy limbs. Its head was small, featureless, yet the black brush strokes were done in such a way that it suggested a pair of lidless eyes and a mouth that was somehow bigger than the face. Splashes of brown pigment were splashed within the black shadow, suggesting waste and putrescence—this was a thing that had been secreted rather than born into the world.

Jackson turned away, horrified. He didn't want to see any more of this. There was no opportunity for profit here; it was time to leave.

He flailed at the black curtains, looking for the way he'd come in, but there didn't seem to be an opening. He spent minutes rushing around the small space, grabbing at the fabric, trying to pull it apart. Then he attempted to pull the curtains upwards, to create a gap that he might crawl through, but they were stuck to the floor somehow.

Reluctantly, he turned back to the painting. The canvas was blank. Just a black square. It swung gently on its wires, as if someone had passed by, disturbing it. Gingerly, he edged around the painting and found a gap in the curtains.

Forward. Only forward. This time there really was no turning back.

It occurred to him that the internal space seemed so much bigger than the building. Was it a trick of the compartmental layout, or something more sinister?

Don't be stupid, he thought. *Be rational.*

He found himself in yet another narrow gallery, but here there was no painting. Instead, there was a sculpture positioned in the centre of the space. It depicted the same bland man as before, dressed again in his brown suit. He appeared to be wearing a badly fitted wig. His thin-lipped mouth was open slightly, in a wry smile. His eye sockets were nothing more than ragged holes in his face. He was holding both hands out in front of him, in a gesture that could be interpreted as either defensive or an act of supplication. His palms were turned upward, and in each of them was an eyeball.

He wore no shoes. His feet were brown with dirt. The cuffs off his suit jacket and trousers were filthy and frayed. The level of detail was impressive, but for one thing: his limbs were disproportionate. The arms and legs were far too long for his body, giving him an insectile appearance.

Was this deliberate, or simply a lack of anatomical knowledge in the artist?

"Okay...not so scary, this one. Just gross." Yet still he felt unnerved. There was something about the sculpture that spoke of bodily mutation, or an abortive transformation. The gangly limbs, that slitty little mouth, the empty eye sockets. The grisly offerings in each hand.

He leaned in close, inspecting the piece. Was it made from clay? Again, the predominant colour was brown—several different shades of brown, the lightest being almost yellow and the darkest near to black. As he peered at the surface of the sculpture—at the skin of the man's face—he was puzzled by how smooth and malleable it looked; there were not even hairline cracks to suggest that the clay had been dried or baked.

If he touched it, would it be soft beneath his fingers? Like wet mud…or fresh bodily waste?

What a horrible, unwelcome thought… Jackson decided in that moment that he didn't want to know. Some things are best left alone. That was one of Jenny's favourite sayings.

He hurried past the prone figure, looking for the way out.

The next gallery held no art. There was simply a hand-painted sign on the wall that said: *Exit Through the Gift Shop.*

Jackson shook his head and kept moving. Surely this ordeal must be coming to an end—was this the last gallery, and the next section would contain the exit?

He endured another bout of wrestling with the long black curtains until he found a gap, and then he slipped through.

Into darkness.

Absolute darkness.

This was a darkness so profound that it felt as if he were falling, endlessly, into some gigantic chasm. He blinked, trying to acclimatise his eyes, but all he could see was a squirming blackness, which was slowly becoming tinged with brown. Dizziness washed over him, and he stumbled, then fell. His knees slammed into the wooden boards, jolting him back to reality, and as his vision became star-speckled, he was once again able to see.

Another room. Another painting.

No, there was more than one. There were fresh, unframed paintings all around him, on the walls—a jigsaw of images that made up a whole. Parts of something that was so much bigger than himself. Here a slitted yellow eye; there a partial antenna or probiscis; and over there was the cloven end of an angular appendage that could only be a limb. So many pictures, each one a part of something he did not want to see as a complete entity. The walls began to ripple, and it seemed to Jackson that something was trying to burst forth. The paintings shifted on the walls, moving closer together, trying to reform the image of which they were mere fragments.

There was a sound behind him, a gentle scraping, like clumsy footsteps on the rough floorboards.

Somebody coughed softly.

"How do you like them? My artworks?"

Jackson refused to move. He closed his eyes. Tried to seal shut his ears so as not to hear the fragile, singsong voice.

Jenny, he thought. *Why did you leave me all alone in the dark?*

The voice spoke again, louder, and clearer this time, as if it were growing in confidence. "It took me a long time to gather these pieces together—and it cost me so much pain. So much self-doubt as I waited for someone to come and see. But isn't all art an act of faith?"

Jackson shook his head. He was mumbling something but he wasn't sure if there were words or merely sounds.

"Turn to face me," said the voice. "Look upon the artist."

Jackson tried to fight against it, but it felt as if his head was turning on its own. He managed to keep his eyes down, towards the floor, but that was the extent of his conscious volition.

"Look upon the art that you and I have brought forth."

Jackson's eyes sprung open and he saw a pair of blackened feet with only partial toes, the grizzled hems of frayed brown trouser cuffs.

The darkness around him seethed with a raw, fetid energy, and he was aware of the stench of sewage mixed with rotten flowers. He didn't want to look but he no longer had a choice—the artist, the artwork, was drawing him in. He could feel it in his bones, even as they began to lengthen—the joints popping and the tendons tearing.

The paintings on the walls had now stopped moving. They'd come together in a shuddering clot somewhere in the corner of the room, and whatever shape they'd formed was growing, metastasising like a tumour. Soon, he thought, it would fill the space.

"*Look…*"

As Jackson's gaze moved slowly, uncontrollably upwards, he noticed again how impossibly long and thin those legs were, and he was unspeakably afraid of what leering monstrosity might be perched above them, keen and hungry to share with him its vision. It was only when his fingers began to clutch and scrape violently at his face, his eyes, that he understood the true cost of the experience.

Gary McMahon writes intensely personal horror stories. His short fiction has appeared in countless anthologies and magazines and has been reprinted in The Best Horror of the Year, The Year's Best Fantasy & Horror

and Best New Horror. He's been nominated for several awards and even won a couple of obscure ones. He is the author of the Thomas Usher novels, The Concrete Grove trilogy. The End, The Bones of You, and his novella The Grieving Stones was recently adapted into a feature film. He lives with his family in Yorkshire, UK, where he reads, writes, watches far too many films, lifts weights, and trains in Shotokan karate.

Regarding his inspiration for "The Last Gallery," McMahon writes "I was thinking about Goya's Black paintings, and how he'd basically painted them on the walls inside his home. It occurred to me that they might have been some sort of invocation—but invoking what? Then I re-read Ramsey Campbell's terrific tale "At Lorn Hall," and something clicked.

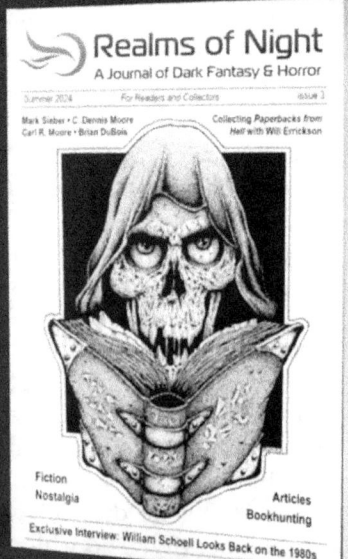

All issues of Black Infinity are still available at AMAZON and other online venues, including the latest:

BLACK INFINITY: CREATURE FEATURES

THE BEAST FROM 20,000 FATHOMS   THE FAMOUS MONSTERS STORY

ROCKET SCIENCE BOOKS

BLACK Infinity 10

CREATURE FEATURES

RAY BRADBURY
JOHN M. NAVROTH
GREGORY L. NORRIS
JASON J. McCUISTON
VONNIE WINSLOW CRIST
SIR ARTHUR CONAN DOYLE
JAMES DORR • WILLIAM MEIKLE
KURT NEWTON • ALLEN KOSZOWSKI
THOMAS KENT MILLER • TOM ENGLISH

FORERUNNERS OF ALIEN:
IT: THE TERROR FROM BEYOND SPACE • PLANET OF THE VAMPIRES

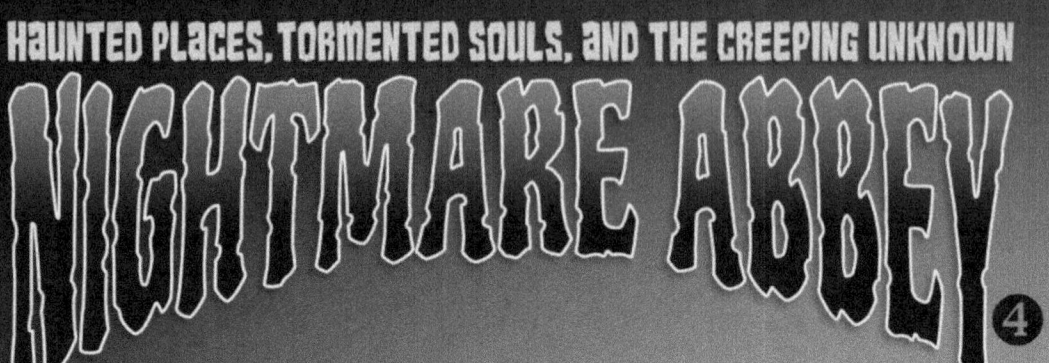

HAUNTED PLACES, TORMENTED SOULS, AND THE CREEPING UNKNOWN

NIGHTMARE ABBEY ④

THE HISTORY OF AMERICAN HORROR COMICS, PART 1

RESURRECTING VAL LEWTON'S *THE BODY SNATCHER*

TITAN OF THE TERROR TALE:
AN INTERVIEW WITH
PAUL FINCH

STEVE RASNIC TEM

DAVID SURFACE

HELEN GRANT

RHYS HUGHES

STEVE DUFFY

RAY CLULEY

IAN ROGERS

MATT COWAN

JOHN M. NAVROTH

ALLEN KOSZOWSKI

GREGORY L. NORRIS

JOHN LLEWELLYN PROBERT

ALLEN K. '91

www.ingramcontent.com/pod-product-compliance
Lightning Source LLC
Chambersburg PA
CBHW080744250626
47162CB00010B/3019

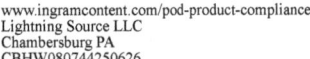